LEXIE AXELSON

the cabin in the storm

AUTHOR'S NOTE

This is a fast-paced romantic suspense. Originally, The Cabin In The Storm was supposed to be a novella. As I continued to write, there were so many twists and turns that I couldn't keep it to novella length. I completely fell in love with Gavin and Coraline. It's different from my other works, and it was so much fun for me to get lost in Sleepy Coldwater! I hope you enjoy their story.

CONTENT WARNINGS

This book contains content, themes, and situations that may be triggering for some readers, such as rough and graphic sexual situations, stalking, childhood trauma, attempted suicide (mention), graphic violence, death, depression, grief, breath and primal play, and pain kink.

If any of the above is triggering, please do not proceed—your mental health matters. This book is intended for mature, adult readers 18+.

PLAYLIST

You Look Like You Love Me by Ella Langley and Riley Green
Choosin' Texas by Ella Langley
I Only Have Eyes For You by The Flamingos
Bad As The Rest by Jessie Murph
Forever by Jessie Murph
POV by Ariana Grande
The Diner by Billie Eilish
Haunted by Isabella Rosa
Indigo by Sam Barber feat. Avery Anna
No One Noticed by The Marias
Constellations by Jade LeMac
Paparrazi by Lady Gaga
Back To Friends by Sombr

DEDICATION

For those who believe they will never be enough, you already are.

CHAPTER 1
CORALINE

This person. They know my real name. It's not my pen name. It's not my artist name. My legal government name, and they want to kill me. It's pretty straight to the point. Someone is lurking, watching me, and wants me dead.

After sifting through the mail, this one quickly caught my eye. It stood out because there was no return address. The writing was done in cutout magazine letters. Everything about it was *off*. I have to be in Alaska for an event, and I'm unsure what to do now.

Should I still go? Maybe this is all a sick prank.

I bite my lip as I hold it in my hand, flipping it over and over again, hoping there's a clue to whoever did this.

Who have I pissed off lately? I look out my car window, but all I see are service members—Army soldiers—walking down the cemented sidewalk, and families going in and out of the coffee shop next to the post office. I'm trying to see if I can catch any familiar faces, with eyes that hold vengeance directed toward me, but nothing rings a hazardous bell. Nothing is out of the ordinary.

Shaking my head, I let my forehead collide with the steering wheel.

Stop spiraling, Cora.

Is this a sick joke? Who would want to kill me? I draw, for crying out loud. I keep to myself as much as I can. I'm afraid of my own damn shadow.

I'm twenty-seven, and someone wants to kill me? I'm not a malicious person. I always give more than I take. I've never gone out of my way to hurt someone. I...

A group of cruel suspects comes to mind. Is this another way to torment me? To hurt me? As if what they did a few months ago was not enough to drive me into a state of mind where I was drowning?

Are they capable of going to these lengths to harass me? Threatening my life as a new form of torture for their entertainment? Do they not have anything else to do but reach a new low to harm me?

It's sick.

Maybe it's them, maybe it's not. My grip on the letter tightens as anger rushes through me. Sucking in a deep breath, I place it back at the bottom of the mail and stuff it inside the center console. I'll throw it away when I get home. I put my car into reverse and foot on the gas to exit the parking lot. My tires run smoothly over small potholes and rocks. I continue to drive down the road, replaying everything I've ever done, and I can't come to any conclusion.

It's just a sick joke. Don't overthink it.

The phone starts to ring in the car, and I see it's my agent, so I click the green button to answer.

"Hey, Maya! What's up?" I tighten my grip on the steering wheel, letting the stress of that ominous letter leave my brain.

"Hello, Cora. So I booked you a hotel a couple of miles from the event. It's high in the mountains with an amazing view. You'll have to catch a taxi or an Uber to get to the event, but I couldn't *not* put you in this place!" She squeals with excitement as if she were joining me. This is why I love my agent. She's so positive all the time. She doesn't know how much her words of encouragement and support affect me. Even if she can't be there with me to enjoy the experience, she takes care of me.

"Okay, as long as it's Anchorage!" I smile as I tilt my head to the side excitedly, already picturing all the cute stores I'll get to shop inside and the food—

"It's...not." Her voice is merely a whisper; I could've mistaken it for static.

"Wait, say that again. It sounded like you said my hotel isn't in Anchorage?"

Did I hear her right?"

"It's a little small town right outside of Anchorage. It's called Sleepy Coldwater. It looks so much like Juneau but better. I grew up there!"

Sleepy Coldwater? I've never heard of it.

"How far is it from the event?"

"Thirty minutes."

"Maya...that's a little far," I say, my shoulders slouching with stress.

"Fine. Fine. Would you like me to rebook?" Her fingertips clack away on her keyboard in the distance.

I ponder as I turn onto the road that leads to my tiny apartment on the outskirts of San Antonio, a Southern Texas City, where it's mostly always hot.

I do like to travel. I've never heard of Sleepy Coldwater, but it intrigues me. Discovering new places, food, and people gives the introvert in me an anxiety attack, but maybe pushing myself to break my shell will help me grow out of it.

"How amazing is the view?"

I OPEN the door after a movie-and-dinner date with a guy I met on a dating app. As soon as I enter my living room, I slip off my black heels one by one and sigh.

The date went perfectly, and he almost kissed me. When he dipped forward with closed eyes and puckered lips on my front porch, I almost jumped away from him. I'm not ready. I turned my head and sprinted inside my house. I want to take things slower. I don't want to rush into anything right now. It's hard for me to commit to someone after recent events. The last man I was with took pieces of me, and I'm not sure I'll ever get them back.

I flick the lights on in my two-bedroom townhome. It's very simply decorated for the holidays. A Christmas tree showered in silver, blue, and pearl white ornaments. A grey and white colored tree skirt circled with reindeer underneath, holding zero presents. One couch, one dining table, one television... everything just for a party of one. That's the way it has to be until I can start truly *living* again.

I step into my art room a moment later, where I like to draw, paint, and write. I continue with my nightly routine of wanting to lose myself in something positive and let go of the betrayal that still haunts me. Standing in the doorway, the memories rewind in my head like a broken record player.

I WALK toward my supportive group of friends with a skip in my step as I reach them. They're all standing in front of the piece, which took me about a year to perfect—a painting of a mother and her daughter, reflecting an estranged, distraught relationship.

"Dude, her work doesn't stand out. It's pretty fucking mid to me," Eli, my friend since the first year of college, says over the room chatter. "It's shit art."

I freeze.

"I did not like it...at all. I was doing everything I could to not just burn it until it became ashes," Lilly adds, and my heart chips further. I tilt my head to the side as a lump forms in my throat.

This can't be happening.

They're my best friends.

A massive man softly bumps into my shoulder by accident. He pauses momentarily, most likely to apologize for the collision, but I can't give him my attention. The betrayal that's unfolding before me is like watching a train crash, and I can't look away or breathe.

"Leave her alone. She has time to grow," my husband of five years interjects.

Liam comes to my defense, but his words don't sound convincing.

I swallow the ache in my throat just as the man who bumped into me walks away.

"She's just so weak, like her art and her books," Lilly says in a tone I don't recognize. It's not familiar to me because she's been masking this persona for the last ten years.

"She isn't good enough. I keep telling her to give up and just focus on our relationship," Liam chimes in just as he grabs my best friend's ass and kisses her.

My stomach coils just as bile rises in my throat, staring at his fingers digging into her over her dark purple dress. I can't stop blinking as my muscles convulse as I hold the tray of champagne in my hand.

I think I'm going to be sick.

"She's burning and crashing. No one is going to buy this shit." Eli continues to spill his truth.

"One star for trying," Lilly adds, gripping Liam's hand as though she's done this a thousand times. Red paints her cheeks as she looks at Liam with clear admiration twinkling in her brown eyes. Batting her lashes, she tugs at her lip seductively.

What the hell?

How long has this been happening behind my back?

This has to be a damn nightmare. This can't be real.

I drop the tray of champagne. My hands couldn't stop shaking. The glass and alcohol spray the floor everywhere as everyone in the room pins their gazes at me. The shattering sound draws everyone's attention to the accident. Still frozen from the raw emotions, my bones continue to tremble in place.

"Oh, shit," Liam mutters, letting Lilly go. His hand zaps away from her like she's a disease.

Yeah, oh shit is right, jackass.

"Coraline? Babe?" Liam walks away from a smirking Lilly. She palms her mouth as she saunters closer to a guilty Eli, failing to hide the unremorseful curve of her red lips.

I think she wanted this to happen by the way her gleeful expression doesn't falter.

Betrayal stings my eyes, and my vision blurs.

Jazz music continues to play when he reaches me. He grabs both of my wobbling, cold hands and holds them tight.

"Hey. I know what this looks like, I promise it's not—"

"It's not what I think?" I interject. I look away from my supposed friends and gaze into my husband's brown orbs instead. "A little cliche, don't you think?" I pull out of his callous grasp as tears roll down my face. "My best friend? Lilly?"

It hurts to say her name. It feels like poison on my tongue.

"How could you?" I say, pain intertwining with my quivering tone.

"I'm sorry. She's...been there for me." His brows raise, remorse evident on his face. He's breaking my heart and has the audacity to act like he's the one who is hurting? "Let's talk about this somewhere private?"

"No," I interject. "I don't want to go anywhere with you privately," I snap.

Liam looks around the room as whispers around us grow louder. This is so humiliating.

"It's just that your art isn't doing well."

"I do it because it's what I love to do!" I concede sadly.

I look straight into Eli's eyes as I say the last word I'll ever speak to him again.

"Someone anonymously bought all of my shit art tonight," I tell him loud enough so Eli can hear him as another tear rolls down my cheek.

That's why I was carrying a tray full of champagne. It was to tell them the good news...to celebrate.

"I've given you all of me, even if I didn't have much to give you, you told me it was enough." I take a step back and wrap myself in my arms.

He gets a promotion at work, and his arrogance reaches new heights. Loving him, taking care of him as my art kept us afloat these past few years. I know it barely paid the bills, but it was enough.

I thought I was enough.

"Lilly. Why?" I ask over Liam's tense shoulder.

Somehow, her betrayal is hitting harder.

She can't meet my eyes. Instead, she lets her face fall and uses Eli as cover.

Cowards.

All of them.

Lilly walks over to Liam, grabs his shoulder, and squeezes. I can see my sullen reflection through her manicured nails.

"Coraline. You will never be enough. You weren't good enough for Liam or being an artist. You'll never make it," Lilly whispers, pouting mockingly, making fun of my heartache as she rests her chin on his shoulder.

Liam rolls his eyes and tries to nudge her off, but she doesn't budge.

"Coraline. Please, let's go outside," Liam pleads, reaching for my hand.

I chuckle and swivel my head left to right.

I take my wedding ring off my finger and squeeze it tight. I give him one last unforgiving stare. I want to curse at him and scream my lungs out at him, but I think he's embarrassed me enough for the last time. I walk away without another word. They don't get to see me fall apart, so with my morals held tight to my chest, I stay quiet.

It's what I'm good at.

THE SOUND of my neighbor's Christmas music snaps me out of the horrible memory. "All I Want For Christmas" by Mariah Carey vibrates through the walls, and I can't help but chuckle. She has played it every year on November first for the past four years.

I stare at my iPad and empty canvases sitting on my wooden desk. My art. My passion. My outlet out of this cruel world… and yet I still can't bring myself to draw. My art is created from dreams.

And lately, my ability to dream is broken.

It's destroying me.

Sulking, wallowing, my shoulders droop. I shut the door and head back into the living room. As soon as I reach the couch, I let myself drop dramatically and bury my head, face-first into the Christmas decorative pillows.

Maybe going to Sleepy Coldwater to meet other artists will help inspire me. I think I've disappeared from my art for too long. Whether it will help or not, I want to go and get out of the house and do something instead of watching reruns of my favorite comedy shows.

The betrayal happened three months ago, and after that, I tried to take my own life. The affair was one thing, and it turned into a deep depression I couldn't get out of.

I didn't feel like I was enough for anything or anyone. I was drowning, and nothing could save me. There were no magic words that someone could say to me to pull me out of it. There was no beacon of light. It wasn't a self-pity party of one. It was deeper than that. Depression felt like self-destruction, and I couldn't save myself.

I tried to say goodbye.

But death wouldn't have me.

I'm still here. Still trying to smile and still trying to live.

I'm trying.

Life keeps teaching me lessons in the worst ways possible. My trust has been betrayed more times than I can count. I'm starting to think that isolation has never been a bad thing. Maybe it's a way to protect myself. If you don't open enough to trust, you can't get hurt.

CHAPTER 2
CORALINE

This was a last-minute trip, but I managed to gather some art pieces together that I hadn't shown anyone to take to the Holly Jolly Arty Event. Holly Jolly Arty...how festive is that?

I shipped watercolor pieces and oil paintings. I'm still learning how to draw people. It's pretty tricky getting all the shading done.

After my plane landed, I took an Uber to the nearest restaurant, ate warm, delicious soup dumplings, and spent the rest of the night exploring until my feet hurt.

As I stand in the middle of the street by a black lamppost with a red bow tightly secured around the top, eating a raspberry cheese danish and watching the snow slowly fall around me, I smile. A smile that feels weightless and reaches my eyes and ears. The stars twinkle brighter in the sky here. The people are friendly. There are no cell phones in sight. All the simple feel-good emotions run through me, making me feel like a kid again on Christmas night.

Sleepy Coldwater is a cute small town in the mountains of Alaska. Everyone knows everyone by the way every store owner talks. There are a few schools, one medical center, one movie theater, and many small businesses. I've visited almost every single store deep on the main street of downtown. There's a cute winter coat store with thick fuzzy socks, called Cozy Fuzzy. A bakery shop called Sugar Plum & Butter that sells cookies, brownies, chocolate-covered pretzels, and strawberries, owned by a retired veteran couple who served in the United States Army. They've been married for over sixty years.

I'm in love with this place. The perfect getaway I didn't know I needed. Maya was right about Sleepy Coldwater. I'm glad I came here over Anchorage, even though the commute to the event is longer than I anticipated. I have a chance to do some soul-searching and much-needed healing.

TODAY IS the day of the showing. I'm in the backseat of a taxi, with a frozen pink nose, red lipstick, and rosy cheeks, wearing white mittens. Freezing but excited. My depression can fuck off today because I want to be able to remember why I started creating again without that menacing voice in my head telling me that I'm not good enough. I'm nervous yet excited to meet other artists and people who are also passionate about art. I haven't been to a showing since I found my ex with his hand on my ex-best friend's ass.

I take off my gloves to send Maya a daily reminder that I'm alive and well. It's hard to type with them on; next to impossible. I always check in with her and my older sister, Everly. Ev has told me numerous times how jealous she is that I'm in Alaska before her.

Holding my cell phone tight in my hands, my finger pats the screen as I text Maya.

ME:

Have I told you how much I love you?

MAYA:

I told you. It's stunning, isn't it?

ME:

Yes!

MAYA:

Bring me back a souvenir. Also, I already booked your return flight. Check your e-mail for the itinerary. I forwarded it to you ten minutes ago. NOW.

ME:

Yes, Mom. 😊 I'm surprised you're getting these texts. The signal is extremely choppy here. It's bad. I don't have service ninety percent of the time.

MAYA:

Good. You get to disconnect. Enjoy nature.

The art convention is held downtown. Every street lamp is decorated with warm lights strung from top to bottom. Everyone walking wears a peaceful smile on their joyful faces, along with their winter coats, mittens, and beanies. The snow grows heavier by the second, but I noticed how well the sidewalks are paved for walking. Everything looks so clean and organized, with nothing out of place.

My eyes glow, soaring with glee and caffeine. I palm the viciously cold windows, mesmerized by the snow-covered mountains in the distance and the thick white flurries that keep falling. It's been an eventful drive with breathtaking views. We drive past the Sugar Plum and Butter bakery, and my mouth waters instantly as the familiar smell of freshly baked buttery bread and confections fills the air. I need to stop by after the event.

"Does it always snow like this every winter?" I ask my driver as I continue to watch the flurries fall and stick. We don't get snow in Texas, and if we do, it's rare. Piano Christmas music plays on the radio. It feels like magic. I'm too glued to the town to look at her. My fingers hold the door window. Frosty temperature bites back, leaving warm fingerprints, but I'm soaking up every minute of being in a different part of the world. When I remove my hand, the white prints slowly fade, and I drink in the historic buildings as the car continues to move.

"It does. However, the local news warned everyone a week ago that we're expecting the worst snowstorm in decades. An arctic blast is running through. I hope you have everything you need while riding out the storm wherever you're staying. Oh. Another tip, stay away from—" She doesn't get to finish. Before I can blink, I'm rocketing forward, and my seatbelt tightens over my chest, restricting my breath. The car brakes harshly, the screeching over the tires looming. We're sliding for one agonizing second before the car comes to a stop.

"That was close," she murmurs before cursing under her breath as she stares at the prominent dark figure in front of the hood of the car.

In front of us is a moose with snow blanketing the tips of its antlers. It slowly trudges along, and my eyes grow wide as I take in the animal I've seen in pictures but never in real life. Its dark brown fur coat is thick, and it strolls with long strides. Shaking its head, the snow falls from the antlers and onto the pavement. It saunters over to the other side of the street, where it's nothing but vast land with tall trees. I follow its tracks, my head tilting as it goes. It turns a corner, disappearing.

"Are you alright?" she asks, her voice shaky. "Moose," she huffs, tightening her hands over the steering wheel. She lowers the dial on the radio before glancing over her shoulder. "Marvelous creatures. You'll find them everywhere. Downtown, the hospital, even your backyard." She shakes her head, forcing a lazy grin.

"Yes, I'm okay." My heart rate slowly returns to normal. I thought we were going to crash. With my hand on my tightening chest, I lay my head back down on the seat and take a deep breath. Shutting my lids, I rub my temples.

"Well, the good news is, we've made it to your destination. The Holly Jolly Arty Event." My eyes spring open. I quickly gather my mittens and place them back on.

She points to the right side of the car, landing on a four-story building by the sidewalk with sharp icicles lining the gutters.

"Oh, we're here!" I exclaim as I grab my purse. "Thank you so much."

CHAPTER 3
CORALINE

J climb out, close the door, and practically rush inside
the building. My toes collide with the sidewalk, and I
almost trip, but I regain my stance. I rush each arm through my
coat and hook my purse over my shoulder.

I stand still, absorbing the building from the bottom up. My
lips tilt upwards. I push open the tall, thick ebony doors, and the
warm air is the first thing to greet me. The heater is blasting
inside. I shrug off my top-layered coat and swing it over the
crook of my arm as I take in my surroundings.

The first floor is vast, with brown leather couches in the
main lobby. An elderly couple, hand in hand, walk in front of
me toward a small bar. It's made up of eight barstools and five
round tables that sit up to four. A group of men saunters past
me, dressed head to toe in Sitka camouflage.

"Excuse us, darlin'," one of them says, their lips slanting.

I nod in return, striding out of their way. As soon as I step to
my right, I find a sign with a red arrow pointing to the receptionist. I glance at the clock, walking fast since there isn't a line.
My palms land on the wooden counter, gripping it, as the male
receptionist types on his keyboard. There's a wall full of vintage

wilderness photography shops, all from a photographer named Ariksen.

"Hello," my eyes meet the golden rectangle with his first name pinned onto his top, "Ian."

"Yes, ma'am. What can I help you with?" he asks with a chirp in his tone. His fingers rest on the keyboard.

"I'm looking for the conference room where the Holly Jolly Arty Event is being held."

He smiles and leans over the counter. I take a step back as he raises his arm and points to my left. It's a long, narrow hall leading to large double doors.

"If you head straight down that way, the volunteers for the event will help guide you into registration. They can help you more than I can." He runs a hand over his face. His smile falters before he grips a white cup of coffee with a label that says "Crickets Coffee Shop" and takes a sip.

"Thank you so much!" I exclaim. Pivoting to my left, I hug my black coat closer to my chest.

The familiar excitement makes my blood rush to my ears and causes my muscles to tense when the doors open. Some artists are heading in and out of the room. I see a blip of black tables already fully set up.

"Are you here for registration?" one of the volunteers dressed in all dark green clothing asks. There's a badge around her neck with the event's name and 'volunteer' written in festive font with a candy cane as a paintbrush and an artist's color palette.

"Yes, I'm Cora Brown." Cora Brown is my pseudonym.

Her honey eyes light up, and her jaw drops.

"Oh my gosh, I love your art so much." She gently places her hand on my shoulder.

My heart flips, and a sting hits my eyes.

"Y-you do?" I ask, trying so hard to blink away the grateful tears.

"Yes. Every time you drop new art in your shop, I buy it all! Everyone loves you here."

My mouth falls open.

"Everyone loves me here?" Surely, no one knows who I am. "What's your name?"

"Willa," she replies.

"Well, thank you, Willa, that means so much to me."

Don't cry. Don't cry. Don't cry.

She loves my art? My art has reached people all the way in Alaska?!

This is…I have no words. This means so much to me. I work so hard to complete unique art pieces, and people admire them?

"Here, I'll help you register. The event starts in thirty minutes!" She extends her hand, guiding me to a booth outside. A line is already forming with other artists. Their faces are familiar. One of them spots me and waves me over. I recognize her from social media. I return the friendly grin and head toward her.

Ever since I've been here, my spark is reviving, and the urge to keep painting keeps growing.

I SIT in my little corner with my art pieces, proud, grateful to be here, and my lips can't stop curving optimistically. Lately, my sales have been doing well. When I get back home, I'm going to prioritize my creativity and remember my time here every day to motivate me to keep going, especially on the days when I feel like giving up.

Everything is set up. I sit down at my table and wait for my first meeting. Shania Twain's music plays louder, and my pulse rockets with excitement.

"Hi, Cora! Congratulations!"

My eyes light up. A tall woman with short curly blonde hair

holds a clipboard in one hand. She pats her fingers against the thighs of her light blue jeans.

"Hi. Thank you…for what exactly?" I ask while nervously tucking my hair behind my ear. I stand up from my chair to greet her properly. Her hands meet mine, and she shakes them.

"I'm so sorry. *Hello.*" She points to a name tag on their chest. "I'm Harper. Someone anonymously bought all of your art this morning when the phones were working; now they're down. Typical timing before a storm rolls in."

Wait. Someone bought all of my art…again?

"Really?" I breathe, fighting the genuine yet confused smile. I straighten my spine, glancing left and right. "Wow. Are you sure it was anonymous? I'd really like to meet them." I grip the ends of my top.

"Yeah. They didn't leave a name. Just said they wanted it all and made a huge offer for every single piece you shipped over here. Let me know how to transfer all the funds to your account. Your art is popular around here. Everyone is excited to see you!"

"Thank you. I, uh, am shocked," I whisper, still trying to digest the news.

"You shouldn't be. You're amazing, Cora." She takes out her cellphone and hastily dabs the screen. The room fills as a group of middle-aged women ambles over with giddy expressions. All of them hold a piece of my art from my shop in their hands.

I think I'm going to cry now.

After having my own husband and group of friends, who I considered my family at one point, degrade me and tell me I'll never make it…*it feels good.*

Hopeful. Inspiring. Reviving.

I work so hard. I sacrifice so much time to create.

"Do you have PayPal?" she asks.

"Yes, I do."

"Awesome, show me the QR code so I can scan it quickly. I

don't want to keep you too long. You already have a line of people excited to meet you!"

"You're not keeping me at all. One second, let me just…" I fumble with my purse. I unzip my purse and fumble through my wallet and receipts before my fingers land on my cell. When I take it out, my face drops, goosebumps break out on my skin from head to toe, and my stomach knots as my blood runs cold.

UNKNOWN:

How are you liking Sleepy Coldwater, Alaska, Coraline? Red lipstick looks good on you. Congrats on selling out again. I'll see you very soon.

CHAPTER 4
CORALINE

I stare at the screen, my hands trembling. My thumb hovers over the keypad, shaking as my breath catches in my throat. Everything is blurry as I process the words, re-reading them over and over again because I'm trying to convince myself this isn't real.

There are no digits attached to the message.

I thought these weird threatening messages were going to stop.

I brush my bottom lip with my fingers. I hold them in front of me, not remembering what shade of lipstick I put on before I came here.

Please don't be red.

My heart drops to my clenched gut when I see the staple holiday red shade deep in the crevices of my fingers.

Is someone watching me? Is he or she here? Is this the same person who left that weird letter in my mailbox? How do they know about me selling out again? How do they know I'm here in Alaska? Specifically, Sleepy Coldwater…

Blood rushes to my ears, and everyone and everything gets tuned out as I lock my knees.

This can't be happening.

I can't be getting stalked.

But it's real. I do have a stalker. It's happening, and all logic gets thrown out of the window as I try to process this.

"Is there something wrong, Cora?" Harper asks, concern painting her tone.

My brows knit together as I grind my molars until it hurts. Before I turn to her, I swipe and report it as spam. I refuse to let anything or anyone ruin this day. It's just a sick joke.

"Yes, everything is fine. Here's my QR code," I say, clicking on the app.

"Thank you," she chirps. Her cellphone camera aims at my screen.

"Hey, Harper, did you tell anyone else about my art being bought out?"

"Nope." She taps her screen faster. "Just you, Cora! Alright, I'm going to get going. Payment sent!"

THE EVENT WENT AMAZINGLY.

But now, I'm rushing.

I'm supposed to be at the airport in an hour, or I'm going to miss my flight. Before I left, I walked down the street and decided to rent a small sedan. There were no taxis or Uber's available to take me all the way to the Anchorage Airport because of the storm, so I'm trusting myself to get there on my own.

"I swear, Coraline Rosa, if you do not take off your wedding ring, I'm going to pull it off your finger the next time I see you." Maya's annoyed tone filters through the car speakers.

I sent her a picture of myself standing in front of my table before I started driving.

I dart my eyes to the square-cut diamond on my ring finger.

Looking at it burns as memories of a false love I thought was real mockingly glare back at me. I should take it off. Throw it in a river. Pawn it. Sell it. Give it back to Liam. Or simply take it off...But I still wear it.

I hope I'm not alone in this. I hope it's more common than I think because right now I feel like I'm the only one. Being married for years to someone I thought was going to be my forever life partner, and then for it all to fall apart? Just a few months ago? I'm a bleeding, hopeless romantic who loves with all her heart. Who gives more than she takes, and still it took everything in me to walk away. Even though I knew it was going to hurt, I had to do it. *For me.*

I don't deserve the cliche affair that happened behind my back.

It's going to take me some time to let him go. Every time I try to move on, I think about all the good times we had together —all the great things about him.

What I need to remind myself of, truly, is the real dick he was.

He broke my heart. He made sure to remind me every other day that my curves and weight were too much, always hinting that I should eat less. He brought down my spirit. Yet, even though he would say these things, I love my body. There's nothing wrong with me; it's all him.

He was a lying, cheating asshole who made me feel like something was wrong with me, and I wasn't enough for him. And then with my so-called best friend? Of all people?

"I don't want to talk about it," I reply.

"Okay...how are you still in Sleepy Coldwater? Girlfriend, you're going to miss your flight." I can see the judgmental scowl on her fair skin through the phone.

I sarcastically let out a loud, dramatic gasp so she can hear me over the thundering windshield wipers and howling glacial winds.

"Wow, Maya. I wonder who booked me *far away* from the nearest airport!"

"I know. Who the fuck did that? You should fire them." She burps.

Cringing, I stare at her contact portrait across my screen and glare at it as though she's next to me in the passenger seat.

"Okay, so by your words, I should fire you." I scoff.

I crane my head forward as though that'll get the thick snow flurries to stop battering my car. My eyes narrow, squinting, trying to stabilize my hands on the wheel to stay in my lane. I haven't seen a car drive by since I started driving. Everyone is probably inside. It's so dark out, and the snow won't stop.

"Fire me and see how well that works out for you." I hear the sound of liquid bottoming a glass.

"Now it's making more sense. How many glasses of wine have you already had tonight?"

"First of all," she slurs, "it's the weekend. And second of all, this is my second wine bottle, but who's counting?"

A laugh bubbles out of my lips.

"Apparently you are," I retort. I twist the heating dial on the Honda Civic to the highest setting because I can still feel the freezing temperature outside. How can people endure brutal winters like this? I love the snow, but only when I'm indoors underneath a pile of fluffy blankets.

I dialed Maya as soon as I started to drive. I told her about the event, but left out the part about the weird messages. She still doesn't know about the letter.

"Where are you?" she asks.

It's pitch black outside. The temperature is dropping so fast that it's below zero.

"Honestly, I'm not sure, somewhere in the mountains. The blizzard is here. It rolled in five hours ahead of schedule." I groan.

"Oh shit," she clips.

My heart drops to my ass.

"What, 'oh shit'? There shall be no, *oh shitting*, right now! I forbid it!" I tighten both hands on the steering wheel.

"I just checked the status of your flight." Static cuts into the call. "It's been can—" Her voice drops into nothing but grainy noise.

"It's been what?" My GPS suddenly spins in circles, distracting me. My stomach flips as I watch it reroute.

"Come on, don't you go out on me!" I'll be stuck up here in the mountains because I don't have a physical map on hand; I'm using my cell.

My feet are on the brake, lightly stepping until I'm slowing down to a complete stop at a stop sign. Finally, the GPS reroutes successfully. I exhale, relieved. Instead of taking a right, it's telling me to go left. It cut the distance time by five minutes, so maybe it's onto something. I take a left.

"Maya?" I call out.

"Coraline, are you still there? I—" Her voice goes out again. My gaze hardens at her contact name. "Y-your flight is—"

"Maya! Are you there? Can you hear me?" I shout, just as a pile of snow falls from a tree and lands on my windshield. I duck my head inside the car and swerve.

This is my worst nightmare. I'm pretty sure I'm in the middle of nowhere, and Mother Nature seems to be very angry tonight. I'm supposed to be at the airport by now, but everything is going wrong. It started when I couldn't get a taxi or an Uber after the event. Hell, I didn't even have time to report the weird, cryptic messages from my stalker. I'm on edge. I just want to be home.

"I can hear you." *Static.* "Barely!" she responds. "Your flight has been canceled. I'll book you another, but you need to find," her voice goes out, "shelter! Go to a hotel or—"

The phone beeps three times. I flick my gaze to the screen and see that the call's been dropped. There are no bars, and my battery is running low. But somehow, my GPS is still working. I hit the call button on her contact, but there's no service.

Of course, there isn't—just my luck.

"Crap!"

Another strong wind rattles my car, forcing it to sway to the left and almost hitting the metal guard rail that protects drivers.

Stay calm. Stay calm. Stay calm.

As much as I would love to say I can endure country life, I cannot. It's been absolutely beautiful, peaceful, and majestic to be up here in the mountains these past few days, but being out here in the dark is making me miss city lights.

Now, all I see is black fog mixed with mist. My windshield keeps getting hit by giant snowflakes that even the wipers can't keep up with anymore.

Suddenly, a huge gush of wind blows by, making me steer my vehicle. I almost ram it on the side of the mountain before I'm plowing it back straight again. The storm is getting wilder by the second.

My heart thunders, adrenaline coursing through my veins, making my senses go into overdrive. I'm hyper alert, and I grip the steering wheel so tight it pinches my palm. A truck has its high beams on behind me, blinding me. The driver is flashing their lights, getting dangerously close to my bumper. I speed up, squinting in my rearview mirror.

What is their problem?!

I push on the gas. Maybe this person is in a hurry. I'm going ten miles per hour over the speed limit right now, and it's still not enough for the person behind me. I swing my hand to the left side of my head like a signal.

"Dude, go past me!"

They don't budge. Their horn blares over and over again as they trail my exact movements. My anxiety is about to explode, and I feel a lump in my throat from being so damn nervous.

"Stop! You're going to hit me, asshole!" I whisper-yell to myself.

Then, I feel it.

The truck crashes into the back of my car.

CHAPTER 5
CORALINE

"*A*h!" I let out a piercing shriek.

The seatbelt tightens across my chest as I blink hard. My tires screech as I try to outmaneuver him without crashing into him, but he doesn't let up—the vehicle slides as I make another turn down the mountain. Somehow, I regain control of the car.

How many freaking turns are there? How tall is this mountain? And why the hell is this guy trying to make us both crash?

"He did not just hit me…" I say aloud, quickly glancing in my rearview mirror as the truck mirrors my every move. My muscles tense as I grow furious.

The engine roars louder as I push on the gas. It's such a narrow road, there's barely enough room for two cars. He's making it impossible to escape.

"Take the exit," the robotic GPS voice instructs me over my rattled breaths. My chest rises and falls erratically. Shit, I have to turn *now*.

So I do.

Then my phone pings. Service. Internet. Signal. My lips curve hopefully. I peer at my screen and internally celebrate. I can report this asshole to the Sleepy Coldwater police and look for a hotel.

I have service, holy hell, I—

UNKNOWN:

I told you I would be seeing you soon.

UNKNOWN:

You shouldn't be driving out in a storm like this.
It's dangerous.

It's him.

Everything feels like it's in slow motion. Blood thrums in my ears as I slowly look in the rearview again. I don't stop driving. My fear triggers autopilot.

UNKNOWN:

It's perfect, actually. Coraline Rosa loses
control of her car while driving in the record
storm and dies tragically. They'll never suspect
it was a truck.

Scrunching my nose, I lunge forward and snatch it. Still driving and being chased, I manage to plug 911 into the keypad. An agonizing pause of silence thickens my anxiety before it finds a connection. It rings twice before the call is dropped.

"No! Damn it!" I stare into the rearview mirror and see a silhouette. It looks like a man behind the wheel, but I can't see any more details. It's too dark, and his headlights are blinding.

"What the hell do you want from me, you crazy asshole?!" I scream inside the car, not caring if he can hear or see me anymore. My eyes are pinballing from the rearview mirror and the road before me.

The sound of his truck engine roars louder, the head of this car swallowing the view.

Here he comes.

I dodge him by frantically spinning the wheel to my left, my heart in the base of my throat with fear so paralyzing it's streaming in my blood.

Am I going to die?

Is this how he wants to end me?

When I think I've outmaneuvered him, he hits me in the right corner of the car's bumper harder and more precisely, like he has a goal to get me off the road…and he's winning. I'm in a cyclone. I'm trying to keep up, but I'm no match for the winds, the snow, and the maniac. He won against my desperate efforts. My car spins into circles, and the next thing I know, I'm flying. Airborne. The top of my head crashes into the roof of the vehicle. I'm off the road, smashing straight through the metal barrier and rolling down the side of the mountain.

Oh no!

Please, no!

I scream just as I'm being thrown against my will against the side of the car. My seatbelt cages me inside as my car hits a tree, and then another tree. I can't hold myself up. Everything is out of my control. I feel helpless as I try to hold onto something. The only thing I can do is register my blood-curdling screams.

Every single window breaks, and pieces of glass fly everywhere. Shards are exploding, then carving their way into my body. I'm clawing at everything to make my body stop hitting the inside of the vehicle, but I can't hook my fingers into anything. It's all too much, and it's all happening too damn fast.

As I continue to roll down the mountain and gain control of the uncontrollable spinning, memories enter my head. My life is literally flashing before my eyes.

Christmas dinners. The beach. The first day I held my first art piece in my hand. Traveling, Italy…the future that I've been so excited about, all of my plans are in my head, blurring together, the ache in my soul growing, and a final blow to my head takes me out, silencing my screams and my pain. I close my eyes to protect them from the glass and accept my fate.

Everything goes numb and quiet.

PAIN AND THE COLOR BLACK. That's all that makes sense. There's a ringing in my ear and warmth trickling down my face like a tear that starts from my hairline.

I can't move. My limbs don't feel like they're my own. Something is lying heavily on my chest, unforgivingly, cementing me to the ground.

Then, the sound of an engine buzzing, the familiar icy, strong winds, and the cold air biting my skin are palpable. I want to scream, but my tongue and lips stay still. A metallic, iron tang fills my throat.

Is this blood?

My chest rises and falls faster.

Where am I? What's going on? Am I dead? Is this all a nightmare? Am I sleeping? Why does my whole body hurt?

Suddenly, I regain my senses. All of my limbs come alive. I groan, blinking slowly and hard. As soon as I'm able to keep them open, it's a blurry sky and white orbs that glimmer all around me.

I'm twisted in an uncomfortable position, staring up at the dark sky, but there are no stars or moon in sight—ribbons of thick smoke swirl in front of me. Tears slide out of the corner of my eyes. Shaking, trembling, my finger tips are burning.

Frostbite? How long have I been lying here in the snow?

I turn to my left and see a car that's been totaled, wrapped around a tree, and it looks unrecognizable—crumpled, broken, torn pieces of machinery litter the ground, sinking into the growing snow.

I've been in an accident.

Fear claws at me. I try to move, but I still can't feel my legs. Are they moving? The world spins as exhaustion knocks on my door, tempting me to fall back into sleeping shadows. My vision blurs trees and the raining snow carousels, until I'm seeing everything in twelve different versions. In my periphery, there's a truck.

The same all-black truck that struck me.

I've got to get out of here now.

"N-no." My tongue is numb as I struggle to get the one syllable out.

Darkness and trepidation anchor me further, and I close my eyes against my will. But before I succumb to my injuries, I see a masked man dressed in all black. I can't get any details. He bends his knees, resting his forearms on his legs as he hovers over my face.

My chest tightens as he stares at me. His eyes are as dark as night—obsidian pools void of emotion. I'm as cold as ice when he tucks his gloved fingers underneath his mask and is about to pull it off, but stops.

I tremble all over as the realization dawns on me. This is the same person who wants me dead. I know he's the one responsible for all the threats.

He towers over me, and just when I try to tell him to get the hell away from me, my heart hammers until my head feels light as a feather, and shadows swallow me.

CHAPTER 6
CORALINE

"**W**ake up."

A voice.

It's a woman's voice. She sounds older; her raspy voice is laced with patience.

Flashes of bloodied snow, my car in pieces, me getting flung out of a moving car and buried in snow come back like a slap in the face. Blood pulses in my ears, tremors infiltrating my muscles as the memories play out. Groaning, I expand my arms like wings, fast and ready to fight.

"You're awake," she says, relief lifting her voice. "You're okay."

Everything is warm.

I'm in a bed. Soft blankets, warmth, a fire crackling in the distance. It's not unbearably freezing. It smells good. Like cinnamon and butter, with a hint of nature. As though the smell of tree bark is thick and wrapped around cedar. Opening my eyes, my gaze snaps to a large rectangular window centered on a dark, wooden wall. The snow is still falling harshly. The blizzard is very much alive and hasn't died out a bit. Despite the horrific last moments of my life, the view is beautiful from the bed. It's even better than the hotel room Maya booked for me.

My head feels like it's been beaten.

."Don't move. Take it slow," she tells me.

I track the voice just as I shudder. Moving my head to the right, my cheek softly brushes against a white pillow. It's an older woman, likely in her seventies, who sits in a rocking chair in the corner of a bedroom. Her right hand is balled over a cane as she rocks, nonchalantly. "How are you feeling?" she rasps out.

Like I'm dying.

She's dressed in a thick white top jacket, with straight white hair, wrinkles, and aged freckles littering her face, and a pair of pale, bright blue eyes stare back at me.

"Where," I swallow. My dry tongue swirls in my mouth as I taste iron. "Am I?"

"You're in Sleepy Coldwater. Alaska? Ariksen's ranch."

She says, 'Ariksen,' like I'm supposed to know what that means.

"Who?" I quirk a brow.

She points to the other side of the room, and I follow her finger.

A tall, broad man in a black sweater stares back at me. Fair skin, a strong nose, dark, tousled hair, and a beard with deep sky-blue eyes stare back at me, surveying me with a strong, unwavering gaze. He doesn't say anything. His brows are pinched inward like he's trying to figure me out or like he's worried. I'm not sure if it's both.

He looks older than me. Maybe late twenties, early thirties. He's masculine, his arms and thick thighs are strained beneath his clothes. His large, veiny hands look calloused from where I'm lying—a muted, pale blue, dim streak of lighting from outside beams on him.

"And you're Ariksen? Is this your house I'm staying in?" I grumble, setting my forearms on both sides of me as I try to lift myself higher in a sitting position, but pain stabs me in the ribs. I'm forced back down, and the back of my head plummets onto the cold, soft pillow, softening the blow.

"Everything hurts." I close my eyes, gritting my teeth, feeling desperately helpless. My body feels like a bulldozer ran over it.

"Honey, don't move. You've been in an accident. Can you tell us your name? We couldn't find your wallet in the wreckage," the elderly woman asks me as she gets up with her cane, and Ariksen continues to watch me agonize.

He still doesn't say anything. Just watches me with a penetrating gaze.

"Why does it hurt to breathe?" I groan.

"What's your name?" she asks urgently.

"My name is C-Coraline." I look at my hands covered in lacerations. "Coraline Rosa," I repeat, staring at my hands over the blanket—my mind blanks.

"I'm Merelyn," she introduces herself, but I'm in no mood to be proper. I want to get straight to the point.

"Where's my car? My phone is in there." I croak out as I touch my head. The front of my head is bandaged up. I pull back my hand until it rests on my side. "Who are you guys? I'm going to miss my flight." I palm my sweaty chest as I try to prevent the panic from completely taking over. Gasping, I try to even out my breaths before I can't anymore. "Wait. Don't I need to get to a hospital?"

They both stare at me with wide eyes and pale faces.

My chest heaves—my heart pounds. And a full-blown anxiety attack ensues.

"All flights are canceled. The nearest hospital is hours away." The lady says as she glances at Ariksen, but he doesn't return her gaze. He's still glued to me.

"Stop staring at me and start talking. Say something!" I shout at him desperately. "Someone crashed into me! Someone is trying to kill me!"

"Honey, calm down." Merelyn instructs.

"Calm down? You want me to calm down? You're telling me I've been in an accident. My head is bandaged. My body feels like I've broken dozens of bones. I'm in a house with two strangers in the middle of a snowstorm, there's someone who ran me off the road, and you want me to *calm down?*"

"Yes," a deep voice cuts in. I whip my attention to the man in the corner. "You need to calm down. We're here to help," he replies. "I'm Gavin Ariksen, and we're only here to help you."

"Well, Gavin Ariksen," I spit mockingly. "Why haven't you guys called the police? Or an ambulance? I need a doctor!" I spiral.

"We did, dear. No one will come up here during the storm. The roads are covered in snow. The winds are dangerous. They said as long as you are stable, you should be okay. I'm a retired surgeon, and from what I can see, you're stable."

"Stable?!"

"Listen, Coraline," Gavin barks, and I rear back. "I know you're scared, hurt, and confused, but I can assure you, it's better to be *in here* than out there," he points to the window beside him, "where I found you. Your heart rate and blood pressure are normal. You don't have any broken bones. A few deep lacerations that will *maybe* leave a scar on your pretty face, but you're going to live," he insists in a commanding tone. "You're alive. Stop complaining."

My jaw drops.

"But I don't know you," I breathe, my voice barely a whisper. "Someone tried to kill me. They ran me off the road, making me crash. And I'm just supposed to trust you?" I squint at him, then flick my worried gaze to Merelyn. Her expression dulls. "I'm not supposed to be here. I-I was supposed to be on a plane back to Texas!" My stomach turns as memories of the text messages I received on the road come back to my mind. What if he's still out there? "I think I'm going to be sick."

I stand quickly. *Too quickly*, as stars dance in the distance, all around the cabin.

"I can't be here. I need to leave. He might find me here! I have to go." I beeline toward the bedroom door, not caring if I feel like I'm going to faint. My knees wobble underneath me as I skitter across the floor in socks. I look down to see I'm in an oversized dark green one-piece gown that reaches just above my knee.

"Who is he? What are you talking about? Stay in bed!" Merelyn advises as she clutches her cane.

"You're freaking out. Calm down," Gavin adds.

"Yes, because miraculously, I'll calm down just because you say to. I don't think that's how it works."

Gavin jumps out of the chair, his cowboy boots thud thunderously against the wooden floor as he races toward me. Still, he's on the far left side of the bedroom, and it gives me an advantage over him so I can beat him to the door.

Luckily enough, it's only a few feet away. Before the older woman can push me back down onto the bed or grab my arm, I twist the black knob and stumble out of the room. That's when I realize I'm in a cabin—made with rock and wood everywhere.

Eight-point antlers on the walls. Photos of nature, birds and animals, flowers, waterfalls, and the aurora lights are framed. I bypass the living room with floor-to-ceiling windows, holding on to the fireplace for balance.

"Sit down, stubborn small woman. You're going to hit your head *again*." Gavin is on my heels, and as soon as I feel his hand coil around my bicep, I'm sliding my arm out of his hold. The next thing I know, I'm in a kitchen with a large marble island.

"I'm fine. Just fine!"

"You're not fine. But hey, be my guest. Open that door and see if there's a taxi parked a mile away by the closed gate, because yes, no one can get onto my ranch without me opening it for them."

I find the front door, and I manage a weak smile on my sore, bruised face. Looking down my body, I re-analyze my stupidity and impulsiveness.

Shit. He's right. What the heck am I doing?

Standing at the front door, I chew on the inside of my lip as my blood continues to throb in my ears wildly. My head is pounding viciously. The stars are multiplying by the second, and I don't have my wallet or even shoes. I look down at my feet and wiggle my toes slowly.

Pivoting on my foot, I face him, out of breath. My chest rises and falls faster. In the kitchen light, he looks…handsome. Too handsome. *Of course, he's hot.* And I hate how I notice his beauty. Attraction ignites like a wildfire when we lock eyes. I physically feel my cheeks flush as he holds my gaze. Blinking slowly, I run my fingers across my temples, nervously, breaking contact. The air between us hums and sparks…or maybe that's the fire's crackles coming from the living room. I don't know.

All I know is that I need to really calm down and lie down.

I'm being stupid. Merelyn and Gavin are only trying to help me, and freaking out isn't going to help my situation.

"Look, I'm sorry," I apologize, shaking my head.

"Don't be. You've been in an accident. Get some rest, and we'll talk more," he tells me softly, his hand reaching for mine. I stare at it like it's going to bite me, yet his soft blue eyes bleed honesty. He wants to help me, I can see it in the way he waits for consent to touch me—to take his hand. There's something about the way he talks and keeps his gaze on my face, clearly trying to figure me out without asking too many questions.

He's a gentleman.

"Nothing makes sense to me right now and—"

The corner of my vision darkens, my hearing slowly going silent as I fall into shadows. The last thing I feel before I'm out is Gavin's arms wrapped around my legs and head.

CHAPTER 7
CORALINE

Screaming.

Someone is screaming so loud it makes my stomach flip upside down. The scream you hear in horror movies. A terror-filled scream that makes blood drain from your face.

As my fingernails claw deep into the thin white sheets, I realize *it's me* who's screaming. Then, I'm facing the wooden ceiling, sucking in large breaths vehemently, as though I've been drowning. My lungs burn, thirsting for air.

All I can do is yell from the horror that fuels my veins. My blood runs cold, but my skin is clammy. This feeling of being chased gnaws at my heart and soul, leaving me trembling and covering my mouth. I pull at it as I try to stop screaming, but nothing changes. I don't recognize my surroundings, which makes everything feel a thousand times worse.

Suddenly, the door explodes open, but I'm too afraid to look at the intruder. I stay screaming, frozen with terror. I'm afraid to move because I fear the man from the wreckage will come back and finish what he started. It's irrational, but I can't think straight right now with so much uncertainty hovering over me like a hopeless cloud.

I pull my knees to my chest like it'll save me from my attacker. Then I feel strong, big hands grip my biceps, squeezing me so tight that I open my eyes.

It's the man from earlier.

The one with the blue, enchanting eyes.

Gavin.

"You've got some lungs," he says hoarsely. "You're okay."

I stiffen, my body still shaking from the tremors. His hold intensifies gently; it steals me away from my panic attack.

He looks at me, worried, and doesn't let his grip on my body falter as the last yelps die out brokenly. I don't know why, but I trust him enough to let him help. It's rare for me to find those types of people. After one conversation with them, I feel safe, and that's how I feel with Gavin. If he wanted to hurt me, he would have already. Those green, highly texturized flecks in his vibrant blue console me, like a warm blanket. They flick side to side vehemently, searching for something deeper.

"I'm…I'm sorry. It was a bad dream." I breathe out heavily.

He blinks at the lamp to my right side and lets me go. He reaches over me, his shoulder brushing against mine, allowing me to get a whiff of his scent—masculine, minty, and natural, kind of like the smell of pine. He pulls the metal string of a lamp, turning on the light.

He watches me intensely as I try to calm myself down with each deep breath.

He probably thinks I'm crazy. Hell, I think I'm going crazy.

I hadn't realized I was crying until he brushes my cheek with the pad of his thumb, wiping my tear away horizontally until it's nothing. I watch him watch me, until the dread dissolves away slowly.

His dark, disheveled locks caress his forehead, as if he were in the middle of a deep sleep. I look down to realize he's not wearing a shirt, only black sweatpants. His chest hair hugs his pecs, and his ab muscles constrict as he breathes in and out. I'm freezing, dressed in layers of clothing, unable to feel my fingers entirely, but he's shirtless. It's probably because he's used to these kinds of conditions.

"I'm sorry for waking you up."

"Don't apologize," he replies instantly, still wearing an unreadable mask.

He shakes his head once and then reaches for my forehead. His fingers lift the bandage, like he's checking if I'm healing alright.

"It doesn't hurt. Not anymore," I murmur. Our bodies are so close I can smell him. He smells...good.

"Great." He clears his throat as though he's nervous. "You don't know me, and I know this must be horrifying. You've been through a lot in the past few days, but it looked like you needed someone to bring you out of that nightmare. I know PTSD when I see it," he says, inching further away on the edge of the bed. "I'm glad it doesn't hurt." He nods toward the top of my head. Then he places the bandage back in its place. He pushes me back down gently with his tight grip on my shoulders until my head falls back onto the pillow. He stands and takes a step back.

"Get some rest. I'll be on the couch," he says, spearing his hair with his hand and turning toward the door. "I'm sure you have a thousand questions running through your mind. I'll answer all of them in the morning, but—"

My anxiety spikes when I realize he's going to leave.

I don't want to be alone. I've never felt like this before. But that nightmare felt so real. Felt so vivid. It was more than just a figment of my imagination. It has to be a memory.

"How do you know about PTSD?" I blurt, cutting him off.

He stops walking and lifts a brow.

"What I'm trying to say is, have you had nights where you wake up screaming?" I ask.

I'm not surprised I've already developed some sort of fight or flight response. It has to be a symptom of my head injury.

He pivots on his feet until his attention is pinned on me.

"Worse." He folds his arms across his chest. "Nights where I wake up unable to speak."

I swallow. There's an underlying pain attached to his deep voice. Even though his sleepy tone is doing a good job at hiding it, sadness flickers through his eyes. That's when I see a clue into his life. Looking down, I spot a tattoo of the Navy SEAL trident on his bicep.

Is he in the military? A veteran?

"I'm going to get going. I have—" He takes another step toward the door, but I can't help it. I'm in a cabin in the middle of a snowstorm, terrified that the man who ran me off the road is still here, lurking.

"Wait, where's Merelyn?" I ask, truly curious. "Why are you sleeping on the couch? Is Merelyn occupying the other bedroom?"

"There's only one bedroom in my home. I live alone," he answers simply before he draws out a yawn.

"But where is she?"

There's a storm? I thought the roads were closed, and that's why I couldn't get to a hospital.

"She lives right next door on my land. Feet away. Goodnight, Coraline. Leave the questions for the morning."

I purse my lips together. The thought of going back to sleep and going back into my nightmares again terrifies me. Gavin notices my hesitation and does a double-take at me and the door, and starts to walk away.

The sound of the wind howling through the window before me calls my attention. I look at it and watch the snow patter harshly on the window glass.

He stops walking, and his back muscles tense up. He turns to me and has a softened expression.

I look at the ivory lampshade that sits on the wooden night-stand by my bed. There's a pile of aged books with tanned yellow paper and a notepad with a pen.

"I was dreaming about the car wreck. The person who forced me off the road in the first place."

His eyes pierce through me like daggers. I've struck his curiosity, and he watches me like he's testing me.

"Do you remember what he looked like?" he asks.

I shake my head.

"No. He was in a mask. It looked like he was going to take it off, but then I fainted."

Thunder draws my attention toward the window.

"Do you know why you would be getting chased?" he asks. "Do you know why this person is trying to kill you?"

"No." Furrowing my brows, I shut my eyes. "I don't want to be alone," I murmur as I sit up and swallow nervously. "That person who was chasing me down the road could be out there, watching me." I nip my bottom lip until it stings. "What if he tries to finish me off? What if he breaks in and hurts one of you? What if—"

His palm covers my mouth, silencing me. It was hard, almost like a slap.

"Hey!" I shout in his palm, but it comes out muffled as he continues to press down on my lips.

"No more fucking what-ifs. No one else lives up here. The roads will be closed for the next few weeks. Maybe even a month. No one is getting hurt." He removes his hand.

Slouching, I glare at him. Deep down inside of me, I know I needed that to snap me out of my anxiety.

"Weeks? A month?" I gasp. "I don't have a month here, Gavin."

I claw at my bedsheets again, and groan when I realize my

rib pain is back. I take in a sharpened breath and squeeze my eyes tight. Maybe if I take shorter breaths, it'll hurt less. I glance toward him again and wince.

"I don't know what to tell you. The phones are down. I have no internet. There's no signal. My ranch is hidden deep in the woods. Hell, I can't remember the last time I saw an airplane or helicopter fly overhead."

My heart sinks.

"How do you live out here like this?" I ask, trying to withhold my judgmental thoughts. I'm a city girl through and through. I can live without the busy streets and buildings, but no internet? No cell signal? In the Alaskan wilderness?

He takes a step forward like he's going to take a seat in the corner of the room where I first met Merelyn.

"Gavin, baby? Where are you?"

A woman calls out in the distance—her voice is different from Merelyn's. She sounds younger with a high-pitched tone. Does he have a girlfriend?

CHAPTER 8
CORALINE

"*O*h, is that your girlfriend?" I ask. "I thought you said you live alone?" My brows knit together as I turn my attention toward the door. The knob twists slowly.

He clenches his jaw and mirrors my gaze. His jaw flexes at a woman wearing the same sweater he wore yesterday, stumbling in, flushed, with messy bed hair. She's not wearing any pants. Her long, fair legs stride toward Gavin. She's barefoot with red-painted toenails.

As soon as she gets to him, she tiptoes, balancing herself on her feet so she can press her lips against his cheek. The woman is beautiful, tall, and radiates a glowing aura. He pulls away from her slowly and gently, apparently uncomfortable. He takes another long step as his lips thin. Her light green eyes light up when she looks my direction with flushed cheeks.

"Oh! She's awake," she says as she shifts behind Gavin, trying to make herself smaller. "I'm sorry, I thought you were still asleep. I'm Georgia." She waves her hand from side to side nervously.

Who is she to Gavin?

Who else has he failed to mention?

"It's alright," I say. "Do you live here?"

She parts her mouth, but Gavin cuts in.

"I'm going to sleep," he grumbles, flexing his jaw. "Georgia was just leaving." He tilts his head toward the opposite side of the room.

"I wanted to say my last goodbye before I head out." She looks up at him, her long lashes dancing as she blinks. "I have to go before sunrise…unless you've changed your mind? I can hole up here with you until the morning." She grabs his hand, pleading with him. "Before she wakes up." Her tone pleads as her eyes glimmer and dance with lust.

Before who wakes up? Should I leave the room so they can have it to themselves? Georgia clearly has no shame in throwing herself at him in front of me. I shift around the bed, gripping the blankets, trying to look busy to give them privacy.

He continues to look through her, not a word comes out of his clenched jaw as the snow falls hard behind them. Tall trees line up through the window, battering against each other with the strong winds—not a single building in sight. Only mountains. Not another neighboring cabin nearby. He really is in the middle of nowhere, Alaska.

There's an awkward audience of one sitting three feet away from her as she waits for his response.

He shakes his head once.

"You want me to leave? Right now?" She pouts, and he deadpans. He's emotionless, but the way he grabs the door to haul her out of my room tells me a lot. I don't think Georgia is his girlfriend.

When he shuts the door, I keep my eyes locked on the beautiful view outside. We don't have mountains in central Texas, and every time I gaze at the Alaska scenery, I'm in awe of its beauty. I settle deeper into the blankets, covering my legs and abdomen, still trembling from how cold I am.

Rolling my head left and right across the pillow, I toss and turn in bed and shut my eyes, listening to my new white noise—the blizzard winds. Then, I hear Georgia curse. Then curse again and again. I lose count after ten times. She's pissed because she wants to stay.

Is he really making her leave? I thought the roads were closed?

I hear her yell at him some more, loud footsteps thud away, and then she slams a door.

Who are these people?

THE LAST THING I remember from last night is Georgia slamming the door after being rejected during a very awkward conversation between her and Gavin. There has to be history there with the way she reacted.

Stretching my arms, I look to my right and see a massive figure on the couch.

It's Gavin, asleep on his side. His head rests on a pillow, and his chest rises and falls slowly.

He stayed the night in the same room?

Did he do it because I told him I didn't want to be alone?

He's...shirtless. His muscular back is to me, and I can't help but track every dip in his muscles. He's physically fit. Why is he sleeping without a shirt? It feels like we're snowed in the middle of the Tundra.

He has five intensely pink, aged scars that go down from his shoulder to his lower back, almost like slashes. A beautiful, detailed skull with a spider starts from his shoulder blades and ends at his lower back. Then there's a quote tatted alongside his ribs that makes its way toward his back in Gothic font. I try to read it, but then someone rings the doorbell, making me gasp, and I palm my mouth to stifle the scream in the base of my throat. Gavin stirs slowly, and I watch his back muscles taut, but then they relax as he shuffles. His legs slide out from the cushions, and he plants them onto the ground, while he bows his head and massages the nape of his neck. Dog tags with a silver chain settle in the middle of his chest, over a detailed raven perched on a sword tattoo.

I sit up, awkwardly, peeking through my hair strands, hoping he missed me gawking. At the end of the day, we're strangers, and I still don't know how I got here exactly. I'm afraid of him. I'm scared of everything right now.

Rising to his feet, he slides his palms into his black sweatpants. Sweat drips down his chest onto the hair above his groin. He palms his face, from his nose down to his bearded jaw, like he's trying to wake himself up. He grabs a T-shirt from the corner of the couch and slides it on.

I stare at him...I mean, truly stare at him this time, not caring if he catches me looking anymore, and take in how Godly handsome this man is. God took his time sculpting this man. His pointed nose is slightly pink, probably from sleeping on it. His bright blue eyes stare at the window outside, watching the snowflakes crash against the window unforgivably, where I catch vibrant flecks of dark green in the corners of the irises. Despite the grey weather, his fair skin is kissed deeply by the sun. He's handsome without even trying.

"You didn't have to tell your girlfriend to leave. I'm the one who's imposing here." I clear my throat. I tuck my knees to my chest, underneath the thick blankets, and wait for him to reply. We exchange glances. My heart skips a beat when we lock eyes.

His lips thin.

"Good morning," he says.

"Morning," I reply.

He sighs as the doorbell rings again.

"One, she's not my girlfriend, and two, you're not imposing."

"If she isn't your girlfriend, why is she here? I thought you said there are no neighbors and the roads were closed?"

"I guess we're already starting with the one hundred questions," he scoffs. "She's a live-in nurse for Merelyn for the most part. She helps take care of her daily. I leave a lot for work, so she keeps her company and makes sure she's okay, and takes her medication, stuff like that, when I can't."

"Who is Merelyn to you? Is she your mother?"

"No. She's not my mother, but she's the only person I consider family. I'll be back."

"Gavin!" Merelyn shouts as the sound of a door closes.

Before he walks out, his shadow looms over me as he stands in front of my face. He makes it harder to stay calm by the way his fingers push the hair out of my face, and he runs his thumb softly over my bandage. He lifts the gauze for a quick second, then places it back down.

"There's only one shower and bedroom, by the way. Shampoo and soap are inside." He leaves the room. The door barely makes a sound as it clicks shut. I wait a few more minutes before stretching out my sore muscles and using the restroom.

CHAPTER 9
CORALINE

After draining my bladder, I see shampoo, conditioner, an unused loofah, lotion, a toothbrush, and floss, all laid out perfectly for me to use. It's all new.

I strip off my clothes, and when I spot the bruises and healing cuts over my body, I shiver. My head still hurts, and I'm sensitive to light. These headaches I get won't go away, and I just know I have a TBI.

I need to get to a hospital after the storm passes to be checked for any additional injuries. I hold myself and tear my eyes away from my reflection. Dark half-moons are under my eyes. Even though I've slept for what feels like forever, it isn't enough.

I tear off the bandages from my forehead and toss them in the small black trash can sitting in the corner. The deep maroon slash I have begins at my temple, into my hairline, and ends in my scalp. *Ouch*. The cut is already scabbed over and stitched. I must have passed out when Merelyn or Gavin did them because I don't remember it. My hair has oil residue from whichever antibiotic cream they rubbed on me.

I neatly place my clothes on a wooden shelf above the toilet.

I survey myself in the bronze framed, rectangular mirror mounted above the sink. Deep black and purple bruises freckle the left side of my ribs. I swivel to my right to get a better view. I guess that explains the pain. I gently line my fingers against them, tracing them, testing how fresh they are. Luckily, I can touch my skin, and it doesn't sting.

My hair looks like a knotted mess. My thick black hair strands don't know which way to go as they defy gravity and stick out in all directions. My teeth and tongue feel gross. God, I need a shower.

I turn on the shower by twisting the silver knob. Once it reaches lukewarm, I step into the tub.

At first, I went straight for my hair. Cleaned my body and moved more gently over my cuts and bruises. Now that that's finished, I want to stay under the soothing water as long as I can. I turn the water off. The knob creaks until I can't turn it any longer. The water stops running and drips down the showerhead as I pull the shower curtains aside. Standing in front of the foggy mirror above the sink, I lean over and swipe it with my palm to create a window for my reflection. My dark hair clings to my collarbones.

I look way better after that shower.

I line the toothbrush with toothpaste when a drop of red falls into the sink bowl, then another, and another. Shit, I must have nicked the cut on my head when I was washing my hair. I steal a glance in the mirror when I spot a pale woman with darkened undereyes, blue lips, wearing a loose white satin dress behind me. She's looking straight at me, holding my scared gaze. Her skin looks like it's glowing. She reaches out to touch my shoulder, and I lose it. It all happens in a second. A string of horror ripples through my veins, making me scream—the tube of toothpaste crashes to the ground at my feet. I whirl around, hugging the towel tighter to my naked, wet chest.

The woman is gone.

Blood pounds in my ears as I try to control my racing heart. Goosebumps erupt all over my body as I blink hard and fast, checking every single corner of the bathroom for the woman. The door is still closed. It wasn't Merelyn. It wasn't Georgia. And it definitely wasn't Gavin.

Who the hell was behind me staring at me through the mirror with a dead expression in my restroom, because I refuse to believe I just saw a ghost. There's clearly a rational explanation for this.

I open the door and head straight for the dresser.

"*Oh hell no*. No. No. No. *No*," I sing-song, hiding the tremble in my voice as I tie oversized pants over my waist. "I just hit my head really hard, that's all. It's a delusion. A symptom of my possible and most likely concussion? I can't possibly be seeing..." My tongue stills.

Ghosts? Spirits? The dead?

"Please don't tell me this cabin is haunted, too." I shake my head, pacing up and down until I find my shoes hidden by the nightstand. "So there's no internet, no phones, no open roads, and I'm snowed in a haunted cabin with a cowboy? What could go wrong?" I mumble to myself, brushing my wet hair with my fingers.

"Coraline Rosa. Breakfast!" Merelyn shouts behind the door.

CHAPTER 10
CORALINE

"How did you find me?" I ask.

"I was bringing all the horses back into the barn when your car crashed through my fence. I heard the collision, and minutes later, I saw the fire and knew something was wrong, so I checked it out." He pats his lip with a napkin. "You were passed out in the snow with blood all over your face. I'm surprised you're walking and talking fine," Gavin says nonchalantly as he spoons more eggs onto his plate.

"Well, we don't know that for sure because an ortho doctor hasn't looked at me."

"If you broke something, you would know," Merelyn and Gavin say at the same time.

"And why didn't you guys call anyone?"

"I did," Gavin says, as though he's losing patience with me. "When we had service, I called the Chief of Police. He's one of my good friends, and he told me he couldn't send anyone up here. It's too dangerous to reach by vehicle or helicopter. He asked Georgia whether he thought you were stable, and she confirmed it wasn't an emergency. And when you woke up, the phones were down again. It happens every blizzard."

"How convenient," I mumble sarcastically before taking a bite of toast. The strawberry jelly tastes fresh and sweet, the salivation crashing wildly all over my taste buds. My stomach cramps, the acid already breaking down my first solid food in days. I can feel it all as I chew. I hum as I swallow.

"Yeah, it's convenient that I found you and you're not dead. A bear could've beaten me to it and dragged you to feed its cubs. Or the person you claim was chasing you down the road could've finished you off," he snaps. "When I found you, there was no truck, no strange man. You hit your head pretty hard, so maybe—"

"Then you must have scared the man away, Gavin," Merelyn interrupts his asshole rant, flashing him a scowl. He clears his throat and continues to shovel eggs and beans into his mouth, no longer glaring at me.

"I'm just saying that driving in the middle of a storm was stupid," he continues to berate me.

My jaw drops. This man is grumpy as fuck, and I'm supposed to be spending the next few days with him? He might be handsome, but he's a jerk.

Or he's just incredibly outspoken.

"That's fine, you don't have to believe me. Yes, it was stupid. I guess I'm stupid then. I know someone is after me, and I need to talk to the police, so whenever the phones are running again, let me know." Pushing my feet to the cold ground, I push the wooden chair back until it's screeching against the floor. I rise to my feet fast and pivot toward the bedroom I've been sleeping in.

"Dick," I mutter under my breath.

As soon as I get to the hallway, my stomach growls with a vengeance.

Fuck.

I whirl around and face the dining table again. I amble

toward it as Merelyn watches silently. I catch Gavin's eye twitching in my periphery as I fish the plate off the table.

I'm taking this with me. Despite how angry I am, I'm still starving, and I won't deprive myself of free, delicious food. I just don't want to be near him if he's going to be a terrible ass of a host.

"Sit down. You're going to hurt yourself," he grumbles, licking his lips.

"I'm fine, thank you."

"Sit down. And eat." He lowers his tone like a deadly warning.

"Sweetie, please sit. We don't get many visitors up here," she encourages, her cold palm on top of mine. I freeze and gaze at her freckled hand. My shoulder drops as the gesture warms me. Why am I letting him get to me? I mean, it was stupid to get myself lost high in the mountain tops. "Gavin's social skills need a little work, but I promise we're harmless," she tells me as a small smile crests her face.

"Speak for yourself, Mer," Gavin retorts.

His knee knocks the base of the table a second later.

"That was my shin," he gawks at her.

"I know it was your shin. That was my foot's subtle way of telling you to zip it," Merelyn replies, tilting her head to the side like a jab.

I can't help it, but a smile pulls at my lips at their quarrel. I let out a defeated sigh. I'm going to sit here for Merelyn. As soon as my hand touches the base of the chair, Gavin rises to his feet. I watch him round the table and pull the chair out for me.

I nod as an awkward thank you, pursing my lips, then I sit. He tucks in the chair and then heads back to his seat. As soon as he sits down, he reaches for a small pot of black coffee and pours it into my empty mug.

"There's hazelnut creamer," he says, pointing to a small ivory plate with miniature hazelnut creamers with his finger. It sits in the center of the table with a glass mason jar of strawberry jam.

"Hazelnut is my favorite. Thank you." I peel it open with my fingernails, then pour it into the mug. The white creamer swirls as I add three more.

So he can be a gentleman when he chooses.

"Want some coffee with your creamer?" Gavin asks as he eyes me.

The whiplash this man is giving me. He's nice one moment, and then he opens his mouth, ruining it.

Flicking my annoyed gaze at him as I hold my mug, I spot his cruel smirk. Rolling my eyes, I take a small sip, the warm coffee waves over my tongue and down my throat. God, coffee feels so good on icy days.

"So you got jokes." I cock a brow, setting the mug down. "I want to see the crash site."

I've been holding that in since I sat down.

Merelyn freezes; the spoonful of fluffy scrambled eggs shakes as she slowly blinks my way.

"I mean, someone has to be looking for me by now. My parents, my sister, and friends?" I continue. "I need my phone, regardless of the signal."

Gavin straightens his spine as he continues to chew breakfast and glances at me.

"How far is it from the cabin?" I ask.

"Like a twenty-minute walk."

"I'm going. Maybe I can find my cellphone while I'm there."

"No," Gavin tells me with a scowl.

"You can't keep me locked in this cabin. If I want to look for my things, I can do that."

He scoffs.

"Go ahead and be my guest. You won't last five minutes with how cold it is right now. I'm not leaving my house unless it's an emergency. The winds and snowfall are brutal right now."

Shit. Maybe he's right. I can't go out there alone.

"Where's Georgia?" I ask, genuinely curious.

Gavin shrugs.

"Must have been something I said last night," he replies coldly.

She tried to shoot her shot with him, and he rejected her.

"She's next door, probably helping me organize my house. I have a hoarding problem," Merelyn replies. She slowly scoots her chair back, collects her fork and butter knife, and places them on her empty plate. The glass and utensils chime together as she stands, but before she can take a step, Gavin helps her. Towering over her, he takes the plate from her hand and hands her her cane instead. He saunters over to the kitchen and puts the dishes in the sink. Merelyn slowly walks to the living room.

I'm almost done with my breakfast, and then I need to find a way to convince Gavin to take me to the crash site.

As soon as I turn around, a shadow of a figure, resembling a woman with long black hair, flashes outside the dining room window's wooden curtains. The woman disappears into thin air, my mouth gaping open as I hold back a scream. Blinking, an eagle crashes against the window hard. The sound of its beak and nails scratching the glass momentarily catches my attention. The loud thudding boom startles me, forcing me to yelp and jump in my chair. Its wings slowly batter as it picks itself up and flies away. My palm covers my trembling lips as I watch it travel deeper into the trees through the raging snowfall. I'm surprised the window didn't crack or break with how hard it hit it, and I'm shocked that the bird was able to get back up and fly.

"T-there was someone in the window. It looked like a woman," I call out, losing my appetite. First, I saw someone behind me in the bathroom, then on the porch? What the hell is going on with me?

"It was an eagle that hit the window, Coraline. We live in the wilderness, and lots of wild animals stop by. It happens." He closes the shutters.

My tongue clicks. He doesn't believe me.

"I'm not talking about the eagle! I saw a woman walking by just before." I point in the direction she went with my finger, my heart racing.

I turn to Gavin, who has his hands on his waist, his long fingers hovering over his belt. He looks at me momentarily and then glances toward the front door. He unlocks it, opens it, and peers with only his head outside, looking left and right. I stand, doing the same.

The wrap-around porch is empty. Nothing but two rocking chairs sway in the wind next to a small, round table with drink coasters—no tall woman with black hair in sight.

"No one is here," Gavin replies as he closes the door.

"But I swear I saw a woman with long, straight black hair."

"No one is here but you, me, Merelyn, and Georgia," he reiterates. His hand snakes into his left pocket and takes out a pack of Marlboros. He takes one bud out and pinches it in between his teeth. I track him as he walks out of the kitchen, heading out toward the back of the house, as chills skate down my spine, still trying to process what I just saw. His hand spears through his long, dark hair, combing it, before he places a brown cowboy hat on top. "I'm going to check on my horses."

CHAPTER 11
CORALINE

After breakfast, I went back into the bedroom and ended up taking a nap.

Mission: find my car and cellphone is the center of my mind right now. I'm stubborn. I have always been since I was a child. I don't care if I need to find it alone, because as the minutes go by, getting frustrated by the simple fact that I can't call my parents or sister is driving me up the wall.

I walk into the living room with the winter clothes I found in the dresser. Surprisingly, I found some that fit me. I dressed myself in a light blue, soft sweater that reads "Sleepy Coldwater, Alaska" in cursive font, with mountains as the art. It presses softly against my skin, beneath a thick, layered silver coat. I finish up by tying the string to the waistband of my blue jeans.

As soon as I look at the door, the lights flicker. Flashing fast in a strobe-like pattern.

My skin immediately crawls. The air around me turns colder than usual, and the hairs on my skin rise like static. My thoughts immediately race to the black-haired woman on the porch and in the bathroom.

Am I seeing things? Is this a part of my brain injury? Or am I seeing…phantoms? Ghosts? Spirits? My heart skips a beat as I watch the light bulb continue to struggle to stay lit. The smell of butter and pecan from the burning candle fills my nose, distracting me momentarily as I watch the ceiling.

"Gavin? Merelyn?" I shout, my chest rising and falling fast with shaky breaths. I wait for their voices, listening over the sound of my heart and blood thrashing in my ears. Seconds turn into an agonizing minute.

Where are they?

I keep walking around, looking for Gavin or the older woman, but there's no one. The slam of a door makes me jump in place. I whirl around toward the direction I heard it come from. My attention lands on a long, tall door on the opposite side of the living room. The fireplace is lit, crackling viciously just as the electricity goes out, leaving me in a darkened area.

I take a step closer to the front door when I spot a note on a neon-colored yellow paper.

HERE ARE SOME MEDS FOR YOUR BODY PAIN. I'M
OUT WITH THE HORSES.
   —GAVIN

The door keeps slamming against the wall, pulling my attention away from the note. I saunter over to the door, bypassing the living room. As soon as I grab the knob, a gust of freezing air whooshes against my cheeks, making my hair flail all around me hard. I look toward the cold draft and see a wooden staircase leading down to a basement.

Oh, what the hell.

THERE'S STILL no sign of Gavin or Merelyn inside the cabin. After five minutes standing in the living room awkwardly, I grew tired of waiting for them to show up. So now, I'm holding onto a glass candle I found in the kitchen. There was a lighter right next to it in the pantry.

I'm using it to help guide me through the darkness of the basement. I know I shouldn't be prying hard into his home like this, but if there's an open window he missed, I need to close it. As soon as I reach the bottom of the creaky stairs, the yellow glow of the candle leads me into a vast, open room with boxes and neatly arranged furniture. The walls are empty, and the basement looks equivalent to a garage or storage room. Organized but dusty. There are decorative boxes. Each is labeled for its specific holiday season.

When's the last time Gavin was down here?

The temperature dips further, and the strong winds can be felt now that I'm down here. I locate the open window. It's in the corner by the drawers. It's cracked open an inch wide. Shivering from my head to my toes, I grip the window and pull it down. I lock it by turning a white knob before I pivot on my heels, heading back upstairs, before my hip crashes into the desk.

It stutters, my hip bone throbbing with a ruthless heartbeat.

"Ouch." I breathe, my face twisting into pain as I lean my palms on the corner of the desk.

I glare at it when I spot a piece of paper poking through the cracks of the top drawer. As I rub my hip, I eye it closely.

I slide it open and find a newspaper. I grab the tinted yellow paper in one hand, and it reveals a pile of journals. I bite my lip nervously and turn to the door over my shoulder, making sure I'm still alone.

Just the occasional strong gusts of wind that continue to pummel through the cracks of windows are the only sounds I can hear.

I turn back to the journals and run the pad of my fingers over the leather cover. I know my limits and boundaries, and I respect privacy. It seems like an incredibly intimate object. I wouldn't dare read it. As a writer and artist, I know how intrusive that can come off.

I place the newspaper back on top of the journals, and the headline catches my attention. The first half is ripped off, leaving only the last paragraph entry.

SERIAL KILLER STILL NOT FOUND

PLEASE SEND IN ANY TIPS TO THE LOCAL POLICE TO HELP CATCH THE MAN WHO IS ALLEGEDLY LINKED AND RESPONSIBLE FOR THE UNSOLVED MURDERS OF THE TWENTY MEN AND WOMEN IN THE TOWN.

The paper shakes as my hands continue to tremble from shivering so hard. Before I can turn the page to analyze the photo of the man, I'm screaming.

"Coraline. Gavin doesn't let anyone in the basement. Not even me."

I spin around, hiding the newspaper behind my back.

Merelyn stands at the bottom of the stairs, cane in hand, looking at me with curious knitted brows. Her hand coils tighter on the cane as she surveys me up and down.

"I-uh. I'm sorry about this." I tuck the newspaper back into the drawer and do the walk of shame toward her. "There was an open window. The winds were pushing through the crack, making the door slam against the wall, so I came down here and closed it," I tell her honestly.

I meet her narrowing blue eyes. She's clearly suspicious of me but gives me grace and doesn't start an interrogation.

"Come upstairs, dear. Georgia is going to remove the stitches from your head before the sun goes down."

CHAPTER 12
CORALINE

"*A*nd that's the last one," Georgia says with enthusiasm as she scissors the last one. "You took it like a champ."

She pats my shoulder, then discards the stitches into the trash can. She gives me a tight, dry smile as she tugs off her blue-green gloves and tosses them with the rest.

It didn't hurt as much as I thought it would.

"Thank you." I run my hands down my thighs. "Where's Gavin? Shouldn't he have been back by now? It's getting late." I suppress the worry in my tone.

"He likes to spend time with the horses." Georgia huffs. "I'm going to get going. The nights during a snowstorm are the most brutal," she says and heads out of the living room. She stands before the front door, bracing her beanie on top of her head and pushing it down until it covers her ears. "I've got to make sure Merelyn gets to bed okay."

"I left a meal for you and Gavin," Merelyn adds just as she hooks her arm in Georgia's. "I cooked it before the electricity went out. It's still good to eat. Please make sure my guy eats if you see him tonight," Merelyn says as her face lightens, pleading genuinely. She speaks like a motherly figure. Every time she mentions or looks at Gavin, her expression softens with a hint of sadness glimmering in her gaze.

"He can be stubborn that way. He's always working and taking care of others that he forgets to take care of himself," she adds, zipping up her jacket.

"Thank you, Merelyn. That's very kind of you. I'll make sure he eats."

❄

I'M EATING IN SILENCE, a dinner full of unanswered questions running through my mind as I finish the last forkful of grilled chicken and broccoli. I stare at his empty chair with only the sound of my chewing to fill the tense void.

Where is he? He won't let me go to the crash site, but he can leave to God knows where?

And why is there a newspaper about a serial killer in his basement? Is he just really into true crime?

Wait.

What if the man who is after me is The Sleepy Coldwater Serial Killer? What if I'm his next victim? Maybe Gavin…

Oh gosh. I need to get out of my head.

Collecting my spoon and plate, I head into the kitchen and wash the dishes. More heavy snow hits the window, followed by sleet and ice. Then, there's a boom of lightning. The thunder rattles the entire ranch-style cabin home, making the light come back on for a second before it goes out again.

That same gust of cold wind is back, ghosting my skin, making the hairs on my nape rise. As I shut off the sink water, it feels like someone is watching me from behind. The aura of a shadow lurking somewhere I cannot see.

Frozen from head to toe, I whirl around to check if it's Gavin.

I can see my breath detailed in a white puff of air swirling above my lips as the cold continues to bite me back with no remorse. *There's nobody here.* There's no one in this haunted cabin but me right now.

His living room is so…plain. It needs a warm touch. Isn't it Christmas time? Where's the tree? Where are the pops of classic red shades representing the holiday?

If I'm going to be stuck here for a few weeks, I want to keep busy and help around the house, if I can. But most of all, I need to find my cellphone and figure out who's trying to kill me so I can report it to the police once the storm is over.

I dry the last dish with a hand towel in circular motions. I place the dry, cleaned bowl back where the rest of them are in his cabinets, right above the toaster. Just as I close it, a man covered in blood all over his face reflects in the cabinet glass.

Fear. Hatred. Darkness. All three emotions are written all over his strained face. His eyes are pure black, radiating with vengeance.

I yelp loud and high.

I turn around fast, gripping a kitchen knife in my hand, and hold it in front of me, ready to spear the intruder. When I glance in front of me, the man is gone. There's no trace of him anywhere as my head dips left and right, searching every corner for his existence.

My chest violently rocks, blood pounds in my ears as my hands shake around the black handle.

"What the hell is going on with this cabin?"

CHAPTER 13
CORALINE

I haven't seen Gavin in three days. He only left that one note, and the feet of snow keep growing by the day. It's piled up so high against the back door that it almost reaches the roof. The electricity came back on in the middle of the night two nights ago.

An unnerving sensation runs through me.

Today is different. It feels different. The nightmares don't stop. I wake up every single night, feeling like someone is watching me in every corner of the room. Goosebumps erupt all over my skin as the wind howls angrily through the cracks of the windows.

What if The Sleepy Coldwater Serial Killer is here? What if he knows where I'm staying, and he knows I'm alone since Gavin left me? What if he's here to finish the job? What if the reason why Gavin's been gone so long is because my stalker hurt him?

Oh no.

I think the reason why I'm still alive after I survived the car crash is because Gavin found me, scaring off my attempted murderer before he could finish what he started. I'm in his debt.

Slipping on snow boots one by one, I decide to look for him. Merelyn grows more worried by the day since he hasn't come back from 'being with the horses'. After I dress in a heavy coat, jeans, and snow boots, I head for the front door. I take a deep breath before I turn the knob.

I'm not sure why I'm already feeling a sense of worry when it comes to him, but I can't help it. He's been a sarcastic asshole to me since we met, but I don't want anything bad happening to him. I'm still shaken from the flashes of people who disappear into thin air, to the empty cabin, and the mystery of the lurking threat. I don't want to be alone right now. I can't leave anywhere. I'm stuck in a home full of ghosts. When it comes to choosing between being alone with spirits while a stalker hunts me, or a cowboy who refuses to smile? I'm choosing Gavin.

Who knows what lengths this person will go to kill me? What if he hurts Gavin and Merelyn if this person finds out they're harboring me?

Trees start to bang against the walls of the house. The lights flicker once again, making me freeze and stare at the withering electricity. I grip the doorknob tighter just as another bang thuds behind me, making me scream.

"Ahh!" I yelp and turn toward the origin of surprise. At the same time, I watch lightning strike a tree right behind Gavin's house through the living room floor-to-ceiling windows, causing it to fall over in the backyard. Time comes to a stop for me.

"Oh, fuck this." I shake my head.

I open the door, motivated to find someone with a beating heart. As soon as I do, harsh glacial winds slap me in the face unforgivingly. Its cold breeze is unremorseful, and I instantly regret my choice to leave.

I close the door behind me just as the bells continue to chime. The blizzard is still in full force, so painfully freezing, I feel it in my bones. I start walking, and the sky is a deep shade of grey. The snow buries my foot when I take my first step. I struggle pulling it out, marching through it, soldiering on as the winds and snow pelt my body.

I look to my left and then my right, trying to see if I can make out a barn full of horses or the crash sight in the distance, but I see nothing but snow flurries circling all around me. I decide to go right. I coil in on myself, my arms wrapped around my biceps to create another barrier of heat. Looking back at the cabin, and then to the tall trees I'm in the middle of, makes anxiety ripple through me. This may have been a dumb decision.

I've already committed. I have to keep going.

Branches hit my sides as I venture further. My feet get stuck every other minute, but eventually, I make it to a clearing.

Still…no barn or Gavin in sight. I keep going, walking into more trees for what feels like forever, until I spot a tire. I track it, my eyes going north until it lands on another tire and then another. My heart skips out of my chest when I see a beat-up, crumpled vehicle.

"It's my rental!"

I rush toward it, hopping over branches, almost tripping over my own heel, when I hear something crack behind me. My brows raise curiously. I'm hoping it's Gavin, but when I turn around, there's no one. Trees, more trees, and snow whirl around in the storm.

Before I can keep venturing, something catches my eye in my peripheral vision. A tall, thick shadow steps out from behind a tree. Is that Gavin?

"Gavin?" I call out, but the shadow doesn't respond.

"Gavin, is that you?" I walk toward him, biting my freezing lip. I can't feel my face. I squint my eyes as if that'll help me miraculously see better through thick flurries.

"Gavin!" I shout once more.

Suddenly, the shadow reveals more of himself and starts to run, straight toward me.

A wave of unease crashes into my soul, and my eyes widen.

It's not a human.

It's an animal.

A small moose appears through the fog. Its black eyes look straight at me. It's chewing on something, looking anything but spooked. I'm the one who feels like their soul has left their body. I thought it was the one after me. I instantly feel relief. I sigh, my heart rate evening out.

Placing my hands on my thighs, I lean over and chuckle. It's so cute. It doesn't even have antlers yet. Brown thick fur, two pointy ears that stick out above its head, and extremely long legs—almost too long for such a small body.

"It's just a baby moose. It's just a baby moose," I chant out of relief, but then I realize what that entails. Horror spreads through me. "It's just...a baby moose. *A moose that's a baby...*" Another sound of a twig snaps nearby, and my brows raise. "Oh, shit."

If there's a baby nearby, then that means its mother is too.

A tall, massive older moose slowly guards its calf by moving in front of it. It huffs, making a grunty sound before it's heading toward me with its head down, using its antlers as a weapon. *It's charging me.*

I can't outrun an animal.

Oh my god.

Gavin warned me about the wildlife out here, and I didn't listen.

I whip around and sprint toward the open field. I run, the icy air burning my lungs, but I don't care. I peer over my shoulder, hoping it's a symptom of my brain injury, but no, it's not. It's not a delusion. I hear the thud of this moose's hooves on the ground, and it keeps closing the distance, not giving up.

I keep running, and don't dare to look over my shoulder

again. My hair gets caught several times in the branches as I weave through the trees and head straight for the wreckage. I ignore the pulsing pain in my scalp as the sounds of its footsteps grow closer and louder. I've read somewhere that moose attacks are not uncommon in Alaska, but can be fatal. I'm not ready to die and definitely not like this.

I lean down, my hand curling around a rock. Grunting, I hold it over my shoulder, ready to launch it, just to scare it away, not hurt it, but when I turn around, it's gone. My lungs burn, my chest tightening with each shallow breath. Adrenaline is simmering in my veins as I hold on to the rock so tight like it's my lifeline.

Standing still, I search for it and its calf in every tree.

It's really gone.

With every passing second, I wait for it to pop out again— charging me, but it doesn't. I guess the moose gave up and granted me mercy. I don't waste another second.

Still holding onto the rock by my side, I rush toward the wrecked vehicle. I skim through the snow until I find the driver's seat. The car door is closed, but all the glass is shattered. I peek through the open window and search for a purse, bags, or anything that I can take back to the cabin. But most importantly, why can't I find my cell phone? It's been a few days, so it might be dead.

Great. My cellphone is nowhere to be found, but something glistens, calling my attention. Dipping my upper half into the car, I grab my ring with a wedding band attached to it. I pinch it, twirl it around, and set it back on my ring finger. It fits like a perfect glove.

I find the ring from Liam—my cheating, despicable ex, whom I can't seem to separate from in my heart fully and a sting hits my eyes. I hate it when you fall in love because it can be scary. The one person you promise yourself to and build a life with, stabs you in the back and isn't even sorry about it.

Then, I find my wallet. A familiar warm feeling makes my heart swell. This is my sister's wallet. I miss her so much. I never miss our weekly check-ins. She knows something is wrong, and I wouldn't be surprised if she has the National Guard looking for me right now because I know how crazy protective she is. I open it, and sure enough, my identification cards are tucked inside. I pull out the Texas-issued one first and find my name on it. The black-and-white portrait of me is unscathed right next to all my information.

Coraline Rosa. 5'1. Hispanic. San Antonio, Texas. Organ Donor.

The ground begins to vibrate. The sensation runs up my legs as I continue to tiptoe into the car. Then, the sound of something cracking sends a shiver down my spine. My eyes widen as I push myself out of the vehicle.

A bolt of fear strikes deep into my gut when I spot a pack of wolves in the cracked rearview mirror. One of them stepped on glass, leaving a small trail of dark red underneath its paw. The wallet slips from my trembling hands. The one in the front is the biggest. Massive, light ocean eyes, sharp and texturized, with a white and silver coat. She's beautiful. If it weren't looking at me like I'm its next meal, I'd pet it. With a snarl, the wolf flashes me its sharp teeth. Its tongue swipes its lips as it takes more slow, calculated steps my way. The rest of the pack start to howl behind it and bark at me like they're ready for the command to take me out from their leader. All of them disperse, circling me as they bolt left and right on their paws. They jump with excitement, vividly hungry, and they've chosen me as their next meal.

"Go!" I shout. "Go away!" I warn, flailing my hands in front of my chest.

A deep and low rumbling overpowers their growls and the sound of my blood thrashing in my ears. I would turn my head toward the origin, but I don't want to look away, and then I'm getting blindsided by jaws. All of the wolves make a high-pitched whimper, their gazes suddenly off me and somewhere else. They all scatter and follow the silver-tailed leader. I track them as they amble in the direction of the woods.

The mysterious loud roars send reverberations through the ground, rattling my boots. I flick my gaze to my feet, then back to the last spot I saw the pack running through. They're gone. Whatever this sound is, it's scaring them off. They've disappeared through the trees with no more signs of wildlife.

Is this an earthquake?

Before I can move or think, I get the answer to my own question. It's not an earthquake. It's an avalanche. Hundreds of feet of snow are falling off the peak that's right by Gavin's ranch. I see it every morning I wake up, and right now a piece of it is falling straight on top of me. I abandon the car and trudge through the feet of snow.

I run like my life depends on it, because it does. I keep going with tears rolling down my face, the sound of the snow falling behind me growing louder and louder. I'm not running fast enough!

The snow envelopes me, sticking to my body. I find myself unable to lift my knees smoothly as I stumble deeper into white ice. It's burying me, swallowing my screams, crashing against my back, forcing me to hold my breath.

I couldn't get away in time.

"No!" I shrill, but the sound doesn't go anywhere, staying trapped inside more ice.

I'm still alive.

I'm still alive even though I'm buried. Fighting through it, I do my best to make space to breathe. But the more snow I push out with my hands, the more that comes rushing back in, coating and violently rocking against my face. I keep my mouth closed so I don't swallow it. I swing, kick, scream—fighting until I can see the sky again, but nothing but more white keeps trampling my face. Panic settles in as I keep probing for something to pull me out, but I keep coming up empty. I'm sinking deeper into the snow every time I jump in place. Blinding white envelops me. I flap my arms up and down, holding my breath as I try to make an opening, but nothing happens.

Everything burns on the inside as my lungs scream at me, desperate for air. With every flail, I let out a strangled cry. I don't know how long it's been, but it feels like hours that I've been screaming and fighting. Growing weaker, my vision dims with darkness as I slip into unconsciousness, still attempting to resist death.

CHAPTER 14
GAVIN

Coraline's desperate voice echoes into my ears. Even though she's only been in my house for a week, I know her voice like my favorite catchy song that's stuck in my head; no matter how many times I try to forget the melody, it's still there. It's distinct. Light, airy, and sweet.

But she's also annoyingly stubborn and has a habit of making really stupid decisions, like going against my advice and trying to look for her cell phone that's most likely buried in feet of snow, broken, or flew out of the car and is on the street she lost control on. During a record-breaking blizzard. I wasn't exaggerating when I said lots of wild animals roam my property, but I guess she's intrigued to challenge me and curious to be eaten.

Her scream sounds more guttural and uneasy with each strangled blare. There are no words, just sounds of clear desperation and urgency. I swing my hunting rifle over my shoulder and stalk faster. The horses should be okay for the rest of the blizzard. They're safe, well-fed, and warm. My boots crunch over the thick snow. I'm wearing my black winter balaclava and winter hunting camo gear.

The visibility is slim to none due to thick white fog. Running through it, I head straight to where I think she is, but then her screams stop, and it gives me a sick sensation in my stomach. Something about how her sounds stopped has me on high alert. Her voice is coming by…

No.

She better not be where I think she is!

My heart sinks, and I begin to run faster. I push through the trees and gaze at the river that is in the corner of my land—the one the horses like to spend time around during the summer. Sure enough, there's an avalanche of snow burying the car.

She's in there.

I know she is.

Fucking hell.

This woman really does have a death wish.

CHAPTER 15
CORALINE

Someone's arms are around my body, and I'm being pressed against something warm. Everything burns and aches as I heave to the side. Weakness pulls me back to the floor, and I gaze at the white light from before. With each slow blink, my vision stabilizes.

Gavin.

He's above me with flashes of worry in those celestial, cerulean eyes. His beauty is irresistible. It's unfair the way it makes me forget about the no flirting or dating rule I set for myself after what Liam did to me.

I reach for Gavin's face and run my hand against his perfect jaw, feeling the pricks of his beard against the palm of my hand.

"Am I alive?" I blink slowly, trying to stay awake, but it's hard with the way my body feels like it was run over. I swallow as I try to suck in breath after slow breath.

It feels good to breathe again.

"Yes, Coraline. You're alive." His brows narrow. His relieving smile morphs into a deep frown the longer we lock eyes. The harsh lines around his eyes deepen. Then his full, red lips are moving again. "Alive and still a stubborn woman," he scolds. "Why are you out here? What the fuck were you thinking?"

Before I can respond, reality pulls me further in. The avalanche. The moose and the pack of wolves. A slap in the face with how dangerously beautiful Alaska can be. Now, I'm in pain, and *I'm so damn cold*. I can't feel my hands or feet, and I can barely process a single thought. I guess I deserve it for being impatient.

"You weren't thinking," he reminds me. "Listen to me next time, goddamnit."

Groaning, my hand falls back to my side—soreness bleeding from my chest down to my frozen toes. I'm going in and out of consciousness.

Gavin lifts me in the air and presses me against his hard, muscular chest. Shadows of darkness are calling my name every other second. Large, thick flurries roam around us, and I'm tempted to reach out for one.

"Stay awake," he rasps. "Don't fall back to sleep."

I nod lazily, my forehead brushing against his steel-muscled chest. Instead of closing my eyes, I focus on the snowfall.

It swirls down from the sky, ghosting my face, and swirls in the air.

It looks like magic.

Seeing snowfall has always felt like a wonder of the world to me. Like a version of heaven on Earth. Living in South Texas, I don't get to experience it often, but when I do, it distracts me from everything. For a moment, I forget about my daily problems, responsibilities, and insecurities. Everything good and bad vanishes the longer I get lost in its essence. *It's not just the weather to me.* Snowfall is a gentle, minuscule reminder that seasons change just like chapters in a book.

It won't stay dark forever.

Sometimes, when I get stuck on how I'm feeling inside, and there's only pain that feels like I'm burning alive, I forget it won't always be constant. The page will turn. The skies will clear, and there will be light again, even when it seems my story feels like it's going nowhere.

Being in Alaska is making me feel like I've put the brakes on an isolating train ride with no specific destination. The mountains call my name when the city lights drain me.

"H-hey," I murmur, looking at Gavin's Adam's apple.

He keeps his focus on the cabin, face forward.

"I found my car." My lungs seize the words in my itchy throat. *Cough.*

"But I didn't find my cell. There was a pack of—" *cough.* "Wolves and then—"

"Don't talk. Just stay awake for me," he quips like an order.

Gavin kicks his door open as I continue to shiver against him. The familiar bells chime against the rich wood. The frostbite all over my frail body is slowly torturing me. My shivers are frantic and desperate, clinging to him desperately.

As soon as we get inside his cabin, the temperature is no better. He sets me on his couch, my back falling into the cushion.

"S-so c-cold," I say, coiling into a fetal position, trying to soak up any heat my body has to offer.

He rushes to his fireplace, throwing more logs in. The fire rises, an orange glow growing larger, illuminating the living room. I'm too focused on clinging to the couch that I hadn't realized I was drifting into sleep again.

"Coraline," he calls me.

His shadow spreads over me. A second later, he springs me to my feet with harsh purpose. He claws at my shirt, forcing me to lift it over my head.

"Hey, w-what are you d-doing?" My teeth chatter, but I manage to get all of my questions out. Of course, no response from him. He continues to pull off all of my clothes, leaving me in my bra and underwear. Then he slips his own shirt off and throws it on top of my clothes, creating a pile.

"Hey, what the hell, G-Gavin?" I try to push him away, but he doesn't hesitate for one second. He embraces me tightly, holding me to his chest. My muscles continue to convulse as I try to push him away. I fight him off as much as I can, but it's not doing anything against his steel hold.

"Stop. Get off me!" I shout into his chest, but that familiar simmer in my veins comes back full force. He moves his hand down the small of my back, up and down, creating friction and another spark I need to ignore.

"Body heat is the best way to battle hypothermia. I'm going to hold you until you think it's good enough. Until you stop shaking. Okay?"

"You-you're trying to get me warm?" I ask through my jaw that threatens to lock up on me.

He nods.

"S-sorry." My teeth continue to chatter. "You're right." I loosen up, letting myself fall into him, pressing my cheek against his thundering heartbeat.

He doesn't say anything else. He continues to hold me, and even though the gesture is sweet, his eyes and expression reflect a more bothersome expression—almost as if my almost dying *twice* is an inconvenience for him. I hold onto his skin, continuing to shake and concentrate on the flames next to us.

"Are you in the Navy? Or were you in the Navy?"

There's a picture of him on deployment in a submarine.

He doesn't answer me. Just keeps holding me like I'm nothing but a job to get done. Gavin is massive. Tall. And most of all—warm. He embraces me tighter, my shivering going in and out. Just when I think I'm all good and ready to let go, tremors vibrate my body. With my fingers pressing against his chest, I press my frozen nose tip against his chest hair, unashamed. He still manages to smell so fucking good for pulling me out of the snow.

"That's a trident, though. Are you a Navy SEAL?" I ask, shutting my eyes, rubbing my cheek against his hard pec, and trying to focus on getting the questions out.

"Was," he breathes, still staring at the fireplace.

"Ex special operator. That's impressive." I smile against him, but he only stiffens.

Maybe he doesn't like to talk about his time in the military.

He never loosens his grip on my back. He keeps holding onto me, and my shuddering finally comes to a standstill. I blink slowly, catching myself almost falling asleep while standing in his arms. I don't know how much time has passed, but it feels…good. I haven't felt this safe in a long time. I haven't held another man like this, so intimately, who wasn't my husband. And it feels peaceful.

He has to be freezing, too. I run my hand up his back, returning the friction. My palms smooth over the thick scars I saw when he was in my room.

"What happened here?" I tilt my head to meet his gaze. When my chin rests on the middle of his chest, my heart leaps. He's looking at me. And for the first time, it feels like he's letting himself look at me, *admire me*—the muscle in his jaw flexes. Our flesh connection doesn't last long after I catch it.

He clears his throat and loosens his grip. Stepping away, he throws another log of wood into the fireplace.

Something I thought was dead inside me already yearns for his touch. His attention. His scent.

Maybe I'm lonely. Perhaps I'm still angry over Liam and Lilly's betrayal. But I liked Gavin's embrace. I liked it when he looked at me even more. Tugging my lip with my front teeth, I smooth my hands over my flushed face and inhale. I sit near the fireplace until the flames are almost catching me with crackles, knicking the air.

I can't have this attraction. I don't get to. I'm still married, and my morals remind me that it isn't right to want another man's attention when I'm still legally bound to someone else.

We're separated technically...

He grabs my clothes, one by one, from the floor, and leaves. I'm still in my underwear and bra, with peaked nipples drawing through the thin satin layers. I'm half-naked in his living room, and his gaze has never strayed to my breasts or lower. He heads toward his laundry room and disappears into the hallway, while I'm left alone with my thoughts.

Did it bother him that I noticed his scars?

I have so many questions, but one plagues me the most.

How did he get to me so fast?

Fear creeps inside me when the most haunting question is waving red flags I wish I could turn the other cheek to.

Is he...the one who chased me to my attempted demise?

Is Gavin the one who caused my car to crash?

Is he the one after me?

He just so happened to be there both times.

No.

There's no way he would do those things to me. Yes, Gavin holds so much mystery, but he doesn't seem like the murdering type to me. The way Merelyn talks highly of him has to count for something.

A door slams in the distance, and I turn my head toward the hallway. I rise to my feet until I'm standing by the fireplace, hugging myself, too afraid and nervous to move. He's the first man to see me without a shirt and pants. I'm curvier than I used to be, and Liam reminded me of that every chance he got. While it was dinner time, or when it came to shopping for clothes. He constantly reminded me that I didn't meet his weight standards. That my stretchmarks on my hips, stomach, and ass would catch his attention to the point that whenever we would have sex, I would turn off the lights because I was afraid he'd find another thing on my body to complain about.

I haven't loved myself since he betrayed me—*loved life*. I didn't know there was anything wrong with me until Liam constantly criticized me. Now I feel a bit insecure, standing before Gavin like this, because what if he has the same thoughts?

And why do I care?

He emerges from the hallway in a change of clothes. He's no longer wearing pants. Instead, he's in dark grey sweatpants that hug his long legs and a loose flannel with long sleeves over a white shirt—a gold chain with a cross over his chest.

He comes back with oversized clothing and a blanket in his hand. He gives it to me, but doesn't make eye contact. There's his familiar cold shoulder again.

"Take a warm bath." He grabs a smoke from his back pocket and heads toward the front porch.

Why is he always so grumpy?

"Do you ever smile, Gavin?" I tease, grabbing the clothes and wrapping myself in the warm, fuzzy blanket.

He quirks a brow and deadpans. Of course…he doesn't say anything and holds an unreadable gaze. Those dark green, vibrant specks in his eyes glow against the blue, and I swear I could get lost in them if he looked at me longer than five seconds.

"One day, I'll get a smile out of you." I take my clothes and head for a shower. He stills, staring at me with a cigarette hanging out between his perfect white teeth and sharp canines.

CHAPTER 16
GAVIN

$\mathcal{I}$'m a man at the end of the day, and something inside me has awakened. When I held her in my arms, I felt like I wasn't in the cabin anymore but somewhere else. I felt something.

And something when you've been a numb soul all your life is everything.

I enjoy being alone. I enjoy reading books before I go to sleep. I enjoy living in the mountains where there isn't another soul for miles. Just nature, the sounds of the earth moving every day.

I want to worry only about Merelyn and myself. I avoid judgment. I avoid human connection like it's the plague.

What I didn't anticipate was that I had to fight the urge to enjoy the way my lips wanted to curl up and match Coraline's beaming smile after I pulled her out of the avalanche. Or the way her cold body shuddered against mine near the fire, pulled heartstrings I never thought I had. All I wanted was for her to live today.

She upsets me.

In the beginning, we didn't get along much, but I'm determined to change that. I don't know what to do with myself with a beautiful woman like Coraline so close to me.

But...before she went into the shower, all I wanted was to bark out all the reasons why venturing onto my land during a storm was one of the most stupid ideas she's had since being in my home. And I couldn't do it.

I held back, and I don't do that for anyone.

I'm sitting on the couch, a Shiner beer in my hand, waiting for her to come out.

Waiting for Coraline Rosa.

Her name is perfect. Beautiful.

Like her.

I'm not stupid. At the end of the day, I'm a man. A man who notices how naturally and effortlessly majestic she is. My fingers got lost in the threads of her long, black, thick, wet hair when they weaved through my fingers. Her skin is so glowingly soft, a beautiful soft brown tone that I could spend endless hours admiring. She has these cute little freckles all over her shoulder blades and neck. I counted them while I held her.

There are twenty in total.

It's like she doesn't know how gorgeous she is and the effect she can have on anyone.

Steam clouds seep through the cracks of the bathroom door. She has the heat on high. I can hear the shower running, with occasional splashes of water hitting the tub. There's a towel already inside, ready for her to use.

For the first time, I don't want to go to bed early. I don't feel the need to grab a book and read until I fall asleep. I want to have a conversation. I want to get to know her. I want to know everything before she leaves.

The shower knob squeaks, and the water stops. My fingers tighten around the glass before I bring it to my lips and take a nervous sip. I haven't felt like this...ever. I thought I was broken. Incapable of wanting to share my space with someone else. Yet, here I am, hoping my long, overgrown mustache and beard don't turn her off, or if I let my callous attitude get the best of me. I don't want our first bumpy days to taint how she looks at me.

My back straightens when the bedroom door opens. I haven't slept in there since I found her looking like a fresh corpse in the snow.

Her footsteps become louder as I sit still, tense and clutching my chest, hoping my heart will stop beating out of it. She appears from the dark hallway, dressed in my clothes because I've run out of Merelyn's old ones. She looks amazing in my black shirt and joggers, even though her petite body makes my shirt look like a dress.

I laugh. My eyes crease as I watch her cheeks pinken. She holds herself by the hips, her arms folding over each other.

"Why are you laughing?" she pouts.

"Because my clothes fit you perfectly. Can't you tell by the way you're dragging the pants?"

She rolls her eyes.

"Still sarcastic, I see."

"Still fucking stubborn, I see."

Her lips part.

"Don't worry, I thought about telling you how stupid, irre-sponsible, foolish, and dumb it was to go out when the blizzard is at its peak, risking your life and how—"

"You *thought* about telling me?" she snaps, clicking her tongue. "You're doing it right now."

My jaw clicks shut.

My social skills are shit.

"I'm sorry." I clear my throat. "Let's start over. Will you let me start over?"

She stares at me for a pregnant moment, then her chin dips.

I want a do-over. She's stuck with me for weeks. And we might as well start getting along. I crave her attention, her laugh, and her smile. I don't plan on leaving her alone in the cabin again unless it's an emergency.

She stops in front of me, and her hand stretches forward.

"Fine." She sighs. "Starting over. I'm Coraline. Coraline Rosa."

I take her small palm in mine and squeeze, ignoring the crackle in my chest and the spark heating when our flesh connects.

"Gavin Ariksen." Our hands rock for a couple of more seconds before she pulls away.

"Well, Gavin Ariksen," she sings, her voice teasing. "I really need to talk to you about a lot of things." She fishes the beer out of my hand and takes a swig. My dick jumps in my sweats, watching her confidently drink it, seeing her lips where mine were a second ago. She falls and sinks into the couch opposite me.

"What is it?"

"How about starting with the fact that your home is haunted!" her shrieking voice pitches.

She thinks my cabin is haunted? That's a first.

"It's not."

"Yes, *it is*," she replies. Looking around the room, she inspects the ceiling. "Do you have cameras? I don't see any."

"I don't need cameras. I have a security system in place." I say, confidently. I raise my shirt, my Glock sitting tucked in my waistband. Her face tightens. "My security." I cover my weapon with my shirt.

"Another thing," she raises the beer and takes another long swallow. I watch her throat roll, "I was chased by a mother moose and a pack of wolves. I will never go out there again." Her eyes bulge.

I chuckle, my chest rising and falling hard. She's dramatic, but I like it.

"Who is trying to kill you, by the way? Are you in some sort of trouble? Owe someone money?" Even though there's humor laced in my tone, I'm genuinely upset at the thought of someone trying to hurt Coraline. To go to these lengths. She seems like a sweet girl...a little naive, but doesn't warrant that type of hatred and insanity. That's why I think this idea of someone running her off the road is almost unbelievable. I hate to say it, but her story is skeptical. I'll keep that part to myself.

"I don't know!" she quips, her voice cracking with a sullen croak. Her eyes turn glassy as she runs her fingers against the healing gash on her face. "I don't know who is trying to kill me. It all started about a few weeks ago, when I received a letter bearing a simple threat. *I'm going to kill you,*" she mocks. "It was so comical to me that I didn't think much of it. But now, ever since I came to Sleepy Coldwater, I've been getting texts from an unknown number. And now? He ran me off the road. My rental car is wrecked. You found me before he could finish me off. And now I have scars on my body." She pushes me away, and her posture collapses. "I'm scared," she whispers. "I'm so fucking scared, Gavin." Her weary gaze drifts in my direction, then flickers back to the beer in her hand—a flash of fear written in her brown irises.

I don't like hearing her voice tremble like this.

"I don't mean to be that guy who tells you it's all in your head, so please don't get offended. I don't think anyone is out there right now. No one could survive that storm outside like that with no shelter or heat."

"You have to believe me, Gavin," she pleads, leaning forward. "I know I sound crazy. I feel like I've been going crazy." She swallows nervously. "From the accident. Seeing figures disappear from your home into thin air. This is all so weird to me," she murmurs. "Has anyone died here?"

I stiffen.

I don't want to talk about death. I know it's been a while since I've talked to someone as beautiful as her, and I'd rather talk about anything else than the history of this place. She shifts in her seat when I don't answer, drawing her brows tight, her cheeks flushing. Her beautiful honey eyes drift toward the crackling fireplace instead.

"Sweetheart, do I scare you?"

She turns back to me wide-eyed.

"Why?"

I shrug.

"Because everyone is."

Everyone is scared of me. No one comes onto my land unless they need something. No one cares to talk to me because of my history. A history that will send this beautiful girl running out of my house in the middle of the night if she finds out.

She blinks slowly.

I can see her pulse pounding away on her dainty neck.

"Get some sleep. I'll take the couch, and well, you can take the bed."

I take the beer from her hand and give her mine to help her to her feet.

"I don't think I can," she says, her hips brushing against mine as she heads toward the hallway.

"Go to sleep, Coraline. It's late."

"Gavin. You saved my life twice." I stop walking. She pauses and flicks her nervous gaze to me. Her chest reddens as I wait for her to finish.

"Thank you," she says.

My brow rises. Where is this going? We're standing right outside my bedroom. The sound of trees scratching the outside walls joins our deep, shallow breaths. She smells like my shampoo, with a hint of something sweet.

"For what?"

"For everything. For helping me. For talking to me," she says, looking straight at me. My chest swells until it's full of warmth and good feelings.

"Talking to you?" I ask.

"Yeah." She smiles with sunshine. "You listen to me. You really look at me. And it's been a really long time since someone has."

We stand there, only an inch of thick tension dripping in between our rising and falling chests in the middle of the hallway. Her diamond ring on her finger glistens against the distant fire from the living room. It shines like the biggest cockblock it is, reminding me that she's taken. I saw it on her after I pulled her out of the snow, but I didn't ask about it.

"Doesn't your husband see you?" I ask, placing my hand on the wall beside her head. My palm sticks to it, helping me balance myself. "Where is he? Why isn't he here in Alaska with you?"

She takes a step forward, closing the distance. Everything hardens inside of me from head to toe, keeping me from falling into her. I swear, the way she's looking at me has me wanting to stay up all night listening to her talk about anything and everything.

"He's not here," she shrugs.

I don't know why I care. I don't know why I was hoping she'd say she's single. It pulls me out of the trance she naturally encases me in. I'm not that type of man. I don't go after taken women.

"Goodnight, Coraline." I take a step backward, drinking the last of the beer. The bitter taste runs down my tongue and into my throat.

"Goodnight, Ga—" Her face pales. Her eyes grow wide, her mouth frozen in time as I watch her track something behind me.

"What is it?"

"Right there!" She points behind me. "I saw something!"

I turn around and glance over to the kitchen. There's no one.

"What did you see?"

The island is empty. Merelyn and Georgia are asleep next door. Nothing is out of place. The doors are locked. I place my hand on my gun, just in case the fucker she talks about tries to break in. She comes up close and slightly presses her chest against my back.

. "I saw another one of those disappearing shadows! Gavin. Your house is haunted!" Both hands flail over her head, wildly.

Jesus. She really won't stop with the ghost thing.

My head dips back as I palm my face, smoothing over my mustache and beard. I stare at the ceiling, holding back.

"No, it's not."

"You're telling me you've never experienced anything weird happening here? Lights flickering? Doors slamming? Random shadows moving on your porch?" She pours out question after question like I'm being interviewed.

"Everything has a scientific explanation." I sigh.

"Like what?" She slaps her hand against her thigh, impatiently.

"The lights flickering—the storm. The door slamming? The wind. Yeah, Merelyn told me she found you in my basement. Which, stay the hell out of there." She rears back at my calloused tone. "And the shadows moving? It was an animal. Elk, Moose, deer, hell, it could have even been a bear," I quip. "It happens daily out here."

"And so you're back to being an ass." She crosses her arms against her chest, rolling her eyes.

"I guess so." I grind my teeth.

"And here I thought we were finally getting along."

I shake my head, feeling defeated.

"I'm going to take the couch."

"No!" She pulls my hand back. I stare at her hand wrapped around three of my fingers. My nostrils flare the longer I fight the hot wave of fire.

"I just mean you should take the bed."

She is so damn stubborn, but telling her no is the last thing I want to do, and if I say yes, all I'm going to be thinking about is wanting to taste her, steal a kiss, or watch her sleep.

"No."

"Gavin," she insists. "*Please*."

Her shoulders fall, her fingers convulse around her sides, clearly rattled with nerves, and her face is pale. She's still shaken by everything that happened today. She almost lost her life, and if I thought someone was trying to kill me at every corner, I wouldn't be able to think straight, either. I honestly wouldn't sleep until I buried them.

Fucking fuck.

I'm not good at comforting or expressing emotions.

"I'm not taking the bed," I say, heading for the trash can. I toss the beer inside and palm the island, leaning over it. I turn to her.

Her expression falls into disappointment. She pivots on her feet and turns, heading into my room.

"I'm taking the small couch in the corner of the room."

She peers over her shoulder and smiles.

CHAPTER 17
CORALINE

I can be a brat. I know I can. I can tell I get under Gavin's skin easily. I can also confirm with myself that his cheeks flushed red when we were in the hallway.

He's attracted to me.

And I am to him.

He's…hot. His voice makes my heart skip a beat. Those light blue eyes bring me peace, and just the way he moves, his muscular shoulders sway, full of confidence and control. He's a gentleman. In the beginning, he came off as a grumpy asshole, but there's a switch, and I'm not complaining or asking why.

Everything about him attracts me like a moth to a flame, but I know if I get too close, I'll burn.

I see how Georgia can't take her eyes off him, how upset and hurt she was when he turned her down. There has to be history there.

I also noticed his handsome face turn stone cold when I admitted I'm married. I hated myself after I said it. I wanted to explain everything. How yes, I'm still married, but I'm also technically single.

Fuck Liam. I feel pathetic for still wearing a ring that holds false promises and broken memories when I know he probably wore his ring proudly while he had sex with my best friend.

I still care about him. Regardless of how deeply he cut me. I still care, and I hate myself for it. Maybe it makes me stupid, but I think more than anything, it makes me human. I was loyal to him, and it hurts. I've been moving on, rightfully so, but it doesn't mean the dream I had, to be married to someone I thought I could trust, died with him right away when his affair came to light. I wish it did. I wish the feelings and memories never existed. Liam did a number on my confidence. I don't have any left, and I'm trying to get it back.

When Gavin asked if I was married, I couldn't lie. So, I kept half the truth. I don't know if I'm ready to look at another man with irrefutable lust, but I'm doing it now, and there are ounces of guilt residing in my loyal heart. Liam's been trying to reach out to me with flowers and chocolates to ask for my forgiveness ever since we separated, but I blocked him on everything possible, so he resorts to mail. I can't block him from using the postal service, and I don't have enough money to move, so it all ends up in the trash.

Tossing and turning underneath the blankets, I stop when I face a sleeping Gavin. He's on his back, his white shirt hugging his ab muscles.

Damn it, why does he look even sexier asleep?

Fuck me and my morals.

I stare at the ceiling, placing my hands on my chest, and count sheep as the sounds of the snowstorm lull my anxieties away. The high-pitched winds, the sound of ice pelting the windows, and the occasional strange creaks and thumping off the cabin. It all turns into white noise.

Maybe Gavin's right. Perhaps the guy who was after me ran off when he saw Gavin for the second time. Either way, when the snow clears, I'm filing a police report and getting the hell away from Sleepy Coldwater.

My fear is slipping away with Gavin's help. I haven't seen another spirit appearing out of the walls, and I don't feel that eerie sense of being watched. The dreary undercurrent of this place is gone, and instead, a spark that brews with the beat of my heart replaces it.

My sore body begins to melt into the mattress and soft blankets as I drift away in my head, growing sleepier by the second.

It has to be lonely up here for him.

He says everyone is scared of him, and my curiosity grows.

I mean, he can be a grumpy ass.

My stomach turns as butterflies flock in my gut as I remember the way his chiseled body felt against mine when he used his own body heat to warm me up. The way he stayed respectful when he undressed me melted me.

I blink at him through the darkness, the moon peeking through the window against his face.

Maybe we can be friends?

A rush of nirvana pulls through me and grabs me by the throat. The longer I watch him sleep, I picture him close up again, replaying the way he held me, and the way a look of desire flashed across his stony face.

Yeah…

I like him.

I WAKE to a loud sound that only resembles an explosion. I jolt against something hard. I'm too tired to open my eyes, so I nestle further into the soft, cloudy, fuzzy blankets. I haven't slept this comfortably and peacefully since Liam's betrayal, and that was months ago. I slowly drift deeper into sleep again when the fuzzy blankets move…

Wait. It's not fuzzy anymore. They're hard. Like rock-solid hard.

Like a muscular man, hard, and my heart does that stupid thing where it skips a beat when I'm around a specific person.

My lids fly open.

I'm right.

Gavin is asleep, *beneath me.* He's facing the wall, so I get a glimpse of his perfect, strong jawline. Several silver strands intertwined in his dark beard catch my attention. One of his arms is hovering over my waist, his fingers on my hips, gripping me in his sleep.

When did he get into my bed? And why?

I don't mind it all, but how did this happen?

He twitches in his sleep, and his other hand grazes my arms, keeping me pinned to his abs. His rough, calloused palms leave sparks in their wake. My nose brushes against his hard stomach —his scent running into my senses, and his cologne mixed with his natural smell still remains strong. It's becoming my favorite scent lately. The kind that makes me want to savor it and not let go.

"You were crying in your sleep," he mumbles. His deep voice reverberates through his chest while he keeps his blue eyes sealed.

Oh?

"You asked me to come into bed with you."

"I did?" I hold my gasp. "So you listened to someone who is half-conscious?"

"It was the only way I could get some rest. So yes, Coraline, I did," he mumbles with annoyance in his tone.

Ass.

My brows knit together as I remain still as a statue, trying to remember.

It all comes back to me.

I woke in the middle of the night, having another nightmare. This time, I dreamt of a masked man chasing me through the snow, wielding a butcher's knife.

I remember waking up to Gavin's hand on my shoulder. The rest is a bit fuzzy, but I vaguely remember asking him to come into bed with me. He stood silently as I waited for his answer in the dark. I guess I fell back to sleep before I could get his reply.

Five minutes go by, and I hear light snoring coming through his sleeping face. He's too handsome. The kind that's unfair because he could make any girl melt with just one glance.

He's back to sleep. There's a soft, baby silver-blue glow peeking through the window blinds. The sun is rising. The whistling of the windstorms is still present, acting like white noise to my thundering heartbeat. I don't want to move.

I blink slowly and raise my head to face him. My leg is swung over his middle, and the only reason I know this is because something hard pokes through his sweatpants and spears my midsection. When I brush against it to stretch, a low, feral, deep groan slips into my ears. His chest vibrates against my cheek, and heat creeps into my face when he makes that desirable deep growl. I freeze my movements, too afraid to wake him. The man intimidates me whenever he sets those blue eyes on me. I can't handle it if he wakes up now and all my morals go out the window.

It's getting bigger.

I flick my gaze up to his, but I only catch his side profile, the bottom of his bearded jaw, and his wavy, dark hair, sprawled messily. He's still asleep. His chest rises and falls slowly and deeply.

It's his 'morning wood'.

Jesus. He's...*huge*. His length is long and thick. His sweatpants accentuate his hard cock. I'm fully awake now, with a fast heart rate and a fire ignited in the pit of my stomach. Heat travels to my cheeks, chest, neck, and between my thighs.

I make a whimpering sound, tugging the inside of my mouth with my teeth.

"Gavin," I murmur softly and airily, so I don't scare him. I slowly back away from him and inch to the other side of the bed. I shift my hips and raise his hand over my head to place it back to his side—even though it's the last thing I want to do.

It's freezing, which means the fire from the living room must have burnt out a while ago.

He slowly turns and fixates on me. A warm smile pulls on his lips, and his sleepy eyes look me up and down.

"What is it?" I ask.

He clears his throat and gazes away at the other side of the room. While his eyes look anywhere but me, he reaches for my bicep and pulls my shirt back up. Half of my breast was exposed, and half of my nipple peeked through. He raises the strap over my shoulder and covers me back up.

"Oh."

He stands from the bed, and his bulge is bigger than before—holy monster thick dick. I feel like I'm seeing one for the first time. In a way, it does feel that way. I've never been with a man with this length before, and that's because his clothes are straining it. I thought Liam's was average, but this? I mean, I've only ever heard my friends talk about being with hung men, but this?

"Oh," he mirrors my shocked tone, gazing at his boner. He rounds the bed and moves past me.

"It's okay," I reassure him, trying to kill the awkwardness with a forced anxious grin. "I know that happens sometimes." I rock on my heels anxiously, shaking my head.

What a stupid thing to say, Coraline.

He swings open the door and takes one last look at me. He deadpans, a flicker of restraint when he curls his massive fists into balls as he tries to hide his growing bulge. Geez, it's getting bigger? A tingling sensation swims down my body.

"Yeah." His eyes darken before he walks away.

The door clicks shut.

CHAPTER 18
GAVIN

"*I know that happens sometimes.*"

Coraline's flustered cheeks and airy voice linger and pinball in my head like a song on repeat. A mesmerizing broken record I'd gladly listen to.

Yeah, blood seems to rush to my core when there's a beautiful woman I could have only conjured in my dreams, who ends up in my bed with her soft arms tangled around me.

I've slept with strangers before. Plenty of gorgeous women from my time in the military with names I can't remember. I don't know their names on purpose because it's a rule I set for myself since I was a young man.

No words. No names. No stories.

Just sex. Condoms. And no kissing.

But Coraline is breaking my rules one by one without even trying, and it's pissing me off.

It's pissing me off because I want to talk to her. I want to know what her lips will feel like on mine. I want to memorize the shape of them and the way her skin feels. I want to know every single detail about her entire life before the snow stops falling.

This way of thinking is unnatural to me. It's foreign and weird to feel something flip inside my stomach, but this time, I'm not running from it; I'm chasing after it.

I told Coraline I needed to use the bathroom and to please, for the love God, don't leave the cabin without me. I come out of the shower with a white towel wrapped around my waist and step into my bedroom. I dress from the bottom to my waist. I swipe the wet droplets still dripping down my chest, then run the towel through my hair.

Today, the blizzard stops.

I plan to carry on the annual tradition I used to do when I was a kid.

Shed hunting.

It's a hobby of mine.

I walk outside my bedroom door, and smell…

Is that pancakes? Breakfast food? Maple syrup? Coffee?

Is she cooking? For me? *For us?*

Swinging each stiff arm into my sweater, I walk down the hallway, my mouth salivating when I find a kitchen I don't recognize. It looks like Santa Claus retched everywhere. There are shades of bright classic red, emerald green, pearl white, and pops of silver-blue. Standing before the stove, Coraline flips a pancake with a spatula and sets another atop a pile of pancakes on the countertop, wearing a weightless smile. I haven't seen her this cheery since I found her.

My heart seizes in my chest.

These decorations shouldn't be here. I shouldn't be looking at them like I want to burn my whole house down. I haven't seen them in decades because they've been stored in the basement, untouched, *for a reason.*

"Good morning, Gavin. Want some pancakes?" she asks, swiping her forehead.

I don't know how to feel.

Confusion is the first thing to slither into my mind.

Christmas wreaths cover every inch above the wooden cabinets, their ivory lights twinkling slowly—nutcrackers in every corner. The thumping in my chest switches to my ears. Opening and closing my mouth, I can't form a single word. My palms smooth over my shirt across my abdomen, dismantling the wrinkles.

"What the hell is this?" I snap.

Coraline freezes. My cold tone disintegrates the warmth she oozes with every flick of her wrist as she cooks. Her dark brows knit together as she assesses me, almost afraid to make a move, or I'll pounce on her like a hungry predator ready to execute his prey.

"Making you breakfast?" she squeaks innocently. She slowly turns the gas dial until the stove fire is out. "I made pancakes and grilled bacon I found in the fridge. There's coffee still fresh and hot in the pot. Don't worry, I didn't put any creamer in it because I noticed you don't like it." She grabs a plate from a cabinet above her head. "More hazelnut for me." Tiptoeing, her fingers hook two glass plates. I drink her in from the side as perspiration breaks out across my chest. Her thick curls are more voluminous, and some stick to her cheek as she waltzes around the kitchen, moving back and forth from the stove and island. It's tied up in a bun with little strands of hair poking out. She's wearing my mother's apron and using my dad's signature butter knife we made together to top the pancakes with butter—cooking surrounded by my parents' decorations.

It's too much.

This is all too much at once.

Something inside of me snaps in half.

"Stop." My jaw ticks.

Her beautiful, cheery, weightless smile disappears, and I already feel like an ass. But I've never held back.

"What? Why?" she asks, holding a plate in one hand and a

knife in the other. The syrup and butter pool around the pancakes' crispy edges as she keeps them aloft.

"Just stop. Stop moving. Stop cooking. Stop."

"Gavin, is everything okay?"

"You went into the basement again?" I accuse her roughly. My emotions are overflowing, beyond my control, intercepting everything. I'm used to being in control here in the cabin. And I'm losing it.

"Yes, I did." She sets the plates down on the island and pats her thighs. "I thought just because Christmas is over, it doesn't mean we can't pretend, right?" That smile is back, but it's forced. The ivory lights glimmer in her eyes. "I slept through the holiday when you pulled me out of the accident." She sucks in a breath. "Cooking and cleaning for you is the least I can do, and Merelyn mentioned you haven't touched those boxes in years, so I thought—"

"You thought what?" I bark and take a step toward the kitchen counter as she tracks my face, raking up and down vehemently. She visibly shrinks into place. I feel bad, but it's not enough to change the tone. I dart my gaze toward the knife in her hands, and my stomach immediately knots, seeing it again. I softly take it out of her still hands and place it into the sink.

There are so many reasons for the way I'm reacting. So many reasons and stories behind every single thing in this cabin. All of this stays in the basement for a reason because it feels like a portal into the darkness I've kept shut for a long time. Giving her my back, I palm the sink and try to breathe before I crash.

"Gavin. I'm sorry. I didn't mean any harm. I just know that it must be lonely up here for you. I'm stuck here for some time, and I'm trying to help out as much as I can," she murmurs.

I turn around and find her slipping off the apron and hooking it on the pantry door.

"I'm not fucking lonely. I'm not someone to fix," I hiss.

"Don't go into the basement. Don't touch my things. Don't make me coffee. Don't cook for me, don't do anything," I quip coldly.

She stares at me, deadpanning. The silence is growing thicker by the second. Shit, I hate seeing her frown like this. And I hate that it's affecting me this much. I don't want to care about the way she feels about me; she just met me, but it's hard when everything about Coraline is effortlessly magnetic.

There's no way in hell a woman like her could be interested in a man like me. I need to pull away from her. There's no future with anyone because I refuse to give up this place I call home.

"I'm heading out."

I need space and room to breathe.

"But what about breakfast?" she asks and points to the plate of stacked pancakes and bacon.

"I'm not hungry," I tell her as I place my hat on top of my head and exit the house. Cold wind, snow everywhere, nothing but wilderness tuning out the chilling chaos I've managed to keep buried.

CHAPTER 19
CORALINE

I'm snowed in with the Grinch.

I'm sure of it.

I feel defeated. Every time I think we're getting along, taking two steps forward, we're going three distant, impatient steps back. I didn't mean to break his boundaries by going into the basement. I truly wanted to help. After last night, I wanted to do something nice for him.

His place is quite dull for the holidays, so why not lighten it from moody to cheery with decorations, bright colors, and twinkling lights? Sleepy Coldwater seems to go all out when it comes to Christmas.

Why did he seem so triggered?

And why is he going out there right now?

There's wildlife everywhere out here. I've had more close calls in one hour than in my entire life. I'm hesitant to follow him outside because of the wolves, moose, and potential avalanches.

That's why he stays armed in case anything happens.

What if the asshole that's after me could still be here, lurking and waiting for another opportunity to kill me?

I know Gavin doesn't believe me. Maybe he thinks I hit my head too hard and I'm making everything up.

I stand in the middle of the kitchen, tugging on the inside of my cheek with my teeth, going back and forth with myself. I watch the flames swirl in the fireplace, debating if I should head to Merelyn's when my hair gets pulled back harshly.

Now he's yanking my hair? How the hell did he get behind me so fast? I thought he went outside toward the back? How did I miss him? And why the hell is he pulling my hair?

I whirl around, getting ready to screech insults at Gavin, maybe even slap him across the face, but my mouth stays open when nothing but air greets me, my hand staying stiff as a rock by my side.

There's nobody.

My pressed lips fall into a concerned frown. My blood runs cold when I realize I'm alone and that hellish sensation is back.

What the?

I physically felt someone's fingers in my hair, their edges and shape of their flesh against mine—grazing my scalp right before a thick section of my hair was pulled.

With a pulsing heartbeat, my eyes widen as I search for Gavin, Merelyn, or even Georgia, but no one is here. A sinking sensation of dread and fear washes over me. Goosebumps light up my skin as I blink around the room slowly, investigating every corner for an explanation.

I know I felt someone's hand on me.

I know I did.

I don't think I'm alone.

And I don't think a living person did this.

Was it the woman I saw in the bathroom after my first shower? Or was it that man I had nightmares of last night? The same one with blood all over his face in the kitchen cabinet's reflection? Either way, I don't want the answer.

Blood thrums in my ears as I swallow anxiously, and I pedal

backwards slowly until I'm in the living room, just waiting for something to pop out. My eyes are glued to the walls, the windows, anything and everything, waiting for a figure to present itself.

Screw this. I don't want to be alone when questionable things are happening in this cabin. I've never believed in ghosts. Sure, I love watching paranormal horror movies, but I've never had an experience to make me think spirits are real. I think I'm being haunted.

After my stay, I think I can say I'm a firm believer in the paranormal.

I guess I won't get to eat the breakfast I've been cooking for the past hour.

I quickly swing on a coat I find on the coat rack. It's thick, black, and goes all the way down past my knees, surprisingly fitting me enough to cling to my body. This must be Merelyn's. I follow Gavin outside and track his footsteps in the snow. It leads me straight to him.

Easy.

I find him just in time before he disappears into the trees. Tall and moody, walking with a signature distinct pace. His massive shoulders sway with every strut. He's smoking a cigarette. With his two fingers, he flicks it until small pieces of ash soar into the air. For someone who seems to smoke frequently, it doesn't stain his home or clothes or follow him home, which is refreshing.

I don't know why I try with Gavin, but I can recognize when someone is hurting. I notice it in the way he can't smile or laugh. He's someone with a story. A history that made him guarded, timid, abrasive, and tainted. Someone who can't seem to pull themselves out of the dark. It's the way I've been for the past few months, fighting to get out of my depression.

We have a lot in common that way, but how long has he been trying to get out of the dark?

"Why are you such a jerk?!" I blurt as soon as I'm in range for him to hear me complain.

Yikes.

I'm getting straight to the point, but after getting to know him, I don't think he minds. He might even prefer it.

He stops moving. I don't bother bringing up what just happened in the kitchen with my hair. I don't need to make him think I'm delusional, too. He might kick me out of the cabin at this point if I keep bringing up the abnormal encounters. I believe it's best to keep this to myself for the remainder of my stay.

"I mean, look," I palm my hips. "You said you want to start over, but every time I think we're making progress as room-mates, you push me away and leave. What? Are you going to disappear for three days again? Leave me alone in the cabin while you do God knows what?"

"Don't talk to me as if I owe you something," he snarls. "I owe you nothing. You're in my house," he points to the cabin, "cooking my food, sleeping in my bed, putting up my mother's decorations! I'm sorry I gave you the wrong idea about me. So let's clear up my reputation so you don't get the wrong idea." His Adam's apple bobs. "I didn't have to do anything for you that night, and I still don't."

I rear back, feeling more unwelcome and like an inconvenience than ever before.

"Don't be mistaken, sweetheart. I'm not a good man. I pulled you out of that wreckage because it was the right thing to do. I could have left you there."

"Wow, *my hero*," I spit slowly and sarcastically with a cruel bite to my words. I ignore the way heat crept into my cheeks when he called me sweetheart. How does he manage to be still so hot even when he's being a grumpy asshole?

"I'm trying to be nice, but why do you make it so hard to get to know you?!"

"Maybe because I'm not worth getting to know. There's *nothing to get to know.*"

His eyes narrow, and his cruel frown drops into something unreadable. I rear back as I watch him curse to himself. He rearranges his brown hat on the top of his head, lifting it into the air as he uses his fingers to rake through his hair. It's as though he let candor slip through the cracks of the wall he likes to hide behind.

"Maybe because I don't know what to do with you when you look at and talk to me." His nostrils flare while puffs of air swirl out of his mouth every time he breathes. "I don't know what to do when you're cooking in my kitchen, looking the way you do. Or when you come out of my shower wearing my clothes. You intimidate me. No one comes up here. I'm not interesting—I'm dull. What you see is what you get."

I intimidate him? Me? There's nothing to intimidate him with. He's the one who makes me nervous with one glance. I hope the snowfall is masking my blush.

"Gavin." I shake my head as I continue to soak his words in. I want to say a thousand things.

Don't be intimidated by me.

You are anything but dull.

Why doesn't anyone visit? Surely you have friends.

I knew he was lonely, but he doesn't want to admit it.

I close the distance in seconds, climbing out of the feet of snow more easily than I thought. When I close in on him, I palm the tree he's leaning on until I'm facing his stressed and remote expression, breathing in his minty, magnetic scent.

I hate how good he smells. I hate it because every time I hear his voice, look at him, smell him, it's hard to force the fact that I'm still married out of my head. I'm technically single, but it still doesn't feel right to acknowledge the tension brewing between us. My attraction toward him guilts me.

"What is that supposed to mean?" I ask softly.

"It means…" He shakes his head and leans on one side of his hip. "It means, why do you want to get to know me? You're going to leave soon." His fingers lurch to my chin until he's tipping it upwards. I submissively let him direct my body as I stand. "Talking leads to attachment. And attachment leads to disappointment." He breathes against my lips teasingly, then pulls back with disdain written all over his face.

"That's an awful way to look at things," I counter.

"It's the reality."

"I think you've protected your peace a little too much in these mountains." I huff. "Where are you going? Are you headed toward the same place you were hiding for three days?"

"You ask a lot of questions," he grumbles. He takes another drag and blows the smoke over his shoulder, keeping his eyes trained on mine. His gaze falls shorty to my lips before he pulls away.

"I'm curious," I point out. It's not a lie. I want to get to know him even when he's being hot and cold all the time.

"I have stuff to do today. I don't have time for your inquisition."

"Like what?" I lift a brow. "Where are you going? To make a snowman?"

He's so serious all the time. He makes it so easy to get under his skin. It's actually fun.

"Shed hunting."

Out of all the things I thought he was going to say, that wasn't one of them.

"Shed hunting? What is that?"

Gavin gives me a long sweep from head to toe before he concedes. He turns around and continues to saunter away, looking more relaxed than he did in the kitchen. I push off the tree and soldier into the snow until I'm right beside him.

"Slow down, I have little legs," I complain as I try to match his fast pace. "My legs aren't as long as yours."

An icy wind rattles the leaves and branches. God, he's so tall.

"Fine," I offer. "I'll help you."

"No."

"Yes."

"Coraline, go back to the cabin."

"No."

"Do you know any other word than no?"

"Whatever. So why do you like shed hunting?"

"You're annoying."

"Yes," I tell him, stepping over a branch.

He's given up on trying to convince me to go back, and I cherish the small victory over the long silence. I gaze up at the mountains, wrapping my head around the beauty. Now that the snow fog has cleared, everything is clearer. There's a bright blue lake running not too far from here.

"Every spring, animals shed their antlers. I collect them. That's why I call it shed hunting."

Finally!

He's opening up to me.

"I used to do this when I was a kid. It's...fun for me. Every winter, I get out of the house, search for them, and add them to my collection. I started this tradition when I was five years old, whenever my parents would argue. I didn't want to be around them when they would fight, and we don't live near the city. I didn't have friends nearby. Only Merelyn. So, I went shed hunting."

"Your parents fought a lot, too, huh? My parents are still together, even though they argue all day, every day, like it's a competition to see who can instigate the most fights, wins."

"Yeah, except when my mother wasn't around, he'd take his anger out on me with a knife."

I still, almost tripping over my feet. He says it like it's a regular part of childhood. He keeps walking until something catches his attention. I stare at the back of his head as I spot a scar on the back of his neck.

I remember those scars. I spotted them all over his back when he slept in the corner of his bedroom with me. Are those from his father?

He bends down, pulls a shed of antlers out of the snow.

"A three-pointer. Where's the other one?" he mumbles to himself. "If I get lucky, I can find the other one nearby." He takes a long stride to the right away from me. "Anyways, they're dead. Died before I could understand the meaning of death. I never understood what it feels like to have a family. Merelyn is the closest I'll ever get."

How the hell is he so nonchalant right now?

His father would stab him.

No, that can't be what he said, right? I want to ask him to repeat himself to make sure, but I hold back.

"What animal is this from?" I ask, trying to push down the rock in my throat with a long swallow, rolling with the topic change. I don't want to imagine a five-year-old Gavin, afraid and lonely, getting stabbed by his own father. It hurts.

"A Sitka black-tailed deer."

I nod like I know what that means and force a smile anyway through glassy eyes. He's opening up about something personal. It's a window for us to talk. This is an opportunity to share something, too.

"I'm getting stalked," I blurt.

"You told me."

"I have a feeling the man after me won't stop until I'm dead."

Gavin looks at me over his shoulder.

"If this person tries to get near you again, I'll kill him. It's simple, Coraline. You worry so much, all the time."

I don't know how to respond, so I give him a reluctant nod. Is he starting to believe me?

"Gavin."

"Yeah?"

"Have you ever thought of leaving this place?"

"It crosses my mind every time it snows," he scoffs with a lazy grin. He exhales—a puff of white swirls from his parted lips. "But no. I could never leave Merelyn up here alone. She's also rooted herself here, with no plans to move. She's more stubborn than I am, and this is my home."

He stands back up and hands me the antler. I look over it, studying every crease and edge—the scratches. It's an older animal with history written all over it.

"This is beautiful."

"Keep going, Coraline. Tell me more," he says, walking faster. His boots easily push through the mountains of ice. He finds another one, this time it's smaller. We add it to the growing pile in my arms.

"My husband cheated on me with my best friend."

He doesn't say anything. He doesn't stop or flinch, but I think he likes hearing me talk, even if he won't admit it…I think he secretly likes my company.

"I stopped drawing after that. I was sad for a long time."

"When did this happen?"

"A few months ago." This time, there's no overly emotional tone to my voice. It doesn't hurt to talk about it. "I came to Sleepy Coldwater after receiving an invitation via email. I was going to pass it up because this year was rough on me mentally, but—"

"You're here," he finishes for me.

I nod.

"I'm here."

He stops and glances at me, making my lungs seize. I'm ashamed of how quickly this man pulls me in like gravity.

"Good," he says. His voice is rougher than what I'm used to. Empathy flickers through his eyes as he stares at me longer.

He closes the distance, facing me, looking deeply past my blood and bones until I feel him inside me—something warm invades my swelling chest, and the need to feel how his lips would feel on mine enters my head. But then Gavin breaks the moment with a fast blink, catching himself before he can say or do anything more. He turns around, his tongue dragging against his lips before he gives me his back.

Was he thinking the same thing as me?

I press my lips together, trying to fight the fire he's ignited.

"You're stubborn, but you're a good person. I know you are."

"I'm not perfect."

"None of us is," he says.

During one of the most challenging moments of my life, I shut down completely. I didn't want to talk or see anyone. Even when my sister reached out to help, I couldn't get out of the hole I was sinking into. I didn't give them a chance to be there for me.

Since coming to Alaska, I've found something to hold onto.

Hope.

My foot hits something hard. I look down and spot another shed. I yank it out of the snow and smile.

"I found its match!" I bristle, excitedly, twisting it around in my hand.

"Would you look at that?" He turns around and ambles toward me. He grins. Holy shit, Gavin's smiling. And it's the kind of smile that's infectious. I can't help but mirror it with my own. I miss being able to smile like this, but around Gavin, it's instinct. I don't even realize I'm doing it too.

"You're finally pulling your weight around here. I don't have to throw you out of my cabin today."

"You know you can say, thank you, right? Say nice things?"

"It's not a part of my vocabulary."

"Right." I roll my eyes before I take more antlers from his

hands and add them to my collection. I stick out my tongue playfully, and I swear I spot a small smile, but he turns around before I can define it.

"What do you do for a living, Gavin? Rescue girls from wreckages?"

He chuckles.

"And you're a veteran, correct? You were in the Navy?"

"Yes. I served 15 years in special operations before I got out. I loved it. I didn't want to leave the teams, but I was forced—*ordered to*. There were multiple reasons. The main reason was that I got injured and could no longer do my job." He takes something out of his pocket. It's a knife. He twirls it around his palm. "I wanted to leave Alaska for good, but Merelyn needed me as she got older. She's too prideful to say it, but I know she needs me. She has no one. No children or family nearby, but me. So I moved back home to the cabin. I'm a fisherman now, looking for Salmon, King Crabs, Snow Crab, and Halibut. I'll leave for days to weeks on a boat with a crew."

"That's why Merelyn needs Georgia?"

He nods.

"I think Georgia likes you."

I don't know why I feel a curious pull toward Georgia's and Gavin's relationship. But there has to be history there.

He doesn't say anything.

"Do you like her?"

Nada.

"She's pretty," I add, pulling teeth.

"She's not the one I want."

"So, there is someone! Who do you wa—"

"And you? What do you do for work?" he intercepts.

"I'm...well..."

How am I supposed to top that? He literally risks his life for a career. It's a very physically demanding job. Is he going to laugh when I tell him I paint for a living? Will he say it's stupid and impractical, just like Liam would?

"Spit it out."

Here goes nothing.

"I…paint. I'm an artist." I shut my eyes tight, waiting for him to degrade me. Twisting my face, I wait for the cruel words I've grown so accustomed to; they linger in my head with my own voice instead of Liam's.

You'll never make it.

No one cares.

You're not good at this.

It's just a dream. It's never going to happen. You're not good enough.

Give up. Quit.

Colliding with a hard wall interrupts my thoughts. Shit. I open my eyes to find out that the hard wall is actually Gavin's chest. I lose my footing, letting out a high-pitched yelp. I'm falling over; the pile of sheds I was holding onto is now airborne—getting flung into the air. Gavin slings his arm forward, firmly coiling around my waist. I lurch for his other arm, barely able to hook my hand around him when I'm anchoring him down with me to the floor. Before I can hit the ground, his hand curls around the back of my head, so I land in his palm instead of a log.

Grunting, the air gets knocked out of me. Gavin's on top of me, his chest on mine, his knees settling in between my inner thighs, the tip of his nose softly brushing against mine.

"I'm sorry," I murmur, suddenly unable to breathe when he's this close. I can't think straight.

"You're an artist?"

"Mhm," I hum.

"I think that's amazing, Cora. You have a gift. Don't ever stop."

"But you haven't seen any pieces."

"Don't need to."

Hearing those words fall out of his mouth so effortlessly feels so good. A sting hits my eyes. I try so hard to create—to be different. Art is how I stay alive when I feel so dead sometimes.

"I don't want to stop," I breathe, zeroing in on his full lips, practically begging him to make a move. Screw it. I want to let myself be happy.

Kiss me.

As if he can read my thoughts, he leans closer, his cool breath ghosting over mine. His lids lazily fall over his deep blue irises. They're glowing, but this time, I don't see pain.

He pushes his fingers through my hair, and just when I think he's going to seal his lips on mine, he pulls out a twig from my curls, killing the moment.

"So adding clumsy on top of stubborn and amazingly talent-ed." He sighs, falling to his side so he's off me and lying next to me instead.

"Gavin?" I quirk a brow.

"Yeah?"

"Thank you."

He turns to me.

"Thank you for talking to me." I reach for his hand. When our fingers connect, he doesn't pull away. He watches me thread my fingers with his and squeeze. He doesn't fight it, but he doesn't squeeze back. "I have the urge to pick up a pencil now." I scoff with a smile.

We lock eyes as the air around us buzzes.

Does he feel it too?

"You know, I used to have a passion, just like you. An outlet. Something that gives me life and excitement." His blue eyes light up differently as he shares. "But after my injury," he sighs sadly, "I quit. I quit everything that once made me happy until I found something that inspired me again. Something that gave me hope to at least *try*."

I quirk a brow, wanting to know so badly what his ray of hope was.

Depression is like that sometimes for me.

When I feel like I'm lost in the dark, I search so badly for something to remind me of the woman I'm meant to be. I cling to it like an anchor in a deep, chaotic ocean. Watch it like a shooting star in the night sky. Cherish it like the only sunflower in a badland.

"What was that thing for you?" I ask, getting closer. "What gave you hope again?"

He smiles, tucking a hair strand behind my ear.

"You know, Coraline, you should be afraid of me. Everyone in this town is."

I hesitate, my brows furrowing for a moment, then I relax.

"I'm not." I frown.

Why does he think that about himself? I want to ask a dozen questions, but I want to hold onto this rare moment more.

"I'm afraid of *you*." He holds my hand tighter when I try to retract. My heart begins to pound harder, louder.

Can he hear it?

"Why?" I ask, fighting back the curve of my lips.

"Not yet."

"Not yet?" I ask, confused.

"Not yet," he parrots calmly.

With the way he's staring at me, I get the hint that there's a deeper meaning behind those two words. He doesn't want to talk; he just wants to savor the moment and be in the present.

I smile, wondering what his past holds. I want to know all about it and his injury. I want to keep asking him questions just so I can hear his voice, full of hope, but I don't want to push it. I like watching him open up to me. It feels freeing to be here in the wilderness with him.

He looks everywhere—my eyes, my face, my nose, my cheeks, my hair.

"What are you doing?" I whisper.

"I'm looking at you, sweetheart."

"Why?"

"Because I can't seem to stop."

CHAPTER 20
CORALINE

I'm so bad at flirting. After I left Liam, I took a gamble on my dating life before I came to Sleepy Coldwater. I met a guy who worked at a law firm on an online app, and we matched. The date was going well, mostly because I let him do all the talking. Then, when I was about to break the ice with a joke, I got the appetizer potato soup in my hair when I leaned closer. I urgently grabbed the napkin from my lap, fully embarrassed, but when I took it off my lap and jetted it toward my hair frantically, I hit the ends of the table with so much force, the table lifted, causing his soup to fall all over his lap. Aaand, it was all downhill from there.

So when Gavin looks at me like this, full of desire and a hint of need—I don't know how to handle it. His dark brows furrowed, his eyes sweeping over my lips and face. I've never met any man with beautiful blue eyes like his. His addictive, minty-cedar scent envelops me. All of it is a perfect, enchanting potion I don't mind drinking even if it's poisonous.

I need to get away from him because I'm not good at this anymore. I've been constantly put down so much by Liam and my ex-friends that my insecurities seem to always leak through the cracks of my built-up confidence. I don't know how to accept when something feels good.

The snow will stop falling, and it'll melt away. My time here has an end date. *We both know that.*

Standing up, I gather all the antlers around us, brush the snow off each one, and tuck them into the crook of my arm.

"I'll keep looking for more antlers this way!" I squeak nervously, letting my thick curls hide my heated red cheeks.

"Sweetheart?"

Sweetheart.

That one word makes time come to a stop for me, only because it's coming from Gavin.

"Coraline, wait." His distant voice bristles and echoes through the trees. He rises slowly, almost tripping over his left leg. He regains his stance quickly, pasting his elbow on the tree for balance. I peer over my shoulder as I head towards the stables in the distance. He doesn't chase after me, but only looks at me like he's disappointed.

I hate that I'm a coward. I can tell cutting that moment off is bothering him, and I'm only proving his own point of feeling like he's not worth getting to know when he *truly is*. I'm just too scared to let myself get too close.

"It's okay! I'll keep looking. It's getting dark already. We'll be able to collect more of these if we split up anyway. I'll meet you at the cabin in a few minutes!" I turn around, biting my lip nervously, and scrunch my nose, wanting so badly to facepalm.

I feel bad.

It's a terrible excuse, but not exactly a lie. He takes it anyway and gives me space. He doesn't force the moment. He lets me go, still holding a clenched jaw and a defeated look on his handsome face.

I keep walking, veering farther away from him and closer to the horses. The sound of running water catches my attention. It's wide and shallow, running over all shapes of rocks and fallen tree branches. I'm surprised it isn't frozen. The current is fast and strong, and the water is the darkest blue I've ever seen.

The grey sky darkens. It feels like an hour has gone by, and I haven't found another antler. I guess my good luck charm is Gavin. I keep walking, scouring the snow, looking for a brown tip. I'm about to head back to the cabin when I spot one. I almost mistook it for a branch.

I grab the four-pointed antler and do a happy dance. Gavin will love this!

The sound of snow crunching interrupts my solo celebration. I smile, hoping to rub it in grumpy Gavin's face playfully.

"Look what I got, Gavin." I straighten my spine and watch clouds come out of my nose and mouth. "I told you splitting up was a good idea. I'm going to take this with me to Texas."

I whip my head in its direction, lifting the antler as if it's a diamond or gold bar.

"Do you think it'll fit in my suit—" My grin immediately drops into a scared frown when I realize it isn't Gavin.

It's not the pack of wolves or a moose.

It's the masked man from the night of the car crash. He's covered head to toe in white, seamlessly blending in with the snow. He's standing feet away, walking slowly toward me. Then, he's sprinting fast like he's on a mission and nothing will stop him.

I drop the antlers and make a beeline in the direction I last saw Gavin.

He's here, and he's going to kill me!

"Gavin!" I yelp. I hope he can hear me, and he's not that far away. "Gavin! Help! Please!" I keep screaming until my throat feels like it's going to bleed. With my body running cold, the footsteps grow louder and faster behind me. He's right on my heels.

He is still here. I knew it, but no one believed me!

I sneak a quick glance, fisting my hands, ready to strike, but when I look behind me, the masked man is no longer there.

"What?!" I breathe, veering left and right, inspecting every corner of the woods. Then, I'm crashing into something hard. It completely takes me out, and I lose my footing and fall into the snow. My back collides first, so I'm facing the dark silver sky and trees.

"Coraline!" Gavin emerges from a few feet away. I dart my gaze toward him, blinking away the tears. My heart instantly slows down at the sight of him.

"Gavin! He was here! He was right there!" I point toward the river. He hoists me up by tucking his arms under my armpits. He brings me close to his chest, protectively.

"Did he hurt you?" he barks furiously, scanning me up and down. His hands hook onto my arms as I try to gather my emotions and find my words.

I shake my head, my tongue drying up. "No, I ran into a tree, but I saw him, Gavin! He was wearing all-white hunting clothes and a white mask." My fingers tremble against his biceps. I glance over to the running river, expecting him to be there again, but no one is.

He pulls out a gun from his waistband and clicks off the safety. "Go back to the cabin, now! I'll be back. If I'm not back in thirty minutes, go find Georgia and Merelyn." He points it to the ground as he saunters away from me.

"Gavin. No! Don't go." Fear vibrates through me. I reach out for him, capturing air because he's already walking away from me with a murderous expression and a tight grip on his weapon. I do as I'm told and sprint back to the cabin.

IT'S PITCH BLACK OUTSIDE. My fingers are stabbed in between the window blinds, searching for Gavin or the one after me. My stomach growls loudly as I push myself closer to the freezing window.

He has to be okay. I'm one minute from going to Georgia's when the front door springs open. I whirl around, grabbing a log of wood, ready to launch it.

I thought I locked it?!

Gavin appears relaxed, kicking the snow and dirt off his boots. He shuts the door. I slowly lower the wood beside the couch until it's on the floor. Taking off his cowboy hat, he sets it on the kitchen counter and stares at me.

"There's no one out there." He shrugs nonchalantly.

I scoff.

"I know what I saw, Gavin."

He places his hands on his hips and gazes at me. A look so serious it sends shivers down my spine.

"Which brings me to what happened earlier today. I felt someone pull my hair! Right after you stormed out of the kitchen to go shed hunt. I thought it was you. T-that," I start to stammer, but I regain my composure. "That you came back into the house, even though I didn't hear you return, and for whatever reason, you yanked my hair, but when I turned around, I was alone in the cabin!" Tears prick my eyes. My chest rises and falls faster, my breaths strained.

I'm so tired of the ghosts thing. I want to get the hell out of this place, but I'm stuck here until the road clears.

"I believe you." He murmurs. "I believe you, Coraline."

"Good." I squeak. "That makes me feel better."

"There's no one else here right now but you and me. I won't let anything or anyone hurt you, okay?"

Heat flares from my chest to my cheeks.

As I look into his eyes, I nod.

"Come here, I want to show you something," he calls me over with a swipe of his fingers. "Put your coat back on," he fishes my coat off the rack and holds it up, waiting for me at the front door.

"We're going outside?" I stroll over to him, eagerly. "What if he's out there?"

"Yes, we're going outside, and if he's out there, I have my gun on me," he replies. My heart begins to race as I give him my back. Just being close to him makes me flustered. Shrugging my way into the coat, he gathers my hair in one fist, so my coat doesn't yank it. "Let's go."

"Why?" I ask nervously.

"Follow me, Coraline." He grabs my hand, threading his fingers into mine. I let him pull me outside.

As soon as my boots hit the snow, I see exactly what he wants to show me.

The northern lights.

Beams of green and purple light up the sky. The beautiful colors and twinkling stars take my breath away. My mouth drops open, and the corners of my lips lift. Gavin lets my hand go but stays close to my side.

"I've never seen the northern lights with my own eyes before. Only in pictures and videos." I say, tilting my head back, stunned by its beauty.

"So beautiful and so incredible." My vision blurs. I can't believe I'm seeing this. I feel like I'm falling in love with life again, slowly. My cheeks burn from grinning so hard.

"Yes," he replies softly.

I peer over to him. Isn't he seeing this too?

He's standing right next to me, his gaze locked onto my face and not the sky. How long has he been staring at me like this?

He's smiling.

"*You are,*" he finishes. The green rays, tinged with lavender, beam across his handsome face. I match his smile with my own. I'm afraid to open my heart again, but if love feels like this moment, right now, it might be worth a chance.

For the first time since I was in the Navy, I talked.

Like, *really talked* to someone about something other than deployments, missions, fishing, and war. We talked for hours outside, collecting shed after shed, and not once did she complain. I've always done this alone, since I was five years old. My father would get deeply inebriated, and he would pass out on the couch after he would beat and stab me. To make myself feel better, I'd go hunt for sheds for my mother and for me. Today was the first time I did this with another person.

Coraline Rosa.

She knows things about me that no one else does. She catches the little things—like how I like my coffee black and how I can't stay inside more than a few hours because I'm addicted to the outdoors. She knows when I'm thinking about her in ways I desire because she blushes every time I look at her like she's the only woman in this world…because to me, she is.

I'm obsessed already and so fucking fucked.

She makes me smile just by breathing.

I've had to fight erection after erection. Smile after smile. The urge to rip her clothes off and take her against a tree when she pulled me down on top of her. I'm attracted to her in every way I thought I couldn't be with another person. I want to be inside her, not just physically, but in the way I learn everything about her. I want to meet her parents so they can tell me stories about her growing up. I want to know all her secrets and ambitions, because I want to be someone she can trust and lean on for support. I crave her insatiably, desire her as much as my lungs need their next breath. The way the moon yearns for the sun. We're two different people, and I'll keep chasing her even though my attraction to her may hurt us both. She's too enchantingly perfect, and she doesn't even realize it. Her body is a temple I'd worship on my knees all night if she'd let me. She's a rare stone. Her husband lost a diamond. He let a rare diamond slip through his fingers while he chased after coal. He doesn't know what he had...But I do.

Liam is a fucking moron who doesn't deserve her.

I want to make her mine in every single way, because I know she loves it here. She's a city girl, but her soul lights up brighter here, where there are no buildings, no busy streets, no overcrowded cities. She belongs here in Alaska. I'll make her see that before the roads clear.

Coraline has, and will always be, like morphine to me since I first pulled her out of that wreckage, bloodied and weak. And now, after only a few sunrises and moonfalls, I'm a fucking fool for her. I've seen the world and been to over twenty countries throughout my career as a SEAL. And there is no one—not a fucking person like Coraline. No one has even come close to what she does to me.

She is the one I want.

Does this make me crazy?

Probably.

But what I feel for her wouldn't be real if it didn't break my sanity. At forty years old, I don't want to waste my time anymore. I've never felt an instant connection to anything or anyone, but I feel it whenever I'm with her. Coraline doesn't just see my scars, she sees me. She doesn't pity me; instead, she listens to what I have to say. She spent hours with me in the unforgiving Alaskan wilderness, where it's the most fatal time of the year. Hell, it almost killed her.

She's a fighter.

She's still here. Warm. Breathing.

And I need to have her completely without scaring her away.

There's a reason for everything. I'm not a man who believes in hope, and I don't believe the stars align for you to meet your soulmate. No, all of that is bullshit for people with naive hearts.

I believe you want something, you'll have to fight for it, and if that means being calculative, then so be it.

I want her.

But when my secrets come to light, will she stay? Or will she look at me the way everyone else does? Will she see a monster? Or will she see a man who would do anything and everything to keep her safe and happy?

CHAPTER 22
CORALINE

Today, for the first time in a long time, I had the overwhelming urge to pick up a pencil. A paintbrush. My iPad. Even a notebook to pen new stories, bottling up inside my brain. I feel inspired, and I can't contain my excitement.

I felt the need to dream again.

It's also the first time I thought about what it would feel like to have my first one-night stand or to kiss a man I just met. I've never been the adventurous type.

Always too afraid. Always too scared to live. Always insecure.

But when Gavin talks or looks at me, I forget that I'm hurting and sad. I know we just met, but there's a connection. One I can't understand or justify, but only feel. My gut is telling me to chase after this feeling because life is too short, and I want to start living again.

I look up from the thriller book I found on Gavin's bookshelf and sneak another glance at him. We've been avoiding each other throughout the cabin, but stealing glances all afternoon. He's bending down, dressed in jeans, socks, with an all-black shirt that hugs his body so right. The veins in his biceps bulge as he tosses another log into the fireplace. The flames swallow it, and orange sparks filter through. The crackles grow punchier and the flames longer.

The worst of the snowstorm is over. The roads will clear soon, and then I can leave. I flick my gaze to Gavin, who continues to sift through the wood with a metal pike. I know he's doing it to pretend he's busy. He's been avoiding me ever since we nearly kissed outside. Or maybe it's me who's avoiding him, I don't know.

But what I do know is that I don't want to leave without knowing what Gavin tastes like. I twirl my wedding ring on my finger, which I've been holding onto since the separation.

To hell with Liam.

Our divorce will be finalized soon. I'm just waiting for him to sign the papers, which, for some odd reason, he's been dodging for far too long already. I'm not going to let Liam steal another moment from me.

It's time to let go. It's time to go after things I want and right now, I want to kiss a handsome cowboy without feeling guilty about it.

Specifically Gavin.

I slide the ring off my finger. The wedding bands are soldered, so it all slides off with one slow pull. I thought my heart would crack as I did it, but I feel nothing. Nothing for the man I used to hold so high. I don't feel anything because Gavin is showing me that real men exist. Men who uplift my dreams;not slander them into the ground. How is that a man I just met is already outdoing him in every single way?

I slide the ring into my jeans pocket and tug at my bottom lip. Before I can walk over to him, three loud knocks thunder through the house.

It has to be Merelyn or Georgia. I haven't seen them in a few days.

Gavin beats me to it first. He unlocks the door and swings it open. Merelyn stands there, alone, wrapped head to toe in warm clothing, nothing but her grey-blue orbs glowing against her fair skin. The wrinkles around her eyes crease as the tips of her lips curve upwards.

"I brought over Shepherd's Pie!" Merelyn holds up a tray wrapped in aluminum.

"So, Coraline Rosa. What do you paint?" Merelyn asks, genuinely curious. I can hear it in her voice.

Gavin told Merelyn everything from my name to my career, and how I ended up in Sleepy Coldwater attending the Holly Jolly Arty Event as she served us both.

"Mostly oil paintings. I like painting skeletons, flowers, and sometimes people. Drawing people is challenging, and I'm still learning, but I love it. Sometimes, I'll get frustrated during the process, but it's all worth it in the end. I have to remind myself to be patient, but as I said, it's always worth it in the end."

"You love what you do?"

"Yes. It's been a privilege to do this. I love art. It's…my outlet. A passion that reminds me every so often that I'll be okay when I'm feeling like everything is too heavy, I pick up a pencil and get lost. I forget I'm hurting, even if it's only for a few minutes, it helps." I shake my head as I remember the moment I stopped dreaming and creating. I quit because I was forced into a hole, experiencing an unexpected affair. "But I stopped drawing. It's been a couple of months since I created. Life lately has been… cruel, I guess."

Maybe I'm oversharing, but I'm very passionate about what I do. I can't help but get emotional over the thing that consistently saves my life—the one thing I can depend on. Art will never hurt me. It saves me, tugs on my heartstrings, and doesn't stop playing until the darkness fades away. I don't realize I'm tearing up until tears cling to my lashes and my vision blurs, unable to see. I dip my head forward and focus on the last little bit of food on my plate, and push it around with my fork.

I hate that I'm so emotional sometimes. I feel so deeply, and it gets me in trouble. I quickly regain my composure by blinking hard and fast.

Hopefully, Gavin doesn't notice I'm having a moment. But when my eyes land on his face, my heart flips in my chest. *He notices everything.* Shit. I expect him to belittle me because Liam always did. He would constantly invalidate my feelings, making me feel crazy with an eye roll, or asking me to get over myself whenever I tried to go to him during moments of need. I don't know why I stayed for so long, but I felt like all of this was normal...until it wasn't.

Instead, Gavin matches my emotions with a frown, taking me by surprise. He seems empathetic, as he stares directly at me. Something brushes against my shoe, drawing my attention to the ground. I purse my lips, fighting back a cheery grin, when I realize it's Gavin's boot running against my toes, softly.

The gesture is understanding and thoughtful.

"Maybe you can paint me something, yeah? Before you leave?" Merelyn asks, tearing me away from Gavin.

"I would love to! I can draw something with a pencil and paper. When I'm not drawing on my iPad, I'll pick up a pencil and paper and change up my style to refuel my creativity."

"Amazing. Promise?" Merelyn asks with a giddy smile. "Maybe a portrait of beautiful me?" she teases, leaning forward.

"I promise," I reply.

"I can get you that," Gavin says as he lifts his beer to his lips, winking. It's another Shiner Bock. That's his favorite. "A pencil and paper. Whatever you draw, I'll frame it," he finishes.

I flush, and my mouth drops for a second.

"It usually takes me two to three weeks to finish a piece," I admit, shyly.

"Oh, the roads should be cleared in about a week," Merelyn replies. That's quicker than I thought. Gavin flinches while I jump in my seat excitedly.

"Oh, that's great! I think my family is going crazy, worried about me. Does your phone and internet work now?" I ask, straightening my spine, hoping she'll say yes. I'm sure my parents are worried sick. It's unlike me to go a day without speaking to my mother, let alone weeks.

I'm lucky enough to say that my parents love me like they can't live without me. Yes, they fought frequently, but they always put my sister and me first. They always attended every talent show and awards ceremony. They always showed up for any little thing they could. We take annual family trips to the beach or mountains, and I go to my dad's house to watch every Dallas Cowboys football game because I know he's going to BBQ. My mouth waters when I remember how amazing my dad's brisket comes out every single time—the cooler full of Dr. Pepper.

I hope they're not worrying too much.

My heart cracks when I realize Gavin never had any of that growing up.

"Not at the moment, no," she says as she puts a spoonful in her mouth.

I slow my chewing. "Where's the closest phone?" I ask after spooning down ground beef. Gavin narrows his gaze. A grim expression replaces his once blissful smile. His lips are pressed as he chews. "I'm sorry, it's just that I have to know." I grab my napkin and slowly tap my lips. "I need to get going. There are so many things I need to get done. My family needs to know I'm okay. I need to report the accident to the police and hire a detective to find out who has been sending me these messages. I keep having nightmares and seeing–"

Ghosts.

Merelyn interrupts before I can say it.

"What kind of nightmares, dear?" Merelyn places her cold, veiny hand on mine comfortingly.

"One moment, I see myself driving, and the next thing I know, I'm rolling down the hill, over and over again. Or I'll dream about a man wielding a butcher knife, chasing me through the trees. Just your usual nightmares," I say sarcastically. "I'm sure my parents are wondering where I am."

"Where are they? Where's home for you, dear?"

"Texas. I'm from San Antonio."

Gavin clears his throat loudly. A deep sound reverberates in his chest and slices through the suspenseful tension brewing at the dinner table. Is the conversation upsetting him?

He stands, his chair scooting back loudly against the floor. He grabs his empty plate and utensils and reluctantly hurries to the kitchen.

"I've always wanted to go to Texas. Gavin was stationed at Fort Hood for training. Gavin's grandfather taught him how to bull ride as soon as he could walk, before he passed away. He was only there for about six months, but he told me he liked it. Isn't that right, Gavin? Tell her about the local rodeos you were in while you were there."

We both turn to him. He's drinking beer like it's water. He sets it down on the counter with a loud clink. He doesn't bother looking at us when he nods. Instead, his attention is on the porch, looking through the kitchen window. The sun is almost down. Streaks of dark grey reflect through his blue eyes, illuminating his face.

He looks stressed.

"Yeah, I haven't done it in a while because of my injury. I know I still can, but..." He trails off like he doesn't want to talk about it. Grabbing a toothpick, he places it in between his teeth. I wait for him to continue, but he just fixates on the beer and shrugs nonchalantly.

Is bullriding the passion he doesn't get to do anymore?

Is he upset that I have to go? My home is in Texas.

I purse my lips, placing my hands on my lap nervously. He's shutting down again. I know that look, and I don't miss it. I want the Gavin who lets himself smile.

"Where's the closest neighbor? I'm sure they have a phone, right? I mean, I know the blizzard was bad, but—"

A loud crash of dishes blares over the howling winds and crackles of fire. I jump in my seat while my heart leaps to my throat. Merelyn slowly shifts her gaze over my shoulder. I follow her worried gaze, and it lands upon Gavin's cold expression. His chest rises and falls like he's trying to catch his breath. He clenches his jaw, and we hold each other's stare for a good five seconds, but it feels like minutes.

"Gavin, honey, everything alright?" Merelyn's concerned tone rings into our ears, and she tilts her head to the side like she's trying to figure him out.

He gives me one last disapproving glare and then forces himself to turn to Merelyn. He deadpans, becoming unpredictable like the day we first met.

"Going to go see the horses and make sure they're okay. Thank you for dinner." He cups her shoulder softly, not meeting my eyes.

She nods in response. He reaches into his back pocket, pulling out the familiar red and white pack of cigarettes, and walks outside, disappearing into the darkness. He shuts his door harder than normal—the once peaceful mood shifts into something tense.

Why is he so upset? He knows I'm leaving soon. I have to go. It's inevitable.

I turn back to my almost empty plate with a sudden loss of appetite.

"Coraline. The closest neighbor is about twenty miles away. Gavin owns most of this land up here."

All of this land is Gavin's?

Does Gavin come from money?

"Merelyn. How did Gavin's parents pass?"

She stiffens.

"He hasn't told you?"

"No."

"I'm not surprised. He's never talked much." She sighs, taking in a deep breath before her wandering eyes land on mine. She massages her fingers apprehensively. "Dear... the Sleepy Coldwater Serial Killer murdered them."

CHAPTER 23
CORALINE

$\mathcal{I}$ gasp and almost choke on my dinner. Coughing, I reach for my water and down it fast.

The Sleepy Coldwater Serial Killer? The same one from the newspaper?

"What? A serial killer?" I don't want to believe it. It's too shocking and too horrible. No wonder Gavin was so upset when I decorated his home with his parents' decorations. It must remind him of them, doesn't it?

Grief is pain that sticks with you forever; no matter how much time passes, the cut still bleeds.

"That's awful."

Merelyn frowns.

"Yes. Truly awful. I don't want to talk about the details. It was a terrible, horrible tragedy that took its toll on my Gavin. This is the home he grew up in and the home his parents were killed in." She waves her hand over her head. "His mother was my best friend. Her name was Barbara. She was so beautiful. Truly an amazing friend, mother, and wife. Gone way too soon and died way too young. She didn't deserve the way she went out." Her shoulders shrink. Pain is written all over her face.

"Being a mother was her entire world. She loved her son with all her heart and soul. Gavin looks a lot like her."

"And his dad?" The word *dad* is a privilege. It feels bitter on my tongue to ask about the cruel man who gave his son scars. Scars he tries to hide but fails. He doesn't deserve that title after the vile things he did to Gavin.

Her mood drops. The lines on her forehead deepen.

"He got nothing from his father but the love for the outdoors; that's it." By the way her tone sharpens, we share the same ideas about him.

"He told me bits and pieces about what his father would do to him, and I don't like him."

"Yeah, well, no one liked him. I love Gavin like my own son, and I loved Barbara like my sister. She made me promise I would be the one to care for him if anything happened to her. Somehow, she knew her time was running out." Her eyes redden. She stands, gathering her plate, but I grip the dish, stopping her.

"Oh, I got it, Merelyn, please sit down. I can clean up; it's the least I can do. Dinner was absolutely delicious."

She sighs like she doesn't want to give in, but hands me her plate anyway.

"Fine, but I'll help dry and put the dishes away."

Fifteen minutes later, we're finishing up the last dishes in the sink. The newspaper I found in the basement keeps coming back to me. Why does Gavin have it? Is that newspaper related to his parents' murders? The last thing I read was that the man was still at large. I didn't check the publication date.

Merelyn gathers her coat and mittens to head back into her guest house. She throws the scarf around her neck. I glance at his bedroom door, wondering if whatever we have going on between us is over just as fast as it started.

"Goodnight, dear," she says as she slowly walks to the door

and places her hand on the doorknob, ready to twist it. "I really enjoy your company."

"The Sleepy Coldwater Serial Killer," I blurt. Merelyn freezes in her tracks.

"Was he ever found? Is he in prison?"

She turns around and looks at me like I've asked her something haunting. Her pink lips tilt into a small smile.

"Gavin likes you. He enjoys your company, too."

My cheeks flush, and my lashes flutter just as butterflies swarm wildly into the pit of my stomach.

"Oh…" I tuck a hair strand behind my ear and put more distance between us. Why am I acting like a schoolgirl who got caught making out with her boyfriend during class?

"I'm sure he likes everyone," I scoff, shaking my head. "And everyone likes Gavin."

I'm sure Gavin likes Georgia, too, and vice versa. Why wouldn't she? Gavin is undeniably handsome and kind when he wants to be. Everything about this man radiates temptation and disastrous sin in all the best ways. He can be an ass, but his heart of gold outshines his brooding ways.

I walk toward the fireplace in an attempt to hide my lust.

"No, dear, not everyone."

"Why do you say that?"

"Because I see the way he looks at you."

My brows pull in together.

"How does he look at me?"

She opens the door and takes one step out.

"Like he's finally found his reason to live again. Maybe even leave Sleepy Coldwater for good like he's always wanted. Like I want him to. He needs to go but won't because of me."

"I don't think he would ever leave this town. He loves it here."

"*Loved it here*," she corrects me.

"Why doesn't he leave?"

"I think he may be too afraid."

"Why would he be afraid? Wait, Merelyn. I'm seeing things around the cabin."

"Seeing what?" She asks, bewildered.

Biting my lip, I hesitate for a moment. I feel crazy for what I'm about to say, but screw it.

"Ghosts?" I say it like a question.

She looks puzzled, confusion flashing across her eyes.

"I've seen a woman in my bathroom and a man in the kitchen. I feel like I'm going crazy here. Maybe it's a symptom of hitting my head too hard in the car wreck? I don't know." I huff, frustrated. "But there's something paranormal going on."

Merelyn glances away.

"I'm sorry, dear. I don't know what to say or do to help. There's no other man but Gavin here. I haven't seen any ghosts..." She shrugs, trailing off, looking genuinely concerned for me.

"But Coraline?" she blurts before I can get a chance to finish. I noticed she's dodging questions and information, but I don't press. I think she's shared more than enough, and I don't want to step on her toes.

"Yes?" My pitch heightens calmly.

"Don't ever go back into the basement." She says it like it's a threat—a stern order—a non-negotiable demand.

She closes the door, leaving me with more unanswered questions.

Maybe I'm reading way too much into it, but I still think the serial killer question is essential.

Why did he target his parents? What if he's still around? Or what if the person who ran me off the road is actually a serial killer copycat?

No...*that's unbelievable.*

It can't be.

Closing my eyes, I run both of my hands through my hair,

trying to make sense of all of this. That same freezing draft from when the basement window was open brushes against my skin. But I know it's not that because I closed it.

I swipe at my forehead as I break out into a cold sweat. I hold onto my arms as I look around the living room, surveying the leather couch, the fireplace, and lastly the kitchen, but nothing is out of the ordinary. Nothing and no one. No fluttering streaks of figures. No woman with long black hair.

And suddenly, that same feeling of being watched is back, and I know I'm not alone. The most pressing question is…is it a person with a beating heart, or a disappearing phantom lurking?

The sound of a loud boom tightens my chest. I scream, whipping my head toward the origin. My whole body tightens, then loosens, once I see it's not a threat. It's Gavin. I'm safe.

"You scared me!" I scold him.

He locks the door behind him and stares at me like I'm a lunatic. He stands in the corner of the living room, with his cowboy hat and boots, and shrugs off his coat. Then smiles.

"Let's play a game, sweetheart."

"Truth or dare?" He hands me a bottle of tequila as Ella Langley plays softly on his radio. We're both sitting across from each other, taking shots straight from the bottle. It stopped burning after the first three takes. I'm buzzing, feeling loose. I'm not a drinker, but when Gavin offered, I didn't hesitate.

I smile.

"Truth."

"I want to see you naked."

I tilt my head to the side with a smirk.

"You're joking." I scoff out a laugh, but his face is colder than ice. "Well, that was bold of you, honest, and bold." I shiver. "I'm not getting naked. I'm—"

"Married," he clips with a deep tone.

I can't handle it when Gavin stares at me the way someone stares at a shooting star—captivation and admiration glimmer in his expression. He's watching me, without even blinking. Even when he lifts the bottle to his lips again, he doesn't blink, as if he doesn't want to miss one moment. I brush my hair behind my ears. A man like Gavin couldn't possibly be into me. Men like him have ladies throwing themselves at him, but something about Gavin tells me he's different.

"And that's not 'a truth'. *It's a dare.* You're playing this wrong." His hand springs forward, like he's motioning me to stop talking.

"It's a truth, sweetheart. I said, I want to see you naked. No. Not your body. Show me your soul. Your fears. Your joys. Your ambition. The darkness you're ashamed of and the sins you try to run away from."

The fire crackles grow louder, matching my flustered blood bumping in my ears. I was not expecting him to say that.

"So, I'm going to ask again. Let me see you naked, Cora. I want the real you. If that's the last thing I receive before you leave this cabin, I want to see the true you, not the woman masking her pain. I've caught sight of her before, but now I want to see every other version of you."

I sag against the floor as Gavin stays seated in front of me with his legs stretched out in front of him.

"Pretty straightforward and blunt of you." I exhale a heavy breath, trying to mask how this man makes my heart flutter. If he wants every version of me, then I want his, too.

"Fine. But only if you do the same. Show me yours, and I'll show you mine, kind of a deal?" I offer an ultimatum.

"What do you want to know?"

"Why don't you want to talk about your parents? Why do

you not want me going into the basement?" His hands tremble. "Forgive me for asking, but I'd like to know," I murmur.

"Ask me something else." He blinks at me.

"Fine." I look around his cabin and sigh. "Would you ever live somewhere else that isn't this haunted cabin?"

He shakes his head.

"I've lived here my entire life. Merelyn is here. When I joined the military, I didn't come back here for fifteen years. Now that I'm here, I haven't been given a reason to leave."

"So if you find a reason to leave, would you?"

He replies with silence and a soul-searching gaze.

"Well, don't you want to see the world?"

"I've seen enough."

Rolling my eyes, I smile.

"I love to travel. You know, there's this place in Italy. It's called Cinque Terre. It means The Five Islands. *It's beautiful.* The water is so blue." I look up at his wooden ceiling while I picture the hot sun kissing my skin as I remember the train rides. "I went there one time when I backpacked Europe as a gift to myself for surviving high school. I ordered a sweet Aperol Spritz after cliff-jumping into the water. It was," I close my eyes and throw my head back as I reminisce about those reckless yet fun times, giggling, "so much fun. Would you ever want to go?"

"Too many people. Every tourist attraction has way too many people. I don't like it. Why would I want to go to a beach when there's one here? It's just water and sand, then when you get back to your car, you smell like salt and have to wash your-self off, and yet sand still gets all over your car."

"God, you're so grumpy." I giggle again, taking another small shot of tequila.

"I like the way you laugh," he says softly.

Once more, my cheeks burn until I feel the blush in my cheeks and chest.

I can't hold the stare he's giving me. A sensation between my thighs throbs, and I rub them together. Despite the blizzard, I suddenly have the urge to run a cold bath.

"I wish I could hear yours," I point out, raising a curious brow. I hate that he's always alone up here in the mountains. There's a whole world out there for him to see, but he chooses to isolate himself. Why?

I want to know what happened to him.

He takes in a deep breath and takes another swig of his beer.

"Truth or dare?"

"Dare." I'm taunting him to give me a hard one. Instead, something shifts inside Gavin.

"I dare you to tell me what I have to do to get you to tell me why you still tie yourself to someone who did those things to you?"

I peer at him.

"When you went back to that wreckage, you put your ring back on and didn't take it off until today. Why? After everything you went through? Why don't you just cut him off from your mind?"

I glance at Gavin before I can keep running my mouth with unfiltered thoughts. I expect to see a solace, happy expression full of hope, but he's giving me that hard ass, masculine, signature look again.

He's dead serious about it.

"To be honest, I don't know. It's hard for me to let go of things because I still want to be enough for him. *Wanted*, I mean. Even after the affair, I wanted to be enough. I thought maybe there was something wrong with me that made him cheat. I doubted everything, replaying every single fight, all the nights he didn't come home because he was 'working'. But the more I replayed everything, the angrier I got. I guess you can say I'm weak." My bottom lip begins to quiver. "I-I trusted him, and the one who called herself my close friend." The familiar sting hits my eyes, but I ignore it. I won't shed another tear over this. "Betrayal sucks," I scoff before I release a hollow chuckle.

I pause, thinking of all of the amazing pieces I've created while sad or full of joy. Art is everything to me. "If I can't draw, create, or dream… then I'm hollow. After everything that happened…" I pause, taking another swig to give me another coat of bravery to open up. "Art is the one consistent thing—*it saves me*. Without it, I'm alone, and it's been a really long time since I've dreamed."

His calloused palm rubs the top of my hand soothingly. I don't flinch or cower away; I relish his touch. I don't want him to feel sorry for me, but it feels so good to vent.

"You're not alone, Coraline," he says with the gentlest tone I've heard. I blink at him.

"Have you ever felt like that with something?" I ask, genuinely curious about what drives Gavin daily. What makes him feel safe? What makes him excited to get out of bed every morning? Is it the horses?

"Like what?"

"A thing that brings you peace, joy, and infinite hope. Happiness?" I scoot closer to him on the floor until our knees touch.

He swallows before piercing me with a stone-cold gaze.

"Not necessarily."

"Oh?" I breathe.

"Because it's not a '*something*' that makes me feel that way."

His expression hardens. Taking the tequila bottle from my hand, he takes a swig, all the while locking eyes with me.

"Is it someone?"

He doesn't say anything.

"Did you have someone before? A wife or girlfriend?"

He changes the conversation's direction by focusing on the fireplace.

"Coraline. Your ex sounds like a real moron."

My shoulders rise and fall slowly.

"I guess. But I think I was the bigger moron for believing I was in love. For falling for his lies."

"You're not. You wear your heart on your sleeve. It's not a bad thing."

"It is, though," I push back. "It makes me weak. It made me vulnerable—an easy prey for any ruthless, cold, and bitter predator to devour and leave nothing behind. Gavin, the betrayal stuck with me. The hurtful things they said, the broken trust, and my marriage falling apart. All of that..." I look Gavin in the eyes as the waves of his light-blue orbs crash into me like waves of safety. I don't want to tell him I fell into a deep depression, but I think it is important to talk about it. "I wanted it to stop hurting. I didn't want to live anymore after that."

Another nod and the tear slips out. He gets in my face, his scent already peeling the shielded layer I hide behind down. With his fingers, he brushes the wetness away, and I hum softly.

"That's why you stopped believing in yourself? Loving yourself?" he asks. His finger darts underneath my chin, lifting my face so I can face him.

"Listen to me, Coraline." He grabs my face with both hands. "You are so fucking perfect because you're you. He stole your spark because he doesn't have one. He tried to steal the way you dream because he doesn't own that power. You do. He wants you to be miserable because he is. You *think* he got to you, but guess what, sweetheart?" He places his hand on my chest. "Your heart is still beating."

Another tear slips out.

Is he drunk? Or is this all coming from a place of honesty? Either way, I find myself drinking it all in.

"You're alive. And if you feel like you don't want to be, well," he tucks a strand of my hair and places it behind my ear, "I can remind you that the fight is worth it. You are worth it." His tone softens as he gets closer to me. His words hit me right in my wounded heart and into my gut. My neck tightens full of tension as I try to stop myself from getting overly emotional. "If you let me."

I cast a grimace, shifting and flinching on the floor, stopping myself from crying. Is it the alcohol? Or is it Gavin's sweet words that's doing this to me right now? I feel drunk, but not because of the bottle in my hand. It's because of the way he looks at me.

I want to let you, Gavin.

I can't say it, though.

I'm still married and still healing.

"Stop saying these things to me." I swipe my knuckles against my cheeks. "You can't say these things to me."

I stand and walk toward the fireplace. He follows from behind. He places his forearm across the bricks, leaning against them, while I try to detach from this moment—*from him.*

I'm leaving. I need to remind myself of that fact because even if we become friends, I refuse to lean on someone else when I need to be strong for myself. This is a fight I need to face alone. Peering over my shoulder to wish him a goodnight, I stall. He clenches his jaw with a pointed chin as he watches me. He's so close to me. So close, I can't think straight. So I focus on the red, orange, and yellow flames flickering in front of us and pretend he's not next to me, hovering.

"Why can't I say these things to you?"

I shake my head, my nostrils flaring.

"You just can't."

"Why?"

"Because I'll fall for it," I clip, turning around. "I'll start to like you more than I should, and I don't think I'm ready to trust another person. I just met you!"

A grin crests his face.

"You like me, sweetheart? I thought I was a dick?" He takes a step closer.

I roll my eyes.

"You are a dick," I spit teasingly. "Sometimes." My lips lift.

"Dance with me," he whispers.

"What?" I turn to him.

"I dare you to dance with me."

Dancing is too intimate. Too intertwining.

It's not a one-night stand. It's emotional. I examine his hand, his smile, those damn perfect blue eyes that resemble a summer sky, and that body I can't help but want to wrap my arms around like the night I woke up with him in his bed. I need to stay focused and think about all the reasons why dancing with him would be a bad idea. If I do, I'll fall for him. And I can't fall for him when I'm still trying to learn how to trust again.

It's unfair to both of us, and I don't want to have sex with another man, and then get ghosted. I'm not ready for those types of games.

Instead, I dart toward his bedroom for the night. I'm sealing up these walls again, hardening them until they're steel, but I'm afraid it's no match for Gavin Ariksen, so I'm taking the coward's way out and running away.

With a heaving chest, heated veins, and burning cheeks, I lock the door behind me, sagging against it until my ass hits the floor. He doesn't waste a second. He's at the door, softly knocking, but I don't have the energy to fight our attraction. This is as much as I can give him.

"Cora?"

Silence.

"Answer me."

Silence.

"Coraline. We're going to finish the game."

I can't.

"I dare you." He raises his voice. "I dare you to stop being so fucking scared and kiss me."

CHAPTER 24
GAVIN

As soon as the declaration leaves my lips, I palm the door on both sides, tempted to kick it down.

I'm going to fucking break it down in five seconds if she doesn't answer.

I see the way she flushes. I know the way her pulse rockets when I look at her. We almost kissed in the woods, but I knew if I claimed those lips—got a taste, I wouldn't be able to stop. And when I kiss her, I want her to be unafraid.

My sights are set on her because I know she feels it too; she's just too scared to let herself fall with me.

I lose my patience. My sanity. My fucking voice of reason when it comes to her. I lost it a long time ago.

The door swings open fast and hard. It makes the cold air whip across my face.

Her eyes darken. Those fucking honey brown eyes that drive me wild. Brown eyes are the most common eye color in the world, but hers feel like the rarest ones of all to me.

"Finish the game, sweetheart." I take a step closer to her. Taking her in from head to toe, stopping at her chest. It rises and falls faster and harder the closer I get. "I dare you to kiss me."

"No."

My heart sinks.

"Please, sweetheart. I want to know what heaven tastes like. Just once. I'll be a good fucking man who begs." I brush my lips against her cheek. "I'll go slow." I kiss her neck, and I hear her moan, arching her back. "Or if you want, I'll go hard and fast. I'll make it last all night or until you pass out. It's all I want."

I need it. I need her so bad.

"Gavin," she purrs, breathless.

God, I'm a mad man hearing her say my name like that.

Jesus.

I thread my fingers through her hair and pull firmly from the base. Her head dips back, exposing her neck, and she presses her full breasts against my chest. Her perfectly peaked nipples are felt through her shirt, and I want to know what they would feel like inside my mouth. Our warm flesh connects, and it sends a rush of fire straight below my waist.

"I dare you to kiss me...*please.*"

"I'm saying no, because I don't just want a kiss, Gavin. I want more." She tangles her fingers into my shirt and pulls me in closer, rough and demanding. The version of her I've been dreaming about is here in front of me, and I'm about to come undone.

Fuck.

I'm not the only one begging tonight. It's getting my dick hard, making me more damn feral for this woman. "Give me more, Gavin. I want all of you all night," she declares sensually. "Force me," she breathes, her brown eyes lighting up with intrigue. "Take it from me. Take all you need tell me I'm beautiful." Her eyes plead with me, and I wish Liam were here so I can fucking kill him, and then fuck her in his blood for making her feel less than.

I grab her face, my fingers snaking into her thick curls, and pull her in until her breath is ghosting my lips. "Coraline. You are more than just beautiful. That word doesn't do your beauty justice. You're celestial. Out of this world, so goddamn *celestial.*"

She sucks in a breath, her cheeks and neck pinkening. Her nails fumble with my belt, but I let her take control and pull it out of the hooks.

"Do you want me to take you right now against this door?" I push her against it, her breasts bouncing.

"Yes. Tell me what you like."

"I like you. I want to see you tied up and gag you with my fingers and dick. I won't even pull the rest of your clothes off because I don't want to waste a damn second. I'll pull your panties aside, unzip my jeans, and stick my cock in you. Would you like that?"

"Yes." She nods, breathlessly. "I want to try it rough, names, pain. The dirtier, the better."

Fucking fuck.

"You're perfect." I hook my arm around her waist and pull her into mine. Her eyes widen, gasping as she looks down. I grip her hand and thrust into it. "Your existence does this to me, sweetheart. Do you feel how fucking hard I am for you? Do you feel what you do to me? You make me crazy." I thrust against her again. She bites her lip, then swipes it with her tongue. I want her to wrap those full pink lips around my cock. "I'm going to come right now in my damn pants because I'm so fucking pathetic for you."

I'm in a trance. She wants this just as badly as I do—my celestial artist.

"Don't," she pants. "Don't come right now." She slips her hand through my waistband, managing to get past my belt and around my length. I shut my eyes tight as she wraps her hot, soft hand around me and gives me one slow stroke. Then, she leans forward and stops until she's at my ear. "I'm on birth control. I want it all inside me."

Jesus.

This mouth.

I pick her up in a second. Before I can close the door behind us, her lips are crashing against mine, full of need and sensuality. Every brush of her lips sends a pulse straight to my heart, solidifying my obsession with her. In fact, it's been upgraded to another tier after kissing her. She feels just how I imagined she would.

Soft. Heavenly. Perfect. And so damn celestial.

My tongue immediately dominates hers. She wraps her hands around my neck as I dig my fingers into her thighs. I slam her against the wall and fulfill the promise. I pull her pants down, move her panties to the side just enough to expose her weeping pussy, and drive only the tip of me inside. I immediately groan as I sink into her slowly.

I need her to stay in Alaska with me forever. My chest tightens, and the ability to breathe is impossible every time she looks at me.

Like right now, I feel like I can't breathe.

She's here with me. Underneath me. This is real.

She's too beautiful. The kind of beauty that makes you think she would never say yes to a date with me, because she's out of this world, magnetic, and divine.

"Oh, my fuck, Gavin. You're too big." She moans and mewls against my lips. Fuck, she begs so fucking pretty. Using the palm of her hands, she tries to scoot away, but I pull her hair again, keeping her in place, and she smiles through it. "Force it from me, Gavin. Take me. Now." She licks my lips and looks down at our connection.

"You're going to be a good filthy girl and take it, won't you, sweetheart?"

I push more in slowly and groan. She's so damn wet and soft.

She scratches my back, her nails stabbing deep, and I slap the wall from how good the pain feels, knowing it's coming from her.

"Say it. Say you can take it," I growl.

"I can take it all night."

I drive all the way deep until I can't go any more. I'm hitting a spot, and she gasps, her head dipping back, with only the whites of her eyes showing.

"So tight." I plug my fingers into her mouth, imagining her on her knees. She sucks and moans around them. I remove them from her mouth and grip her ass. She takes me completely, as if she were made for me.

If she's going to leave me when the snowstorm is over, I'm going to make sure these memories will haunt her for the rest of her life. She's going to remember how good it felt to be my little whore when she goes back home.

"I'm going to make sure you won't be able to move on from this because every time another man kisses you, it'll be my lips you're picturing. Every time another man holds you, it'll be my arms you'll wish for. Every time another man is inside you, it'll be my cock and name you'll be screaming for."

I pull my dick out and groan.

Fuck.

"Gavin, I, uh, I'm married," she breathes, the fear and trauma evident in her expression. Liam has done a number on her, breaking her confidence.

"Coraline." I pull down her shirt until her breasts are exposed. "Do you want to talk? Or do you want to get fucked? Because Liam's wife is my whore tonight," I declare slowly.

She slams her lips onto mine.

"That's what I thought." I snicker.

She screams against my lips, my length stretching her. I pump slowly, and with each thrust, her breasts bounce, her perfect brown nipples calling my name. I want to suck, bite, and fuck them.

"I'm going to fuck his imprint out of you until you can only remember mine." I trail kisses down her chest until my mouth is on her perfectly pointed peaks next. I pull out and rush back in. Her warm, soft walls grip me tighter. She gasps, moans, and pumps her hips until she's fucking me back, meeting me pound for pound as I suck on her nipple. I go to the other one, equally worshipping her.

"I'm going to fuck any doubt you have of yourself away. That fucker poisoned your mind with his own misery, but you are mine now."

Sex has always been fast and quick. A chore that needed to get done. An itch to scratch. But it's different with Coraline. I don't want this to be over after one round. I want forever. She's different. No one has ever come close to what she tastes like. I'm truly fucked.

"I want you all night, over and over again until you're crying out my name, and you can't remember anything but how good it feels to be mine. Can you do that for me?"

"Yes," she says in a high-pitched guttural moan.

"Good girl. *My good girl.*"

I pull down her panties until they're hanging around her ankles and line myself at her entrance again. Her nails stab into my back as I slam inside. She's cut me open, but I don't care. She can make me bleed and come, and I'll make her clean up her mess.

"Eyes on the mirror, I need you to see how fucking sexy you look. I need you to remember this image. I need you to remember how it feels to be my whore and how you look when you're getting your brains fucked out of you."

I turn her around and walk her to the standing mirror in the corner of my bedroom. Her cheeks are red, her mouth gaped open, perfect full breasts and brown nipples making my mouth water. I press her hands on either side of the standing mirror and slap her ass. Lifting her waist, I sink back into her tight, wet hole, and dig my fingers into her hips. She rises to her toes as I thrust deep.

"Gavin!" She cries out my name like I knew she would. I could hear her scream it over and over again, never getting tired of her sweet voice.

"Fuck, baby, I'm going to finish already."

Holding her up by her hair, I smirk as I angle her face toward the mirror. She looks at herself as she finishes, making me wish I could eat her out and fuck her at the same time.

"We were made for each other, baby."

CHAPTER 25
CORALINE

I feel safe with Gavin. I've only been with one other person, and Gavin is making this feel so right. He knows what he wants, and that is so attractive to me.

There's no judgment. No shame. His kisses are gentle yet domineering. His touch is insatiable, as though he can't get enough of the way I feel on his skin.

No one has ever made me feel like this. So freeing and confident to indulge in my desires. The scruff of his beard pricks my skin while his lips brush and suck against my neck, making me more feral.

His cock feels like it's splitting me in half. It's thrusting against a spot I never knew I had until tonight. Every time he hits it, I can't help but dig my nails into his back and scream. The pleasure is blinding.

We moved from the mirror to the wall.

He has me against it, his pants still glued to his thighs as he rails me. The sound of my back hitting the wall joins our grunts and moans. I'm loving the way he feels inside me so much that I don't know where to hold on to him. I'm in his hair, then switch to digging my nails into his muscular back, feeling his scars and shoulder blades. Then, I switch to his abs, running my palms over him as he relentlessly fucks me.

He lurches forward, holding me up with one arm, as he reaches down to retrieve the tequila bottle I took with me from the living room. Still thrusting, he takes a swig and smirks. My body jolts up and down against the wall, keeping my eyes on him, intrigued by a handsome angelic man who fucks full of sin. He brushes his thumb against my bottom lip for a few seconds before he replaces it with his lips against mine. The instant he does, my mouth opens, and I taste the liquor. He spits it into my mouth, yanks my hair from the back like he's urging me to swallow.

So I do.

"I have to make sure you stay hydrated all night, darlin', because the things I have planned for you might hurt, but don't worry, you'll beg for it." He breathes into my ear, right before he presses his mouth into my neck and sinks his teeth into my flesh, biting me—leaving euphoric sparks.

A fiery shudder vibrates through me as he rips me off the wall and carries me to his bed. In the next second, I'm getting thrown on top of his bedsheets like I'm weightless to him. I watch his dick bob up and down, hard and thick, with our mixed arousal glistening around his veins and tip.

He's sculpted so beautifully. He pulls off his shirt in one quick swoop over his head and onto the floor with a whoosh. A gold cross chain remains over his scarred chest. I mirror his actions, doing the same and taking off every piece of clothing that's left on my body, eager to have him on top of me.

I stop moving when I notice the mood in the room has shifted and slowed. Gripping the bed sheets, I glance at Gavin. His expression turns worried as he pauses for a second, looking down at the floor.

"Gavin, what's wrong?" I ask, breathless.

His chest rises and falls as he stares at the ground. He

exhales, body visibly trembling as he towers over me, straightening his back.

He wears a prosthetic foot that begins at the middle of his left shin and extends down. I swallow, as a flicker of sadness runs through me. Sad because losing a limb is world-shatteringly painful, knowing what he went through to suffer an injury like this.

He waits for me to say something as he walks to my side of the bed.

As soon as he reaches my face, he sits on the edge, cupping my head.

"Is this the injury that made you medically retire from the military? From special operations?" I ask.

"Yes." He nods, unable to meet my eyes. "Don't worry, sweetheart. That's a story for another time. I can still do everything you can."

"I know you can."

"Do you want to stop?"

"Stop?" I cut him off. My stomach knots hearing the suggestion. "Gavin. I want you, now." I stroke his cock up and down and pull him on top of me with my other hand, and cup the back of his head. I already miss his lips, and I'm not going anywhere until he finishes what he started. He secures his palms on either side of my face and settles in between my legs.

I am not a shallow person. I wouldn't look at him like there's something wrong with him for sustaining an injury he didn't ask for. I know what it feels like to feel like there's something wrong with you. And I definitely know it's not the same, but this doesn't change the way I feel about Gavin, and he needs to know that.

Thank fuck I don't have to deal with that with my ex anymore. Because right now, Gavin is kissing and swiping his tongue over me, worshipping and grabbing my ass every chance he gets.

What the hell did I ever see in Liam, anyway? Why did I let him make me feel unworthy, not enough, and believe it?

Gavin is infinity times the man I never thought I could experience. He's beautiful in every single way.

"Gavin, please. I need you inside me, now." I moan as he pushes the tip in and out, teasing me. I need all of him right now.

"I've been dreaming about what you would taste like." He runs two fingers up and down my slit before he pushes them in. He takes them out a second later as I arch my back. I look down to find him sucking his fingers. "And I was right. You taste like a dream, baby."

He licks his way down and flicks my clit with his tongue, eliciting a moan. He pushes inside me, fucking me again ruthlessly as he leans over to his nightstand. I can't focus anymore. I don't care what he's doing; he just can't stop. I'm so close to finishing.

He's lifting my arms together, slowing his pace. I feel a rough fabric around my wrists. They're being bound together by a rope.

"You don't get to go anywhere else tonight, darlin'. Your job is to be my dirty cocktease, taking it over and over again, until I've mesmerized every inch of your divine body."

He squeezes until the rope is digging into my skin.

"What do you mean?" I ask with knitted brows.

He turns me to my side and then slides inside, slamming his hips against my ass. The force is so hard and unforgiving that the bed frame hits the wall.

Thrust.

"It means, you fall asleep, I'm fucking you awake."

Thrust.

"It means I want to paint you with my cum."

Thrust.

"Over."

Another deep, mind-blowing thrust.

Another scream spilling out of my throat.

"And over."

Thrust.

"Again."

His hands wrap around my neck, and he squeezes, taking my breath away. He does it tactically, careful not to damage my throat, but enough so that he is in control of every breath I take. I love being controlled in the bedroom, just not out of it, and Gavin seems to understand when to separate the two. My blood is whooshing in my ears, my breasts bouncing with every hard, fast pump as our skin slaps every time we connect.

Then, he's untying me. When my hands are free again, I go straight for his hair and pull him with one hand cupping the back of his head until his mouth is on mine.

"Touch yourself, darlin'. Touch yourself and show me what I've been missing. Show me how you get off while your eyes are on me," he encourages as he kneads my breast. He's choking me hard and roughly, and I'm loving every second.

I obey, circling my clit with my finger. We meet each other's eyes, and he grins sinfully, darkly handsome.

Everything is chaotic, like he's taking out his demons on my body, and I want to dance with them. He's rough, carnal, and greedy, not even letting me take my eyes off him because he's owning every inch that I am.

Biting my lip, I turn my head for a split second, relishing his movements. His fingers grip the hollows of my cheeks and rotate me back into place so that I'm facing him.

"You look at me when I'm inside you."

I'm gone.

He hits that one spot inside me, and I'm crying out his name.

"Gavin! Oh, god, Gavin!" I mewl.

"Dammit, baby. The face you make when you come is my

favorite sight in the world. Fuck," Gavin croons, holding me tight to his chest.

I grip his bicep from behind and hold on for dear life as he continues to wreck my body, chasing his finish line. He's unrelenting. Brutal yet careful. My pussy clamps down on his thick length, and he roars. Instead of choking me, he lets go. I catch my breath, and he threads his fingers through my curls and pulls. I scream and chant his name over and over again while floating away as we reach our climaxes together.

We're both hot, souls burning, flesh feeling alive, as our tension finally collides and explodes. I've never had rough, passionate sex like that before. He doesn't waste a second more reminding me that tonight is about pleasure. He's tying me back to his bed frame, as I sag into the soft bedsheets, shutting my eyes, letting sleep overtake me with his cum leaking out of me. He keeps thrusting, but I'm too drained to stay awake. Aftershocks of the best night I've ever had rattle my body, and I welcome the darkness.

CHAPTER 26
CORALINE

Gavin was not bluffing. He's a man of his word. Still tied up, I lie on my back, him on top, as he slides himself inside me. I'm still wet from earlier's heated session. The ropes rub against my skin, surely burning, but it just adds more fuel to my building orgasm. He enters me as I blink slowly at him; his blurry silhouette makes my chest swell.

"Gavin," I mumble through tired lips. "What time is it?" I ask. From the indigo grey shades of color that filter through the rectangular window, I know it's dawn.

"It's time you taste how perfect we are together. Open your mouth."

This is, quite frankly, the best way I've been woken up. He pulls out of me. I whine, pouting, needing him to keep going. My hands have fallen asleep from being bound for so long. I pull on them, trying to free myself, but nothing budges.

He places both knees on either side of my chest, stroking his dick. He presses the tip against my lips, stirring our cum on them. When I part my lips to suck in a breath, he pushes inside. I taste myself and lazily grin through his deep strokes. He pushes slowly, stretching my mouth around his monster girth.

"I'm going to ruin you, baby. Ruin you so beautifully, you shatter and break only for me. Ruin you so good that you'll never be satisfied with anyone else unless you're coming on my cock. In every single lifetime, I'm haunting you, Coraline."

He pulls out just enough to let me talk.

"Haunt me. Ruin me. Shatter me," I plead.

He smiles before he goes back in deep until I'm gagging. At first, they're slow, deep strokes. Tears leak down my cheeks as I continue to deep throat him. I can't move, but just lie there and take it as he promised. I feel every vein, every drop of cum, and it arouses me higher. I want to play with myself, but he keeps me where he wants.

"So beautiful when you choke on me, Cora."

He has me gripped by the hair, spearing my throat faster until saliva drips down my chin. His thrusts grow faster and needier. His massive cock tastes so delicious. I don't gag anymore, but let him take what he needs. The sound of my moans and his deep, satisfied grunts turns me up higher. I want him inside me. Arching my back, my legs twist, and toes curl as I beg for his cock to be inside my wet pussy too.

"Don't talk right now. I want to see you cry on it, just like your pussy is crying for me to fuck it."

Then his palm connects with my face as he keeps wildly driving into my mouth. Slapping me as he turns me into his cock whore. He slaps me one more time, then I feel him jerk inside my mouth as I stroke him with my tongue.

"Beg me to let you swallow my cum."

I don't even hesitate at his request. I'm so wrapped in Gavin's spell, I want him all the time now. His hooded eyes darken, looking at my lips, gripping his cock. He's close, and it's not fair because I'm aching down below. He takes out his dick and slaps my mouth with it a couple of times as I mutter my pleas.

"Let me swallow your cum, please."

He rams it back inside until it's at the back of my throat again.

He finishes with a growl. Slowing his pace, he shuts his eyes tight, dipping his head back as he pulses. I swallow him, licking every drop.

He unties me, and I immediately cup his face in my hands and stare at him, locking our gaze together, and needing him to understand that he has me under his spell. My nerves explode. My blood boils into euphoric lust. Flames are wild within both our eyes and souls.

"Fuck, Gavin, that was amazing," I admit, shyly still feeling needy for him. I think I can do this all day. Still naked, bruised, and well fucked, his hand settles on my breasts, kneading them.

"Shower next."

His ocean eyes shine with lust.

"Again?" I bite my lip, excitedly.

"I'm going to fuck you in every room of this house, sweetheart."

FOR THE NEXT SEVEN DAYS, it's paradise. Days of shed hunting, drawing, eating food, tangled in bedsheets, and talking about anything and everything. I feel like we're in our own world up here.

I'm curled up in the Sleepy Coldwater, Alaska sweater, another pair of dark grey sweatpants, barefoot as "Indigo" by Sam Barber feat. Avery Anna plays low and soft on the radio in the corner.

Gavin Ariksen is mutating my brain and blood chemistry. One kiss and taste broke the rules I made for myself so I don't fall for any man.

But how can I not want more after what we just shared all these nights? I want more again, and again.

I stare at his sleeping face, heartbeat after heartbeat. Running my digits through his chest, over every scar, I can't help but want to know every single thing about him.

I want to know more about his time in the military, but he hasn't wanted to talk about that yet.

Gavin is asleep on his side. His hair is tousled, his beard longer than the first day I met him. He's just…intriguing, and I can't get enough.

I look down at the sketch pad Gavin gave me.

He inspired me to dive back into my craft. Being here in this cabin, with Gavin's help, I dreamed again.

After he fell asleep, I poured it all on paper and pencil. It's old-school for me, but I still love the classic art I create with charcoal and a number 2 pencil—a nice break from technology. I didn't have to think too hard when I turned the page. *It was instinct.* A breath of fresh air after feeling like I've been in an ocean in the depths of hell. I knew what I wanted to draw and haven't stopped to take a break. I've been sitting in the corner of the room on the couch, drawing Gavin.

My new muse.

The pencil in my hand reminds me of the woman I used to be. With every stroke of the pencil, I get lost and go somewhere no one can hurt me. My spark is back. Lightly giggling to myself, I continue to shade in my favorite part of Gavin's face. *His eyes.* Every time he looks at me, I melt.

I glance up at him as he turns in his sleep. The white blankets wrinkle as he moves. He frowns, his chest rising and falling faster than before, so I saunter over to him.

Is he having a nightmare?

I shouldn't wake him up even though I want to.

The sound of a door slamming catches my attention. I palm my scream, keeping it inside so I don't startle Gavin awake. He's lying on his side with his back to me, mumbling incoherently. I reach out to tap his shoulders, but another door slam pulls me away.

Regardless, someone is in here.

Is it Merelyn or Georgia? My mind travels to the worst—the one who's been after me.

No, I won't go there.

I place my sketchbook down on the nightstand with the pencil next to it, and open the door to the bedroom. The feeling of being watched returns as I take the first step in the dark hallway. The first thing I see makes my blood run cold, and I gasp.

CHAPTER 27
GAVIN

nother fight. Another senseless argument, and of all days, on Christmas morning. Mother says it's a day of family, unity, and gratitude. Now that I'm eight years old, I want to give Mama something special, but Father says we don't have any money for gifts this year.

So I wanted to find more deer sheds in the woods and make them into a bowl for decoration. I know she'll love it because Mama loves her decorations. Every holiday, she decorates the house to match each season with colors and trinkets. Sometimes, she'll go into town to the local Sleepy Coldwater thrift shop and get things from the store to do DIY decor. I help her when Dad isn't having me work on the ranch, and it's our time together. Mama does everything she can to keep me away from his wrath, but I can tell she's scared of him, too.

Now, it's Christmas. Dad has been angrier these days and won't let me leave the house. I don't have anything to give her today, but I hope we can just spend time together...but it's already impossible.

Dad stayed up all night drinking liquor, and now my mother and I get to be his punching bags again.

"You bitch!" The sound of a loud slap echoes through the walls upstairs. Their thudding grows louder, and I get angrier. I try to *distract myself by staring at the poster on my wall that says: "We want you!" A man in a funny hat is pointing straight at me.*

One day, I'm going to go far away from here and never come back. I want to be in the military—a soldier or SEAL who travels the world.

I hold my knees to my chest, fighting the tears that want to come out. I rock back and forth on my bed and pray that it stops soon. I just wanted to hug my mother this morning since I couldn't get her a gift. The sting in my throat grows, but I swallow the dread back down. I can't cry. Father says crying makes you weak, so I hold it in like I always do.

I sleep in the basement. He created a room down here and built it for me before I was born—before his alcohol addiction started. He wasn't always bad.

"Stop it! Stop!" she squeals, and he roars back at her with more sounds of slaps and thudding.

I've tried to break up their fights multiple times, but it always results in me getting hurt. Mother made me promise to hide every time they fought, so I wouldn't hear. I'm not sure where I can hide since he won't let me leave the house, and I'm already the farthest away from them that I can be.

So I bring my hands to my ears and close my eyes.

Suddenly, the door to my room crashes open.

It's Mama.

She's bleeding everywhere.

"Gavin, honey, don't scream. Don't talk, or he'll find you, baby. Hide underneath your bed, right now!" She hugs me tight to her body and presses her lips to the top of my head.

Little did I know that would be the last time I hugged her.

"Mama, what's going on?" I reach out and brush the red out of her black hair.

My mother's blue eyes stay on me. Tears fill the brim of her lashes and profusely leak down her weary face. She doesn't look the same anymore. She's terrified for her life, and I don't know what to do to help.

"You know hide and seek, right, baby?" She nods frantically. "Hide right now, and get under the bed."

My father continues to kick and bang against the door. The sound of the wood chipping sends more hot tears streaming from me and onto the wooden floor.

"Now!" Mama demands.

I scurry onto the floor and crawl under my twin bed that's pressed up against the walls. I'm barefoot, shaking in my red Christmas pajamas.

"Let me in! There's nowhere you can go!" my dad's raspy voice booms with a darkness I've never heard before. It's my dad, but not him at the same time.

"M-mama, please. I'm scared. Let me go with you!" I plead, but she shakes her head. "Please let me go with you, Mama."

"Promise me, Gavin. Promise me right now, you're going to stay here and not say one word, you hear me? You can't come with me. Be strong, okay? And listen to me."

I nod, letting the tears fall down my face because I can't hold in this unfathomable pain anymore.

"I'm so sorry I couldn't protect you, but after this, we're leaving and never coming back." She forces a weak smile as she threads her bloody fingers through my hair.

"M-mama!"

"Promise me right now?"

She can't leave me. She can't.

"I promise," I say with a trembling whisper.

"Promise what?"

"I won't come out."

"And?"

I swallow, my teeth chattering from the amount of adrenaline that's being pumped into my body.

"I promise I won't say a word."

This makes her smile.

"Come on, come out, come out, wherever you are," Dad singsongs *wickedly from behind the door. "Where are you, Gavin? Are you afraid of me? You pussy!"*

"He isn't in here! Please! Stop!" Mother begs as red drips down the floor from her arms and fingers. It begins to form a bright crimson puddle.

But he doesn't stop.

He never stopped.

I WAKE WITH A GASP. Fury boiling in every single vein, my chest tightening with every single deep, fast breath I'm taking. Sitting up, with perspiration leaking down my chest and stomach. I still remember every detail of the day that changed the trajectory of my life.

I'm not like him. I'm not like him.

I reach for the other side of the bed, eager to run my hand up and down Coraline's back. She's always the first thing that's in my head when I wake up. And right now, I'd like to bury the darkness away by being inside her. But to my disappointment, I'm greeted by empty sheets, her scent gone.

She isn't in here. The room is empty and cold without her.

I bring my knees to my chest and run my hands through my hair. The roads are cleared. She's going to leave me soon, but I can't let that happen.

The sketchbook on my nightstand catches my attention. It's a pencil-sketch drawing...*of me.*

She's drawing again. Creating. Dreaming.

I smile, running my hands across the shading by my beard. She managed to get every single detail, even sharpening the scars on my chest. Fuck, she's so talented and so good at what she does. How could she ever doubt her abilities? Even in this drawing, she managed to capture every single detail.

I feel like I've been in a dream since she arrived, and I refuse to wake up without her in my bed ever again.

CHAPTER 28
CORALINE

When I opened the door from Gavin's bedroom, I spotted a dark figure walking toward the basement.

I can't tell if it's a woman or a man underneath the flickering lights, but it's massive, and its aura isn't welcoming. I know it's not because my heart is pounding to uncontrollable limits, and a sensation of unease washes over me. Dread, fear, and anxiety possess me as I watch it in slow motion. This time, it's demon-like and not a ghost or spirit. It's a dark, black, blurry, massive silhouette. I tread lightly, my pulse rocketing at the base of my throat as I reach for a knife in the kitchen. I pull it from the wooden holder on the counter and grip the handle so tightly it burns my palms.

I knew this place was haunted, but Gavin is in denial about it. Every time I bring it up, he changes the subject and avoids giving me a clear answer. He's avoiding it. I know I'm seeing things, and it won't stop.

Maybe I should talk to it?

"What are you? Who are you?" I cling to the walls as I get closer to it.

I can't believe I'm talking to it. Whatever the thing is, it doesn't respond but continues to float and disappear deeper into the basement staircase.

It all comes back to the basement again!

I halt and glance in the direction of Gavin's bedroom, as my hand shakes against the knife handle.

Rubbing my temples, conflicted, I stand in the living room shaking.

In every horror movie, I yell at the main character to not be a dumb ass. *"Don't follow the noise or investigate a strange encounter"*. Yet, now that I'm in that position, I can't help it. If it doesn't have a beating heart, it can't physically hurt me, right?

Screw it.

All logic gets thrown out the window, and my curiosity gets the best of me.

I'm in the basement, still clinging to the kitchen knife tightly. The ceiling light continues to flicker, struggling to stay on. It's colder down here. The hairs on my arms and back raise as I stand there, searching for the black floating orb. I survey every corner, but there's nothing but boxes, aged children's furniture, and spider webs.

The same drawer where I found the initial newspaper on The Sleepy Coldwater Serial Killer is closed all the way this time. Setting the knife down on a box, I slide it open and find more. Biting my lip, I glance behind me, knowing deep down that what I'm doing is wrong, but I'm nosey.

I pull out the first newspaper I see. It's folded in half, wrinkly, stale, and torn. The paper is yellow with faded black ink. The headline reads:

The Sleepy Coldwater Copycat Suspect Has Been Arrested

There's a picture covered in sawdust and webs, blurring the alleged suspect's portrait. I glance over at the date: January 11, 2025. Dated one year ago.

A door from inside the basement slams. There's another

room down here. It's small, with large, harsh dents in the base of the plain white door.

"Sweetheart?" Gavin calls from the basement staircase. His inquisitive tone is laced with concern.

I throw the newspaper back into the drawer, not bothering to fold it like it was. Heart racing, I hide the knife among the papers and zip around, wearing a mask of innocence and curiosity.

"Coraline?" He descends further down the staircase, this time without socks or shoes. Such a small detail that he doesn't do often. I didn't notice it before. He's still dressed in his pajamas with a plain white shirt hugging his muscular build, and his gold cross chain around his neck. "What are you doing down here?" He's holding back his frustration. I can tell by the way his body pulls taut and his dark brows continue to gravitate toward one another as he pins his worried gaze on me.

"I heard the door slamming again. And…"

He reaches for my hand, linking his fingers with mine. He gently pulls me in front of him so I can lead the way. He follows close behind as I head up the stairs, still holding onto my hand.

"And I saw something floating down into the basement," I admit, shaking my head in shame. I know I sound like a broken record on repeat with the ghosts, but fuck. What else am I supposed to say?

As soon as we get into the living room, he shuts the door to the basement behind us.

"And? What did this floating thing look like?" he asks, folding his arms across his chest.

"You know what. It's nothing." I shake my head. "I-it was nothing." I sigh in defeat. "I think I'm going crazy, what do they call it again?" I giggle half-heartedly. "Cabin fever?" I suggest. I don't want to ruin the way our relationship is blooming with talk of ghosts or murder.

He stares at me, raking my face with his mesmerizing blue

orbs and serious expression. His thumb brushes my bottom lip, left and right, before it settles in the middle.

"You're always so damn pretty," he murmurs. My heart skips a beat as the tune in his eyes takes a turn to desire. "In the mornings, noon, and night..." his cool, sultry breath on my neck sends shivers down my spine. His deep yearning voice is laced with pure adoration. "So damn pretty without trying."

Hot lava strikes my chest and between my thighs, stirring up a lustful craving only he can satisfy. He's so sweet to me.

"I think you're the first real gentleman I've met. I like it."

Before I can blink or think, I'm being turned around and pushed up against the brick wall of the living room.

"You think you want a gentleman, but the way you act when I'm inside you tells me you crave a monster too," he whispers seductively, his breath feathering the shell of my ear.

I nod, peering over my shoulder, cheeks burning.

"Hold onto the fireplace."

My pants and underwear are being yanked down. My ass bounces when he slaps me. I let out a low mewl as he undresses me. Before I can turn around, his hard dick is slowly pushing into me.

I moan, shutting my eyes as he stretches me.

"Oh, fuck, Gavin!"

I hold onto the brick wall as he takes me from behind. Each thrust draws me ever closer to the edge. Fuck, he always feels too good. He stretches me in all the best ways, hitting my cervix until my thighs are trembling. His grunts mix in with my moans perfectly as he holds onto me like he's trying to engrave himself into my skin. A connection so powerful, I feel like I can't breathe.

Who knew being stranded during a snowstorm would end up this way? Sharing a connection with a beautiful man with a tortured past.

I'm leaving, though. He knows I have to go, and I think that's why he's not wasting one second where we can't lose ourselves in our dark chemistry. I try to push away the responsibility to catch up with Maya and my family because he makes me want to stay up in the mountains with him longer.

Right now is different.

We're impatient, feral, and greedy.

And I love it.

Our skin slaps, the fire crackles, and my moans are loud. I scream every time he thrusts. He's hurting me today. His fingers dig into my skin, marking me with more bruises.

"Gavin…it hurts," I cry out, but he doesn't stop.

I don't want him to. I love the pain.

"Make it hurt more. Please don't stop. Oh, I'm going to come!"

He reaches for my hair and pulls it. Forming a ponytail with it, he yanks it like a leash, forcing me to arch my back more and release more strangled moans. Before I succumb to the dark pleasure he inflicts on me, he stops mid-thrust.

"I need to hear you say how fucking perfect you are."

My brows rise, my chest heaving. He's denying me my orgasm.

"Gavin…" I hiss. "Please," I pant.

"No."

Thrust.

"Now tell me how perfect and beautiful you are. Fucking say it."

He pulls my hair again, making my head whip back until we lock eyes. He nestles his face onto my cheek, then his tongue licks my lips. My heart flutters in my chest.

"I'm perfect. I'm beautiful," I say, a sting hitting my eyes. I know what he's doing, and I hate him for it. I hate myself for getting to a place where I doubted myself.

"And?" he taunts, his voice deepening.

Thrust.

I squeeze my eyes shut. He hits deep; that spot inside of me has me shrieking for more.

"I'm enough. I'm more than enough."

Then he strums my clit in circles, and then moves to my slit, coating his finger with my arousal. His hand disappears, and my eyebrows narrow. He's sucking and cleaning my taste off his skin. The sight has me completely blown off the edge, and I'm clenching down on him. I scream his name, and he roars with deep satisfaction. His pace quickens for a moment, his power making my breasts bounce while I balance on my toes, almost knocking me into the fire. He pulls me back to him and just then, his cock jerks inside me.

My mind is completely blank. He kisses my shoulder, the back of my neck, gripping my ass, worshipping every curve of my body. I can't think about anything as I try to come down from the clouds. It's so empowering for me to take control of what I like when it comes to sex. I love being submissive, and his dominance has me in a chokehold.

CHAPTER 29
GAVIN

I'm in the woods. Barefoot in the snow, cold, tears down my face, and covered in Mama's blood. After my father murdered her in front of me, I jetted from underneath the bed and ran out of the basement. Tears were still falling from Mama's eyes when I left; I wanted to wipe them off her face so badly. I was the last person she saw before she took her last breath. It brings me solace that it was I she saw last, and not my father. I swear I saw a little curve of her pale lips before they went lifeless.

I hang onto the bark of the tree, planting my back ramrod straight until it hurts. Frostbite is already doing a number on the bottom of my feet. I didn't have time to grab my boots before I sprinted out of there, terrified.

I made my mom a promise, and I already broke it, but now I need to keep the promise to stay alive for her.

I hold all of the emotions of grief and pure blackened anger. Mama is dead. I'll never get to see her again because of my father. He took her away from me, and yet I still can't bring myself to hurt him if he tries to hurt me.

"Gavin! I know you're out here. I can see your footprints, boy!" he slurs slowly and drunkenly.

Of course, he tracked me fast. I'm no match for a six-foot-four man who hunts every season. Except I'm the prey. Will he kill me slowly like he did my mother? Or will he make it fast?

I peer over my shoulder, just one calculated glimpse won't hurt, right? I think to myself as I shiver all over, both from the overwhelming fear and unforgiving Alaskan winter weather. I don't see anything but vast darkness and snowfall on my left side.

I was never that close to my dad. I was always attached to Mama by the hip. Always looking for her guidance, her warmth, her support, and love. She's the only one I receive it from.

I look over to my right, holding my breath as my lungs burn from icy winds. With blurred vision, I see the cabin in the distance, looking worn out and neglected, with my father's hoarding habit filling our land one garbage pile at a time. If I keep running straight, I should hit the lake that runs through here, and on the other side should be the main road leading to downtown. It's miles away, but I think I can brave it out just a few more hours of this. I should be able to survive the storm.

As soon as I take one step, I'm off my feet and being held in the air by a man who looks like my father, but his soul is long gone. Wide eyes, blackened irises, stone-cold pale expression with no remorse. He's ready to end me.

At least I'll get to be with Mama.

"Found you," he spits with wrath, saliva falling out of chapped lips as he holds his only child like we're strangers. There's a flash of emotion—maybe regret—before he raises his knife into the air and takes aim for my heart. I shut my eyes, hoping it doesn't hurt too much.

"I'll be with Mama. I'll be with Mama," I chant to myself repeatedly, waiting for the pain.

Then, a gunshot rings out.

· · ·

"Gavin. It's me. Wake up, *please.*" Someone's familiar angelic voice brings me out of the worst memory.

Olive skin. Honey eyes. Soft, glowing, long, curly hair. I'm out of hell and surrounded by heaven. And her name is Coraline Rosa. She's here, she's right here with me. I'm not in the woods, scared for my life.

I'm taking slow, long, deep breaths as my arms are wrapped around her naked body. We're tangled in my bed sheets, warm and away from the cold air. Back in my bedroom and far away from the basement.

"You were mumbling in your sleep." She rubs my back in circles with her palm. The more she does, the calmer I feel. God, she's the only one who can do that. She makes a bad day feel like it never happened.

"I'm sorry, sweetheart. Did I wake you?" I groan, running my hands over her breast and down the small of her back.

She nods, hesitation written all over her cute, sleepy face.

"What did you hear?" I ask honestly.

When did I start doing that? And why are the nightmares back and so vividly?

"I couldn't decipher much." She runs her hand through my beard, slowly. She loves doing that. Every time we kiss, she does it. "Something about your dad hurting your mom," she says, merely a whisper. She chokes up on the last word, flinching with a flash of melancholy. I don't say anything. Of course, my trauma spills over to the light. "Your father was The Sleepy Coldwater Serial Killer…wasn't he?" Her forehead dips lower as she asks me a question I really don't want to answer. I pause and give her a slow nod.

I wait for her to cower away. To look at me like everyone else in this small town. But…*she doesn't.* She bats her lashes slowly, looking at me like she always does.

Like I'm worth getting to know.

Patient. Kind. And warm.

I knew it was coming. With all those basement trips she's been doing, I was just waiting for her to say something or run away, but she's still here, and I'm not letting her go.

"I want to see you naked. No, not your body." Hearing her say those words to me seizes my flesh and bones, and my chest swells. She moves closer to me, placing her hand over mine, encouraging me. "Bare your soul to me," she begs softly. "I'm not going anywhere, Gavin."

I close my eyes and grind my jaw until it hurts. Pressing her soft lips to my cheek, she slithers off the bed. First, she slides her legs into jeans and dresses herself as she waits for me to get comfortable.

This woman. God, this patient, celestial woman. How am I ever going to let her go? The answer is, I can't and won't.

"My father," I choke out. "My father murdered my mother before he tried to kill me." My entire body starts to shake. She gathers all of her hair and pushes it to the right side of her neck, and sits next to me.

"Keep going," she encourages, running her hand in circles on my back.

"I ran. I ran from the basement, where my bedroom used to be. Where he ended my mother's life. I ran into the woods during a snowstorm, and he found me within minutes." My vision blurs, but I blink the tears of pain away. I have to do this. If she can bare her soul to me, then I have to do the same for her. "But then my mother's best friend shot him before he could give me one more scar with his knife."

I look at her, and the sight has my heart chipping. Coraline has tears streaked down her face. Puffy lips and red cheeks, I want to kiss away.

"Merelyn," she says.

I nod.

"You're the first person I've told that story to who wasn't the police or Merelyn. You make falling apart easy." I cup her small, heart-shaped face with my hands and bring her in for a lethal kiss. "You make falling apart okay. Are you my safe haven, sweetheart?" I murmur against her chest.

"Yes. I'm here for you in any way you need..." Her tone breaks, then she sniffles.

"Don't feel sorry for me. Don't do that." I curl my arm around her, bringing her closer to me. *I just need to feel her on me.*

"Merelyn saved you?" she asks.

"Yes."

When the shot went off with my dad still holding me in the air, I swear I thought I had blinked, and I was in the afterlife. When I opened my eyes, he dropped the knife and had a hole in his chest, blood running down his shirt and onto the snow. Merelyn stood beside me, like my personal guardian angel, with tears clinging to her lashes. I'm forever in her debt. She's my only family, and the only reason why I came back to Sleepy Coldwater despite the horrid memories.

"I've been scared all my life that I would become like him. He struggled significantly and never got help. They say mental illness can be genetic. So if I stay here, in isolation, I don't have to let anyone in, I won't get a chance to become like him, right? But after he died, everyone looked at me like they did him." I flick my gaze at her as agony rips through me like a tidal wave. Flashes of my dead mother looking at me on the ground with a small smile on her pale face return. "I refused to be even a fraction of what he was and joined the military instead. I worked hard to become just like *my brave mother*. To save those who can't save themselves. I was content for fifteen years. Fifteen years of service, intense missions, and travel, but still, something was missing, *Coraline*. That missing piece in my life is you." I can't help but smile. Fuck, I'm a fool for her.

She stares at me, hearing me out, running her thumb in

circles over my wrist. Then lets out a sad whimper, wiping away her tears fast with the back of her hand before she presses her perfect, pouty lips on mine. We move together in sync like we always do. The movements are lustful healing and slow, relishing each kiss until it's engraved into our brains.

"I think you're giving me too much credit for such a short amount of time, Gavin." Her voice is like a melody feathering my lips. She doesn't know how long I've been wanting this. As I listen to her heartbeat, I gather the courage I need to say what I've been wanting to for a long time. She's everything—a beautiful woman who yearns to find something real in this cruel world.

"Your art speaks words without a voice. It evokes emotions I didn't know I had. You make me feel less alone. And most of all, you make me feel like I can conjure dreams and not just nightmares."

I feel her stiffen.

"Gavin?" She pulls away from me, her smile faltering. Her eyes vehemently pinball left and right, searching for an answer. I don't want her to run away, but I need to remind her how amazing and perfect she is, just the way she is.

"What if we hadn't just met? What if I fell in love with you before you saw me?" I ask, my needy gaze intertwining with her perplexed one. "I've been waiting for this moment for what feels like an eternity. The stars are finally aligning, and I would give anything in the world to keep waking up to you in my bed like this."

She huffs out a nervous laugh and takes loose curls behind her ear. "What are you talking about?" Her dark brows raise as she inches away from me. Her quivering smile stays strong on her beautiful face.

"Don't look at me like that. Don't be afraid." Her pink lips pull into a frown.

A blood-curdling scream shatters the moment. We dart our

gaze toward the sound as a woman continues to shout, her voice turning raspy. It's coming from next door, but it's so loud, and it filters through the cabin.

It's Georgia.

Georgia continues to scream, pleading for help, chanting Gavin's name repeatedly, her tone clearly rattled by fear and helpless desperation.

What is Gavin talking about?

My mind is racing with thoughts, but I'm choosing to be optimistic. Why did it feel like he was confessing to something he's ashamed of?

"What if we hadn't just met? What if I fell in love with you before you saw me?"

That one question is on a loop inside my head the whole time he hastily gets dressed.

Gavin tucks his pistol into his belt and puts on his boots. I race toward the door while he's on my trail.

"Somebody help! Gavin!" Her pleas are distant, echoing off the Alaskan mountains. My veins are pulsing at a high rate, and I flinch at every single noise, on high alert.

"Stay with me, baby," Gavin orders, softening his features as we make a beeline toward the back door of Merelyn's place. I hadn't noticed that I stopped walking, captivated by nature, while trepidation froze me.

"Gavin, the way she's screaming..." I want to put my hands over my ears because the sound is too horrific, too terrifying. She's in trouble, and we're doing everything we can to get to her fast.

"I know, baby, stick with me and don't say a word," he reassures me.

I nod, gulping.

The scream has stopped. Gavin peers inside a window. Merelyn's place looks just like Gavin's, but is a smaller version of the same cabin. With my back to the house, I wait for him to tell me what's going on.

"Stay here, Cora. Stay here and don't fucking come inside unless I tell you to. If you see anyone else that isn't Merelyn or me, you fucking run into those woods until you see the river that goes into town."

My jaw drops. No, I can't be alone, and he can't ask me to leave him!

"I'm not going anywhere without you."

"Do as I say. I have to get to Georgia." He swallows hesitantly. "She's not alone."

My vision is blurring as I plead. I've finally found someone rare, and we're stuck in this madness. I feel a pang of guilt pummel through my chest and into my gut. If I hadn't crashed onto Gavin's land, I wouldn't have brought my stalker to them. Merelyn, Georgia, and Gavin are in the crossfire...because of me.

I suck in a long breath, knowing the one who has been after me is finally here to finish me off. It makes sense. Now that the roads have been cleared, he would take this opportunity to come back. I bet he's using Georgia and Merelyn as bait to draw us in so he has the upper hand to catch us off guard.

Gavin takes a key from a rock and uses it to unlock the door.

"Whatever you do, don't look into this window and don't come in. Do you understand me?" His blue irises darken. The darker spec of blue glows with evident stress, yet somehow he manages to keep his voice and body strained with control.

"G-Gavin." I shake my head, already stuttering.

"Promise me, Coraline. *Now*. I can't risk losing you."

I nod.

"I promise."

With that, he's satisfied, his shoulders relaxing a bit as my heart pounds so hard it hurts.

I want to pull him back; my arms reach for him, capturing icy air as he disappears inside, his hand on his Glock, aiming down, finger hovering over the trigger. I forgot he's a veteran with years of combat experience and a trained operator. I want to follow right behind, but I know I have to listen to him. I don't know how to use a gun. I don't have a knife on me. I'm defenseless.

With my back to the wall of logs, a shed in the back that looks like a mini warehouse captures my attention. I've never seen it before. Maybe because it's been hidden by Merelyn's place. With the angle from Gavin's house, it makes sense why I haven't seen it before. I wait, and I wait for what feels like hours, not knowing what's going on.

Then I hear it.

Another scream, but this time, it's not a high-pitched scream belonging to Georgia; it's coming from Merelyn. My chin wobbles at the sound she makes. I dart for the shed, spotting a shovel that's attached to the door.

I'm sorry, Gavin.

I make a beeline for it. My feet crunch in the snow as my curls rake my face. I grab the hair tie on my wrist and pull my hair back. I can't let them all fight alone when it's me he's after. As soon as I drag it out, the door creaks open. A canvas from the art show where I discovered Liam's affair drops to the ground.

My chest rises and falls faster, taking me by surprise.

I push open the door. The sight in front of me has my blood thinning, and confusion makes me second-guess who I truly need to run away from.

CHAPTER 31
CORALINE

The entire space is full of my art on every wall.

The entire place is full of my paintings and drawings.

Dating back to the first year I started, when I opened my little online shop, to the most recent one here in Alaska. There's a rose bleeding red, and the painting of a field full of tulips I did during the summer time. There's a wall full of shelves with Gavin's military awards and coins sitting on them.

A tear rolls down my face as I run my finger across the canvases.

Gavin.

I trusted him.

Is he the one anonymously buying up my art?

"Where is she?!"

That scream. That voice. I've heard it on numerous occasions. When I'm traveling, booking events or deals, and even when I have no one else to talk to on nights when stress from my family boils over and spills into my personal life. When I found out my husband was having an affair, I felt the most alone during nights when I just wanted to disappear into thin air—a shoulder to cry and laugh on.

It's Maya.

I take off sprinting toward Merelyn's with the shovel gripped tightly in my palm. Nostrils flaring, fists clenched, every step is harsh and purposeful as my heart chips and my world spins with a thousand questions swirling around Gavin's true identity.

How could he do this? Was all of this planned?

I burst through the door to find a horrific scene. I immediately feel sick to my stomach as bile rises in my throat, burning it with its acidity. I can't remember the last time I ate. I'm about to puke at the sight of Georgia dead on the ground with Maya pointing a gun at Gavin's head and Gavin doing the same to her. I instinctively put myself between them, attempting to protect them from each other.

Georgia is lying in a puddle of what seems to be her own blood, staining her clothes and wooden floors.

It's dark, cold, and grim. The air feels dense and unbreathable as the two face off. The feelings I have for Gavin are still very much present, even though I'm internally battling with the truth and spiraling thoughts. I hate that they're both pointing the gun at each other. I can't speak or talk, but only blink as I freeze with fear.

"Maya! What is going on?!" I clip coldly, holding up the shovel over my shoulder. I rush in between them.

"I came here to save you! Do you know who this man is?" She scowls, keeping her eyes on Gavin while blood leaks down her lips.

"Put the fucking gun down, or I'll kill you," Gavin threatens.

Maya huffs, shaking her head.

"Did you know he was arrested for being The Sleepy Cold-water Copycat Serial Killer? Everyone in this town stays away from him."

I turn to Gavin, tucking the past few weeks away, pushing my personal feelings aside, but it aches.

"I took the first flight over here after I heard the crash while we were talking on the phone. I've been looking for you. Your family is worried, your supporters! I tried to get to you, but then an avalanche occurred and blocked the roads, making it harder to reach you."

My whole body trembles as I stand in the middle of them.

"Wait, how do you know about all of that, Maya?"

"I come to Sleepy Coldwater a lot. My family lives here, remember?!"

Still with my palm aimed at her barrel, I stiffen.

I believe her. She did say something like that when she booked this place for me.

"Cora." His tone was like a warning. My head snaps toward him, my heart still breaking from what I saw in the shed. "Don't listen to her, sweetheart."

His voice softens for me. My chin wobbles from the tension. I blink at him as he continues to point his gun at Maya. I don't care if I'm putting myself at risk by using my body as their shield. There has to be a way to get out of this without someone dying today.

"You have all of my art," I squeak out, my voice tremoring. I point to the backyard with my finger, but Gavin continues to stay trained on Maya. I know he knows the direction I'm pointing at. "The art from my last viewing and from the event. Are you the one who has been anonymously buying all of it?"

My head feels light as a feather as I watch him. What I saw in that shed in the back contradicts the trust we've formed.

"You're the one who's been sending me those text messages? The person who ran me off the road?" I yell, walking backwards. He flicks an unrecognizable gaze my way. His expression is full of turmoil and sadness.

"Cora. Listen to me and drop the shovel. Get away from that woman!" he demands, but his orders slip through one ear and out the other, keeping my feet planted to the ground.

Locking my knees, I shake my head as a rock in my throat forms.

"Answer me," I insist as I walk toward Maya. I keep my front facing Gavin, and my back to Maya.

"I trusted you, Gavin!" I cry out, my voice breaking. I glance at the blood seeping out of Georgia.

Who hurt Georgia?

"You can still trust me."

"No! Tell me everything!" I shout, my tongue shaking.

Please tell me I haven't been sleeping with a serial killer.

He squints, narrowing his look at me, but still holding his gun pointed at Maya.

"Yes, I'm the anonymous buyer. Yes, I was arrested when I came back home from the Navy because everyone thought I was the Sleepy Coldwater Copycat, but I was released because I am innocent. I'm not a killer. *I'm not like my father.*" His tone is full of pain as I accuse him. It hurts me to say these things after everything we shared. After he opened up to me, even though I knew it was almost impossible for him to do so.

"It's not enough!" I cry out, stepping closer to Maya's side.

"I didn't send you messages. I didn't run you off the road. I don't want to hurt you! I—"

"Fuck you, you fucking creep! You kept Coraline here without telling her who you really are. You are lying! You're the one who has been after her," Maya shrieks from behind, her voice booming with fury.

Maya has been my agent and close friend for years. I trust her too. She's always been very protective of me. I just met Gavin, and from what I discovered in the shed, things are starting to make a lot more sense, and it all points straight to the man I found myself recklessly falling for—a stranger. A stranger who has clearly been keeping a close eye on me now has me in his nest—a skilled predator with a military background.

"It's you!" I scream, wielding the shovel higher over my head, planting my feet, getting ready to swing. "Were you the one who invited me to the art event?" I accuse him, already knowing the answer, but I want to hear him say it. "You've been watching me for years, haven't you?"

Please say no. Please say no and tell me a perfectly scientific explanation for all of these weird coincidences.

He stops walking toward me, and his spine goes straight. His jaw flexes as he raises his hand, higher, evening out with his shoulders.

"Yes." Hair falls over his forehead as he takes another step toward me.

My bottom lip twitches. Betrayal is drowning my heart until I feel it at the pit of my stomach, gutted, and ultimately feeling incredibly naïve and stupid for letting the first man who was nice to me into my pants.

He was a stranger at the end of the day, and I fell for every single lie.

"You lied to me all this time. All of it wasn't real!" I scorn through the rock in my throat. A tear rolls down my cheek.

Gavin tried to kill me.

He ran me off the road.

That's why he was able to get to me so fast and into his home —a perfect setup.

"It was a trap all along, wasn't it?" Another tear escapes my lashes.

"Coraline, I would never hurt you. I've been in love with you for a long time."

"You don't love me!" I scowl. "I don't know you, do I? You coward."

He shakes his head, letting my angry words roll off his back. My eyes continue to well with unshed tears.

"I'm in love with you." He's still calm and collected, his body still, and his face deadpan. I'm shattered, confused, and full of worry, but he's unshaken. The muscles in his arm flex as he holds the gun at Maya.

He still gazes at me like I'm the only woman in the world.

"Your talent drew me in. The art piece with the estranged mother and daughter? That's the one that made me need to find out who you were. The artist behind the brush. The person wielding the creativity. The dreamer." He tries to take a step toward me, but Maya clicks her tongue, warning him to keep his distance.

"Don't be afraid of me...please, sweetheart," he pleads, voice dripping with an earnest tone. He's visibly trembling, his eyes latched onto me even though a gun is pointing straight at him. "Being with you is the most profound privilege I've ever been blessed with. Finding you that night was the first time I took a breath, and it didn't hurt. I didn't run you off the road. I'm telling you the naked truth." His lips curl with hope.

"I love you, even if that scares you, hell, it scares me." He pauses, walking closer to me as Maya threatens his life with more bewildered shouts. It all sounds like blurred noise as I focus on what he has to say. He doesn't cower or stutter, even when Maya fires a warning shot at the ceiling.

He continues to confess. "It's always been real. Every kiss, every conversation, every glance. I'll die a happy man knowing that what we shared in that cabin was real. It was genuine, and I'll apologize to you every morning, every night, every day, until you believe me."

The rock in my throat grows as I subconsciously lower the shovel.

A warm wave runs straight through my chest. He's being completely vulnerable.

All this time, he was hiding the truth. Maybe he didn't lie, but he disguised it perfectly with his charm.

My knuckles are no longer white from how hard I was holding the shovel. I let his words sink in and seep into my open heart until it bleeds into my next decision. I want to believe him. I need to believe him. This situation is incredibly impossible.

Suddenly, a beam of light and orbs surround him, and I get this overwhelming sensation of peace. It's the ghosts again, presenting themselves as bright glimmering lights, like a beacon of encouragement.

"It was real. What I feel for you is real, and you know it," he says, his voice dripping with ease. His hand searches for mine, and I look at it, tempted to grab it.

"Gavin Ariksen is just like his father. Arrested for being the Copycat Sleepy Coldwater Serial Killer and escaped prison. He brought you here because he stalked you. Invited you. Reeled you in. Fed you lies. Like father," Maya says with a twisted tone to her cold voice. "*Like son.*"

"No," Gavin growls, baring his teeth with each vicious vowel. He continues to stand over Georgia's lifeless body.

I narrow my gaze at him, blinking away more tears rooted in betrayal.

"Don't listen to him, Coraline!" Maya urges me with a desperate bellow.

What the fuck do I do?

"Believe me. Coraline Rosa."

He reaches for me again fearlessly.

Leaning forward, unsure of what to say in this dark moment, my hand slowly outstretched for his.

I replay everything. From Maya's surprising arrival to Gavin admitting his obsession with me. That's when the puzzle pieces I've been given are assembling, drawing me to another awful conclusion.

It's not Gavin I should be afraid of.

He shakes his head. His lids are closing until I can barely see the blue orbs I've fallen addicted to.

"I don't want to scare you. I don't want you to fear me. I want to love you," he reiterates.

Gavin's fingers are on mine. I sob softly, unsure of what to do or what the right choice is, but I'm leading with my heart and the ghosts. As soon as I try to thread my fingers with his, he gets ready to pull me into him, but he gets thrown back by a loud boom.

A shot goes off, and it pierces Gavin in the chest. He loudly grunts as blood sprays my face, getting into my mouth and the tip of my tongue. With an iron taste in my mouth, I scream, reaching out to catch or fall with him, but I'm getting pulled back by my hair and away from Gavin.

CHAPTER 32
CORALINE

I shriek as Maya continues to pull me back by my hair viciously. I drop the shovel, the loud clanging ringing in my ears as I'm dragged closer to her and away from helping him. My feet momentarily bump into the back of Georgia's head amidst the chaos. That's when I see something—a blip of life flutters when I spot Georgia's blonde brows furrow, and her nose contorts.

She's still alive.

My nails scrape Maya's hand until I know I've cut her open, hoping it's enough to let me go, but she doesn't. I frantically search for Gavin, who has disappeared after hitting the kitchen counter.

She shot him. She really shot him.

Did she kill him?!

"Gavin!" I scream hoarsely. His name bounces off every corner of the house, echoing.

"Maya, what the hell are you doing!" I plant my feet and spring forward. I swing my elbow back until it hits her in the nose. She yelps for a heartbeat, then presses the gun into my neck and racks it back.

"Hit me again, and I'll end you." Her threat is a stab to my chest and a permanent end to our relationship.

"Why are you doing this? Why are you trying to kill them and me? How fucking could you?" I shout at Maya, but it only gets the pistol cocked into the back of my head. She hits me, determined to silence me. I shriek from the burning, throbbing pain, feeling completely helpless and betrayed.

"Shut the hell up!" she demands, her vision pinned on me. I see Gavin, who stands to his full height and glares daggers at Maya.

He's still alive. *Gracias a Dios.*

He returns with vengeance tattooed all over his body. I've never seen Gavin so angry. Then she aims the gun at Gavin, but he stands his ground, not surrendering but not making any attempt to diffuse the situation.

"Come any closer, and I'll shoot you in the head." She orders Gavin away.

"Let me go!"

"You think I did all of this alone?" Maya huffs manically. Her voice hardens and seethes in my ear while she holds me at gunpoint.

I don't understand what I did to deserve this. Maya is my friend.

"I had help. Now that our cover has been blown, you can stop pretending, Gavin." The barrel is pressed into my neck, right into my carotid artery. One shot and I'm dead. There's no surviving a fatal wound like that, especially being hours away from the nearest hospital. I could bleed out in seconds. I need to stay calm enough to buy us all some time to get out of this.

"What are you talking about?" I turn to her, glaring, eyes filled to the brim with tears rooted in deception. She's still trying to convince me that Gavin is a part of her mess. Well, I don't believe a single word that comes out of her mouth anymore.

"Am I lying, Gavin? Tell her the truth. Did you tell her why her car kept detouring on the road that night?" She pokes with a grim smirk. "Did you tell her you were the one who sent the invite to the event? Huh?" she taunts with a wicked tone.

I flick my gaze to him. My heart shatters because the look on his face right now tells me she isn't lying about those things. A muscle above my lips pulls, twitching. He's not my enemy.

"Did you tell her what other stuff you specialized in while you were a SEAL? I looked you up, Gavin Ariksen. He's a hacker. Cyber fucking security. He hacked your GPS!"

"I don't believe you," I spit sternly. Something emerges from the shadows. My eyes flick to the silhouette behind Maya. It's a spirit. The woman I first saw in the bathroom mirror when I took my first shower. She has long black hair with the same eyes as Gavin. It has to be his mother. She wields a knife, the same knife I took to the basement, then hid in the drawer of newspapers. I'm going to distract Maya before she can kill me. "I'm going to ask you one more time, Maya. Stop dodging my questions. I don't understand why you're doing this. After everything?" I shake my head as another tear rolls down my cheek. "That's the least you can do before you shoot me, don't you think?"

Maya's expression hardens, a look of poison coming out of her pores. Her mask has fallen.

"You think Lilly was the only person Liam was fucking?"

My heart sinks to my stomach.

No.

I can't picture it. I don't want to picture them together like that. Was Liam more of a shallow asshole than I thought? He had my best friend and coworker? How could I have been so blinded to their affair?

"I'm so sick of your success and self-pity! You don't deserve the opportunities getting thrown your way!" She raises her fist and connects it with my cheek. My lip instantly gets cut open.

"I want what you have, bitch. Lilly is out of the picture, but for some odd reason, he doesn't want to sign the divorce papers. He says he can still work it out with you. He has a plan to talk to you and make things right. Maybe if you come back from Alaska, he'll be able to fix what he broke. He's holding on to false hope because *we belong together!*" She pushes me forward so she can take aim. I fall into a wall, a glass frame shattering from the impact. I prepare for the bullet, with my hands in the air to protect my heart…but it never comes.

Gavin reappears, jumping in front of me and taking me to the ground to shield me. Another shot goes off, I close my eyes, and scream. I can't handle seeing him get hurt again because I care about the man who revived me. I care about him so deeply; I feel him in my soul.

My muse.

I look up and see Maya on the ground with a knife in her back. The figure who held it is replaced by trembling Merelyn. My lips tilt upwards, and I sigh heavily with relief. Merelyn was hiding this entire time.

She missed and hit the ceiling. Gavin retrieves the gun from the floor and quickly empties the chamber. I stand shaking, feeling like I'm floating from all of the madness. Maya has been fucking with me all this time. Maya has been writing me letters to scare me away. She's the one who chased me off the road. It wasn't a man. It was her all along—a crime of delusional passion.

"The phones started working an hour ago," Merelyn says as she gets on her knees to help Georgia. Georgia groans as she lifts her head and settles it onto Merelyn's lap. "I already called the police. The captain should be here any minute."

"W-what's going on?" Georgia murmurs, clearly out of it. It seems that Maya stabbed her and knocked her unconscious.

"It's okay, honey, you're safe now." Merelyn eases her mind. "Help is on the way."

"Okay," she murmurs weakly. I quickly glance over to Maya. She's sprawled out on the floor with the knife still attached to her back. Merelyn stabbed her and then knocked her out with a vase of plants to the back of her head. I hope she's dead.

"Sweetheart, are you all right?" Gavin returns to me, pulling me into his chest. I'm an utter mess. I sob uncontrollably into his chest, smelling his familiar scent, thinking I was never going to be able to again. I push myself as hard as I can into his warm flesh, desperate to hear his heart beat.

"I thought I was going to lose you," I cry. "I thought I was going to die."

"It's not over for us. It will never be over for us, baby. If our fate turned cruel, I'd still manage to find a way to you again. In. Every. Single. Lifetime. I love you, Cora. I fucking love you."

I want to say it back. I need to say it back. I don't care if all of this is fucked. Gavin wouldn't hurt me. Fear and adrenaline continue to paralyze me. Either way, I can't say those three words back. I promised myself I'd only say those three words again when I was sure the next man would be my person. The timing and person would be worth it. Someone who protects me, sees me, and makes me feel safe and beautiful.

Still, he hid something big from me, and it's stopping me from fully falling.

I look up at him as blood continues to pour out of his shoulders and seeps through his clothing. He presses his lips to mine, harsh and passionate. I can feel how much he loves me, even though it might be obsessively, it's still pure. He licks at my bottom lip, demanding entry. I quickly oblige and let our tongues dance together as he claims his dominance.

A shot rings out, pulling us apart.

Maya pulled out another hidden gun.

What the hell? I thought she was out! She has two guns on her?

Gavin springs forward, disarming her as Merelyn falls to the ground with a bullet hole in her chest.

CHAPTER 33
GAVIN

I take the gun from Maya's hand before she can pull the trigger on me. I do what I should have done in the first place and make sure she is no longer a threat to the ones I love, and kill her. I point it between her pathetic eyes and send it. She falls to the floor, with her brain splattered across the walls.

Whoever the fuck this woman is, Coraline trusted her like family. My teeth grind against each other as I hover over her dead body. She almost took me away from the love of my life. I can't even feel the bullet wound in my shoulder right now. All I feel is rage.

"Oh my god, Gavin!" Coraline screams behind me. I don't like the sound of her wails. I whirl around to find Merelyn bleeding out from her chest and mouth. Georgia sits up, still dazed with tears in her eyes.

The entire room spins as I watch the only motherly figure in my life I have left, look at me with eyes begging me to save her. The person who did her best to raise me is bleeding out profusely. It keeps pouring out of her chest and onto the floor like a waterfall. Her eyes are wide, her face already pale, and her mouth is gaping. She's clawing at her wound as Coraline and Georgia circle her urgently.

No.

"Gavin…" Georgia shakes her head, already telling me what I already know.

She's going to die.

My heart breaks. Merelyn is looking straight at me while Coraline plugs her wounds with her hands.

"No, no, no," Coraline repeatedly cries, doing her best to stop the bleeding, but it's not working. The sound of sirens is nearing. I'm on my knees in an instant and lift Merelyn's head until she's on my lap. Her lips are turning pale blue, and there is no more light in her greying eyes.

I can't lose her, not like this, and not right now.

"You hear those sirens, Mer." I force a smile. "Officer Matt will be here soon. I can hear the ambulance. You'd better not go anywhere."

I smooth her white hair back. She hangs onto my hand. Her skin is already running cold.

"We both know my time is over," she murmurs weakly. Her breathing turns short and shallow. Blood is everywhere. On my knees, shirt, and shoes.

"Don't say that. You have to stay awake for me, okay?" I grab her hand, pulling her to my chest. She's right. She isn't going to make it, but miracles happen all the time. The artist I've been secretly admiring showed up on my land, and we spent the most enchanting weeks of our lives together. If that isn't a miracle, I don't know what is.

"You're going to live. You're not going anywhere."

I grip her shoulders when she closes her eyes. She doesn't get to go anywhere.

"I get to tell your mom what you've been up to all these years. It's okay to say goodbye." She blinks slowly, her eyes already trying to roll upwards. Georgia and Coraline continue to sob silently, grabbing towels and blankets to buy Merelyn more time.

"I'm looking at her right now," I tell her, a rock in my throat as my muscles begin to quiver. I force a somber smile as a warm teardrop falls out of my eyes. "I got two mamas," I scoff, my throat and chest hurting.

Merelyn can't leave me. She's all I have left in Sleepy Coldwater.

Her mouth parts, and a weak smile crests her face. She reaches out, her finger tips grazing my cheek. I've always seen her as a mother to me when I lost my own. She's a guide. An angel to steer me to make the right choice, a path of morality, and to give me the childhood that my drunken father stole away. She's slipping away, and there's nothing I can do. I want to scream at the world. I want Maya to revive just so I can kill her again, but this time, I would make it slow and painful.

She can't die.

"You've always been my boy," she murmurs, accepting her fate for us both. She's barely able to form her last words. Her lips close at the same time her hand falls to her side. My eyes grow wider with affliction. I take her hand back into mine and squeeze, wishing she would squeeze my hand back.

She doesn't.

She takes her last breath. Her bleeding chest falls for the last time, coming to a complete rest. I wait for it to rise again, feeling for a pulse in her cold neck, but it doesn't come. I'm back in a familiar hell of grief.

No.

No.

God, this isn't happening.

Coraline sags to the side, completely pale and distraught, matching my emotions. I study her for a second, only wanting her arms to fall apart in. As if she can read my mind, she inches closer.

But before she can embrace me, Merelyn's front door is being broken into by the police. The captain—my close friend, Matt, has his weapon drawn and pointed toward the ground. He spots Maya, then darts his lethal gaze at us. His red cheeks match the color of his hair, while his brown eyes dart and assess the situation.

"Jesus Christ," he mutters. "What the hell happened here?"

I watch Gavin's pained blue eyes stay on Merelyn's bagged body. The pain is too much, and I don't know how to stomach it. She's dead because she tried to save me. Because of someone in my past. *Because of Maya.* His only family up here in these mountains is now gone. A sense of guilt eats at me even though I know it's not my fault, but still. I feel responsible for everyone's pain.

I should have left when I had the chance; maybe she would still be alive. I palm my face in my hands as I choke back the sobs in the back of the ambulance.

"That was the last stitch. You took it like a champ." The paramedic's lips curve into a genuine, friendly smile. I try to return it with my own, but nothing reflects. Nothing moves. I feel numb and horrified by the past few hours.

My best friend. My co-worker. My shoulder, I thought I could cry and laugh on, was the one after me the entire time. She was in love with Liam to the point that it drove her crazy. She hid her hatred for me so well.

I don't understand what I ever saw in him. Hell, I don't know what Lilly or Maya did.

The medic places a warm blanket over me.

"Gavin Ariksen. Half of the town is scared of him, and the other half is trying to date him. He hasn't taken his eyes off you since you came into my care. I don't think I've ever seen him so protective of anyone who wasn't Merelyn. Are you guys together?" She looks me up and down after staring at Gavin. I blink rapidly at her, dumbfounded. I tighten my grip on the blanket that wraps around my chest and stomach.

"After all that's happened, you're asking me about this?" I look at her with evident disgust written all over my face. I shake my head at her disdainfully. I can't even fathom or accept Merelyn's death, and she's asking me about my dating life?

"I'm sorry for asking; that was inappropriate." She clears her throat and stands. She pulls off her gloves. I had to get ten stitches where Maya hit me in the back of my head. Then she pulls out her phone and taps away on the screen. I continue to glare at her. "I've been a paramedic for almost ten years. I've become a little desensitized to trauma. I deeply apologize." She turns off her phone and gives me a small smile. "I'm sorry for your loss."

Those five words don't do anyone's grief justice. Nothing will. I've grown attached to Merelyn in such a short amount of time. Gavin not only lost someone close to him but also the only person he talked to. Georgia was quickly transported to the local hospital. She sustained a significant amount of blood loss, but the medics reassured us she'll be okay.

The paramedic, whose name never settled into my memory, walks away, giving me space and time to think.

Gavin continues to talk to the local policeman, his broad arms resting on his chest. This man makes anything look sexy. That same butterfly flaps in the pit of my stomach, loosening my tense nerves for a second. For a swift moment, I forget about the pain. I forgot about what we just went through. No one has made me feel that way. Only he has that effect on me.

Whenever I see him take a breath, it silences my insecurities. The voice in my head telling me I'm not enough goes mute. My art did that for him, and that's why he felt inclined to search for me. I made him feel seen—less alone. The reality of my art leaves gratitude in my soul. I didn't fully grasp the impact art has on another broken soul searching for the same things I am whenever I pick up a pencil. I can't stop dreaming. If I ever stop drawing for myself, I have to keep going for others. That is motivation alone to keep going. No matter what.

For the first time in weeks, the sun emerges, shining a bright golden light mixed with purple and pink shades against the stone texture of Gavin's house. I glance around the surrounding mountains, drinking in the mesmerizing beauty of the landscape. The mountains. The snow. The trees and the wildlife that call it home. Sometimes, I forget just how beautiful this planet is.

The sound of a cop car's sirens filters through my ears from a distance. I watch the cop slow down as it fights its way through the feet of snow. It stops once it's behind the fire truck. Gavin's land is full of cops, detectives, medical personnel, and firefighters.

A man emerges from the backseat, swinging the door frantically. As soon as he steps out, his feet slip, and his forearm connects violently with the hood of the cop car to keep him upright. My brows narrow at him curiously, and a twinge of familiarity pulls in my heart.

What the hell is Liam doing here?

My nostrils flare, my blood turns hot, and I swear I think I could hit something—specifically, him.

He looks straight at me, and I straighten my back, clawing at my thighs, full of anxiety. He picks up his pace, jogging and tripping over the feet of snow, clearly struggling like he doesn't know how to maneuver through it. He's in a thick coat with jeans and a winter beanie that hangs down the sides of his ears.

"Coraline!" he shouts. I roll my eyes at the sound of his voice.

I turn away from him, giving him a cold shoulder. I don't want to see, hear, or speak to him unless he's going to tell me how he got here so fast and that he's ready to sign the divorce papers. I swear if he had anything to do with Maya trying to murder me...

I'm sure he'll be investigated.

I look toward Gavin, who is already making his way to me. He stalks thunderously as Matt looks at him with a confused look on his face. He keeps his death glare planted on Liam.

"Coraline! I'm so glad I've found you! Are you hurt, my love?" he pants, leaning on the door of the ambulance with his forearm. He tries to pull my hand and thread his fingers with mine in a comforting way, but I pull away and flinch. A gold fleck shines underneath the sunlight. He's still wearing his wedding band.

Fuck him.

"Liam, what the hell are you doing here?"

His face sinks, full of regret.

"I'm still your emergency contact." He continues to pant, out of breath. "Maya told me you were here and that you disappeared! Everyone back home is worried about you. Your mom. Your dad. Your siblings. I've been trying to get a hold of you for months now. I-I still love you. I've needed to say that to you. I'm so glad you're okay, and I'm so damn sorry."

Wow. He continues to lie to me, but I see right through him. I scoff, disgusted.

"Maya is dead. She tried to kill me over you." I tut.

"What the hell? Why would she do that?" he asks, his cheeks reddening.

"Really, Liam? Apparently, she's in love with you. As if my best friend wasn't enough, you got with Maya, too? Sign the divorce papers. I want nothing to do with you. I'm ready to close this horrific chapter of my life."

"I was lost. I was fucking anyone and anything that gave me attention. I didn't mean for any of this to happen. I promise I'll do better. Don't give up on us." He leans in, embarrassed. He doesn't want anyone to hear. "We'll talk about this somewhere more private. I want to make sure you're okay first, and then I'll take you to dinner," he offers.

Liam reaches forward and brushes my hair behind my ear. My stomach coils at his touch. As soon as he lingers, a massive hand reaches forward and punches Liam straight to the chin. He falls to the floor, blood already leaking out of his mouth and nose. He keeps going, assaulting him with plain black fury in his darkened eyes. Gavin's fists are bloody, and Liam's nose is obviously broken by the way it's in a different direction. I can't do anything but watch. The paramedics scatter, and a group of policemen let it happen for a moment.

Gavin lifts him back from his collar and throws him until he collides with the ambulance door, letting out a frustrated whine. Clearly still dazed, he looks at Gavin with fear and shock. Before Gavin can continue to pummel, he's held back by three police officers. One stands in the middle, using his body as a wall to prevent Gavin from killing Liam. The other two hold him back by his biceps.

"Get the fuck away from her, or I'll kill you." Gavin intervenes, standing in front of me like my guardian knight.

"Hey, *you get the hell away from her*. That's my wife! I'm her husband." Liam stands back up, puffing his chest. He stands at his full five feet nine, compared to Gavin's well over six feet stature. I want to laugh. Liam couldn't hurt a fly, and he thinks he can intimidate Gavin? Comedy.

Gavin's angry, clearly seeing red. The veins in his neck and hands bulge. He doesn't have his jacket on because it's covered in Merelyn's blood.

"You don't have any claim on her anymore. I made it very

clear who has her now these past few weeks—every night, *all night.*"

My heart flips in my chest. Gavin's possessiveness drips into his tone. Liam's scowl transforms into one of hurt as he soaks in Gavin's insinuation.

"You don't get the honor of looking at her. If you ever come close to her again, I'll bury you." He grabs him by the collar and restrains him in the air. "Now get the fuck off my land." He snarls before launching him to the ground. He skids across the icy foundation and stops right before Matt's feet. Liam's confidence drops as he settles on his elbows, flicking his gaze to me, then back to Gavin.

I don't care that he knows what I've been up to these past few weeks. I just found out one of his mistresses tried to kill me because he won't sign the divorce papers. Who knows how many other women there are?

"Coraline is still my wife, motherfucker!" he spits, his limbs sputtering as he tries to stand. He slips and falls and lands in Matt's arms this time. He lurches forward trying to attack, but Matt holds him back by his elbows.

"I don't give a fuck. A piece of paper doesn't make you her husband. It's material. It doesn't mean anything." With a confident, sly grin, Gavin walks closer to him and leans into his ear. Liam flinches, his face red with anger. "I *enjoyed* your beautiful wife."

I'm in a trance, watching Gavin stand up for me. My mouth gapes open, cheeks burning, completely breathless, and in shock.

"Let's go, buddy. We have some questions to ask you anyway." Another officer joins in and pulls Liam by the arms. They whisk him away as Liam continues to bellow insults at us, but I can't hear him over my thundering heart. Liam has no effect on me anymore. Gavin fucked it all away and imprinted himself instead with a connection that sparks.

Gavin turns to me with a vacant look on his handsome face. We've gone through the investigation with the cops, but now it's my turn to talk to him about everything.

Where do we go from here?

CHAPTER 35
CORALINE

$\mathcal{I}$ sit in the living room, still trying to process everything I witnessed. I feel free and yet guilty because Merelyn's life was collateral damage. I haven't stopped crying; the tears just keep falling out. I only want to sulk and dwell in guilt in Gavin's arms. I want to stretch out and lie beside him, and ask him to never let me go.

But I'm the reason why he has to plan a funeral.

"Gavin," I choke up, playing with my fingers nervously—popping them one by one as I keep my vision trained on the wooden floors. The same wooden floors we played truth or dare on. The same room where we indulged in brain chemistry-altering, intimate sex. The same cabin where I feel revived after being in the dark for so long. I don't know how to say goodbye. I don't want to, but I must.

"I'm sorry. I'm sorry I dragged you guys into this. I didn't know Maya would do this to me."

"I swear to fuck, Coraline," he quips with an edge. "Don't be sorry. None of this is your fault. I don't want to hear it. Don't guilt yourself," he says from across the room. He's standing, looking at a framed photo of him and Merelyn together fishing.

I nod, brushing away another tear with my knuckle.

"What I want to hear you say," he turns around with reddened eyes, staring straight at me, "is that you'll stay. Stay here with me."

"Gavin…" I breathe, already pulling back from him. The air in the room shifts. The spark that always makes its presence known when we're around each other doesn't ignite.

He stalked me.

"I lost Merelyn. Don't make me lose you, too."

I shake my head, dropping my chin in defeat because I know what comes out of my mouth next is going to hurt him.

"Damn it, Coraline. You feel it too. I'm in love with you."

He stands in front of me.

"I'm in the middle of a divorce. I need space and time to think. I need to be on my own. My trust issues just upgraded a tier, and I don't want you to fix what another man broke. It's not fair to you. I can give you my body, but my heart is…" I shake my head as my vision blurs. Everything just feels like it's too much.

"I have a lot of healing, thinking, and growing to do."

It wouldn't be fair to him and to me if I just ignored every sad bone in my body and the things Gavin did to get me here.

Due to the investigation, I can't leave Sleepy Coldwater for another few days, but my parents are flying in now that they know where I am. I'm going to stay with them in a hotel and book the first flight out of here. I don't want to leave Gavin, but I need to pull myself together. Alone.

"You don't have to do anything. I'll wait. I'll wait for you even if it means I get the broken parts of you. *Wait with me* and stay."

"Gavin…"

He's not listening.

I grab my bag. One of Matt's police officers is going to take me to a hotel of my choosing.

"I have to go. You can't make me stay here."

"The hell I can't. I'll tie you up to my bed if I have to, keep fucking you until I get you pregnant."

I scoff.

"You're obsessed," I clip, rising to my feet. "That isn't love."

"Hell yes, I am. *Obsession can be love.* I've never felt like this before, so I know it's real. It hurts when you don't look at me. It hurts when *you are hurting*. It hurts to say those three words, and you don't say them back. I'll do anything for you. Everything that I do will be for you. You want my heart? I'll cut it out of my chest and give it to you. If you want the snow to stop, I'll take you anywhere you want to go and find the bluest beach there is. You want me to get on my knees? I'll find the prettiest, biggest ring I can before I'm on them. I'll do anything for you, sweetheart." He grabs my hands with both of his. He's shaking. "Make me the wealthiest man and stay, baby."

"Gavin! That isn't fair!" I hiccup, as my tone heightens, slipping away from him. "I can't! You can't love me after only a few weeks! You stalked me! You brought me here to Alaska. You hacked my GPS to bring me to you. This is...*it's unbelievable*. It wasn't normal."

"So you think I'm like him?" His shoulders rise and fall for a long beat. "You think I'm like my father?"

"That's not what I meant." I sigh. "I have to leave."

He runs a hand through his beard.

"I'm not normal. I accepted it a long time ago. If loving you so hard, doing anything to make you mine, and doing anything to keep you happy and safe isn't normal, then I never want to be."

I slowly meet his penetrating gaze. The bright blue irises I could get lost in forever are doing what they always do—put me in a chokehold.

"No," I whisper.

"You screamed *my name* all these nights," he snarls low.

I start to pace around the room, holding my hand over my mouth, deep in thought. *I'm breaking him.* I'm trying not to fall apart myself, but he isn't making leaving any easier. He comes up behind me, tempted to embrace me, but he holds himself back.

"Was this all in my fucking head?" he asks.

A tear rolls down my cheek as I try to hold back my sobs, but I continue to choke on them, failing miserably.

"Don't make me answer that," I whisper.

"Look me in my eyes and tell me you didn't fall in love with me, too?"

I keep my vision pinned to his muscular arms. I can't look at him.

"Stop it," I quip. "I have to go," I murmur somberly.

He scoffs and smiles, but it's anything but blissful. There's resentment and unacceptance written all over him. He walks away, his shoulders swaying as he goes. His boots thud with every indignant step. He grabs a cigarette from his pocket and leans on the wall.

"You can't look me in the eyes, can you, sweetheart?" he says brokenly but with forced confidence. I shut my eyes tight as the tears continue to roll down. I reach the front of the house and look out the window. There's an officer waiting in the driver's seat for me. I need to run. Run away and never come back here like the coward that I am.

"Promise me you'll be okay? Promise me you won't shut yourself out from the world?" I whisper, still unable to face him. "I don't want you to be alone."

He chuckles darkly, sarcasm clearly in between us. I glance over at him and tense up. He lights a cigarette with his lighter. He takes a drag and blows the smoke in the air, and seconds later, he's heading toward the backyard. He turns to me, his lips pressed together, with half-moon circles under his eyes, looking incredibly defeated and tired. Then he's ambling toward me, his strides long and purposeful. That same scent of his that drives me wild filters through my nose.

"Do it. Put a fucking end to my misery. Tell me to let you go."

"Stop it," I scold.

"I've killed for you. I'd die for you, but right now, you're making it hard to live for you. Don't you see? If you think I'll ever stop loving you once you leave, you're fucking wrong. I'll keep watching you. I'll keep waiting."

"I can't stay here."

"*Stay with me, then*. Choose the quiet. Choose us."

"Gavin…I-I don't know what to say." I turn around and walk further away so that I can breathe.

"Tell me, you love me." He takes a step forward, forcing me to stop breathing.

"Tell me you can't live without me." Another step.

He cups my face, and I gaze into his reddened eyes. Our chests collide, and my hands hover over his, but I'm still unsure what to do.

"Or tell me to let you go."

He pushes his face in front of mine so that our noses are touching. He closes his eyes as his brows furrow, and I clench onto his fingers like I'm trying to make him decide for me.

"Let me go," I breathe. His entire body loosens, and he rests his forehead against mine. My heart chips more, and I open my mouth to say something, but no words come out. I suck in another breath just as my frown slips into a heavy pout. The one man I thought I could trust obliterated that hope in seconds. He gave me the push I needed to draw again—to dream, but his secrets are burying me back into darkness. I know he's not like Liam, but stalking me? Pretending not to know who I truly am? Hacking my GPS? It's a lot for me to process, especially after what happened to Merelyn. I'm traumatized, and yet I still ache for him.

"I don't want to break your heart. You cannot force me to

accept that everything you did to get me here was okay. This was always going to end. A winter storm doesn't last forever." I take a step away from him. I don't miss the muscle underneath his eye flexing with despair.

"The lengths I'd go to keep you are limitless. If it takes a damn winter storm to keep you here with me, I'll find a way to make it snow 365 days out of the year." He shakes his head. "But that's not what you want, is it?" He swings the door open and stands with one foot out. "You don't want me?"

I don't know what I want. That's why I'm asking him for space, but I know it's hurting him. I turn away, facing the tall mountains I woke up to every morning. A beautiful view that always took my breath away.

I want him. I want him so dangerously and toxic that ignoring what he did to get me here is knocking on my door, but if I cave in, it won't be fair to him or me.

"We can be friends. Come see me sometime?"

"I'm not your fucking friend. I'll always be greedy over you."

"Gavin." I breathe brokenheartedly.

"The city life isn't for me. This is my home. Alone. Cold. And barren. This is what I'm used to." He raises both arms, insinuating the cabin. His glassy eyes become more textured. He forces a pretend smile.

"Are you going back to him?"

My mouth gapes open. I turn to him, appalled.

"What?"

"Liam."

"No. *Hell no.*"

A possessive edge flashes across his strained face.

"I should have warned you how greedy I can be, but I'll do that now." He takes another drag of his cigarette. Eyes glimmering with possessiveness. "If you let another man touch you, Coraline, I will know, and I will break his hands. If you let another man kiss you, I will cut off his tongue. If you let him have you—what I've licked and worshipped, I'll destroy him." The muscle in his jaw tightens.

I know he'll do it.

"Please. I beg of you. Let me go."

"I can't. I won't. You're mine. You'll always be mine. *You've always been mine.* Even if you're old and grey, married to another man, living halfway across the world, past a different ocean. Even if we don't speak another word to each other in this life-time, you'll always be the one who gives me hope."

My throat tightens. No one has ever said words like this to me before. No one has made me laugh, smile, or feel peace like I do when I'm with him. But the tiny voice in my head tells me that he'll get bored. He'll get bored and see what Liam did and walk away like I was never anything.

"Do you know what it's like to watch your family be ripped apart in front of you?" his voice trembles.

"Do you know what it's like to watch the only family you have left die in front of you? *Twice?*" he roars.

His mother and now Merelyn.

Quivering, I look away.

I'm a coward.

"What if I told you that when I look at you, it feels like home?"

I shut my lids tight. I can't look at him as he falls apart.

"I'm terrified," I whisper. "I'm scared. I'm cautious! I'm petri-fied that the man I spent these past few weeks with doesn't see anything wrong with what he did. It almost got me killed."

The car crash. The GPS.

I open the front porch door and close it for the last time. The familiar bells chime as the cold wind blows.

Without looking at him, I mutter, "Don't follow me. Don't stalk me. Don't look for me."

CHAPTER 36
GAVIN

She left.

I watch the back of the police car, my whole body trembling from head to toe. I'm shutting down completely. I'm tired, wounded physically and mentally, bleeding—grieving, and yet the thought of never seeing Cora is killing me.

I can't take it.

Through the glass shield, I watch the silhouette of thick, soft curls inside the cop car face forward toward the mountains. She hasn't looked back once. I'm not sure if that hurts more than not hearing her say goodbye.

She didn't choose me.

How could she?

Everyone I've ever loved has left me or died.

I did unforgivable things to get her here. I stole her time like a thief...and I would do it again. I would make the same selfish decisions because it brought her to me. I directed her car toward my ranch because the storm was getting too dangerous. I didn't expect her to drive in it, so I made her detour to find shelter. I bought out her art at events because I wanted it all to myself.

Everything I've done has been for her.

I've been following her work for years, and when she stopped creating, I noticed. I wanted to know why, and I did everything I could to find out.

The night she found out her husband was having an affair with her best friend, I was there. We bumped shoulders when she was on her way back with champagne glasses. Again, I purchased it all. Her art helped heal parts of me. Second, she deserves all the love and support. She works hard for it. While her own trusted group was secretly bringing her down, I wanted to remind her to never quit and to keep believing in herself. I have the money. I have the time. I will always be what she needs me to be so she stays happy. If she can't believe in herself right now, I'll be the voice she needs to hear when she shuts down.

I just want to be here for her. Always.

The car makes the final turn heading down the road that leads off my property. They disappear into the woods, and all I see is snow.

The cabin is quieter and colder. Merelyn is dead. Georgia is in the hospital. And my sweetheart left.

I'm alone with my haunted past. Walls of spilled blood. And there's no one who makes me feel the fraction of happiness that Coraline does. I can't go an hour without knowing she's okay. Does she really think I can withstand days? Weeks?

I head toward the cabinet where I store all of my alcohol. My leg hurts from wearing the prosthetic. She took one look at me, and the desire in her beautiful brown eyes didn't falter. Not even for a second. No pity. No sadness. No apologies.

She is the only person I've bared all my darkness to, and in the end, she...left.

Sauntering into my bedroom, the door slowly creaks open after pushing it. I gave her the brown sketchbook so she could draw again. My heart skips a beat as I flip through the pages. I find the portrait of myself. My throat rolls. Fuck, she's an amazing artist and the most talented, beautiful woman I've ever met. No one can compare to her. I hope that being here, she got her stardust back—the light she thought she lost.

Tearing the page from the book, I pin it to the wall on the side where she used to sleep.

I'VE BEEN DRINKING HEAVILY these past few days. The burning taste of bourbon doesn't quench my thirst for Coraline. It doesn't compare to the burn I feel in my chest and eyes at the thought of her in harm's way again.

The investigation is nearing an end.

Maya was responsible for Coraline's torment. The letters, the texts, and the car crash. Liam had nothing to do with it. She acted alone.

Still, I have the urge to kill him next if he tries to manipulate her into giving him another chance. The thought alone has me spiraling deeper. I look at the reflection in the mirror and throw water on my face.

I have to find her. I know she asked me not to, but she doesn't get it. She can't ask that of me because it's not a choice. Loving her is instinct. Protecting her is all I can think about.

The doorbell rings.

Who the fuck is it? I'm not in the mood for more press. Reporters have been standing outside my land, wanting to interview me. I've turned everyone down. I can already predict the headlines. Using my father's name for clicks and money. *The Sleepy Coldwater Serial Killer's Son is Under Investigation Again.*

When they don't know shit about what transpired here, they just assume I'm a killer too.

The only people with access to my land are Georgia and Matt.

Is it her?

Did she come back? Fuck, I'm so damn bad for her.

Drying myself with a towel, I rush out of the bathroom. I clothe myself, throw on my shoes, and stumble to the door. My face falls when I see Matt.

"Well, you look like shit," he huffs, pushing past me and entering my living room uninvited.

I slam the door behind him.

"You also smell like I just walked into a bar."

"What the hell do you want, Matt?" I spit with rage. I don't want to see anyone if it's not Coraline.

"I came here to check up on you."

"If it's not regarding the investigation, I don't want to know. I don't want to speak or see anyone." I stalk over to the kitchen, dragging my feet. Everything is slowly stirring as though gravity wants to anchor me until I'm lying on the ground. I pour myself a shot of liquor. "You can leave." I point to my front door.

My eyes linger on the Christmas wreath that hangs in the top center. I haven't touched the cabin. I left it like it was when she left. The only reason I haven't dragged her back here is because of the gunshot wound to my chest. I'm giving it one more day before I head out and find her. She doesn't get to leave me.

"Coraline is leaving on an airplane with her family. She's already at the airport."

I can't breathe.

"What?"

"She's leaving Sleepy Coldwater. This shitty small town."

"No. She fucking can't."

"Yes, she can," he counters. "And quite frankly, so should you."

I shake my head, feeling the weight of her absence. I lost Merelyn. I lost my birth mother right here in this cabin. I can't leave this place. As dark and fucking sad as it is, my mother still lives through these walls, and now Merelyn will too. I can't leave this place. Anxiety rips through me, and I break out into a sweat.

"Leave this place, man. There's nothing for you here. Don't drown in it."

"I can't leave."

"Yes, brother. *You can.*"

"No, you don't understand...I can't!" I shout, rushing my words out frantically.

And she can't leave this place either.

My mama will be all alone. Her soul still hovers. I feel her presence all the time.

Matt has his hands on both sides of his hips, leaning on one leg as he studies me.

"I'm drunk off my ass. Give me a ride to the airport, now."

"It's a two-hour drive. I don't think we can make it," he replies. I pull out his pistol from his holster faster than I'm processing my own thoughts. I point it at his head and nod at his keys dancing from his pocket. He holds his hands up, nostrils flaring. His brown eyes narrow at me, disappointed.

"Better drive fast, then."

"This is insane. *You're insane,*" he spits, moving past me, still holding his hands up. He won't fight me; I'll blow his brains if he tries. He knows I'm not one to fuck with. We've spent way too many times in a jail cell when we were active because of bar fights. We didn't start them, but he knows I always finished them.

"Yeah, well, you already knew that."

CHAPTER 37
GAVIN

att turned on the sirens. Flashes of red, white, and blue guided us through the snow-covered streets down the mountain. The sun is setting, and I keep looking at the dashboard, watching the minutes tick by as if my life depends on it. The traffic opens up for him as we blast through.

As soon as he parks outside of arrivals, I head out the door and make a beeline for the entrance doors. I don't say one word to Matt as I race out of his vehicle. I'm being an asshole, but that's pretty up to par with my personality.

As soon as I'm inside, I check the plane schedules. My heart sinks to hell when I realize she boarded 20 minutes ago and the flight status has changed to 'departed'.

I'm too late.

The next thing I know, my desperation has me tripping over my prosthetic foot. I fall to the ground, gritting my teeth.

Fuck. That hurt.

"I got you, brother," Matt says as he hooks his arm in mine. Placing it back on, I rise to my feet, itching for a smoke.

I can't lose her.

I know what I have to do.

I have to leave the place that I've called home since I was a boy. I have to let go of the past, because Coraline is my future. But the thought of me leaving the cabin kills me. It's everything. The land, the state, the horses, the two women who raised me there.

It's my life. I'm not meant for anything else. Alaska made me the man I am today. Now that I'm out of the military, I've never envisioned myself anywhere else. I loved being on the teams, but as soon as I lost my leg, I was done. Everything I loved doing was made harder for me—but not impossible.

Coraline makes me feel like life has just begun...and I've lost her.

We both stand there, watching the plane's wheels go airborne. The plane's nose turns up to the right. The engines roar and reverberate against the floor-to-ceiling windows. *That's her plane.* I memorized the flight company.

"Take me home," I grumble. "Take me home before I flip this place apart."

Matt nods with a flash of empathy. "You're drunk. You're angry, and you're grieving. Slow down."

He lets out a deep breath, staring at me. I know he's trying to help, but I'm in no fucking mood. I need to get the fuck out of this airport and back to the cabin. I have a funeral to plan. But then, I see a familiar look in his eyes. That's the same look he has when someone's pushed him over the edge. I know it so well because I've had it so many times when we were in the military. And it's the same look I'd get when we were getting smoked by our leadership after long nights doing shit we're not supposed to.

Here we go again.

His fist connects with my chin. Stumbling over my feet, I'm taken aback by the pain.

"Don't point my own gun at me again," he scolds. Everyone

around us stops walking, their luggage slowly wheeling behind. Laughing, I suck in a deep breath before I cock my hand back and strike his face. He stumbles back, gripping and rubbing his cheek. A bright red mark reflects.

"I can't promise you that."

I got him good, but so did he. The strong taste of blood seeps through my tongue. I run my hand through my hair as two airport security make their way toward us. As soon as they get close, their tense body language fades away.

"Matt." One of them extends their arm for a handshake. Both of them smile as they greet Matt, but when they turn my way, it's that same apprehensive expression I get from everyone in Sleepy Coldwater.

Fear.

They just give me a silent nod, pressing their lips together. As soon as I take one step forward, they scatter backward. My shadow swallows them as I get close since I'm taller than both of them. My father's reputation as a serial killer will always bleed onto me. It doesn't matter that I served fifteen years as a SEAL. It doesn't matter that I do everything I can to stay out of everyone's way and live a quiet life. I'll always be known to them as a walking time bomb.

Huffing, I walk past them and head back to Matt's car, with a soulless body that echoes and yearns for one woman who made me feel like a normal man.

"Shit." I groan in the passenger seat of Matt's police car. Shifting in my seat, I lean forward, eyeing my cabin in the distance.

"What is it?" he asks, keeping his eyes on the road.

"I left the gate open."

Matt squints as he drives down the dirt road to the house. I already know something is wrong. I feel it in my bones. Sure enough, as we pull up to the front of the house, there is something different and horribly wrong. The first thing that stands out is the shattered windows. All of them are broken; the shattered glass floods the wrap-around porch.

"Fuck," Matt murmurs, his eyes growing wide in shock. His hands rub against the wheel as he grips it tight. Tension rolls off of me and onto him. As soon as he parks, I bolt out of the car and amble as fast as I can to my house. Matt turns off the engine and follows right behind.

The sound of our boots crunching through the grass overpowers the rage in my chest. I can't hear the sound of my heart beating erratically. The front door is already ajar. Pressing my palms against its center, it creaks as it springs wide.

"Let me go first," Matt offers, his weapon already drawn.

"No," I insist. "I don't think anyone is here anymore."

"I'll make sure of that," he says as he pushes past me. He surveys the kitchen first, then heads into the living room as I stay planted at the front door. I wait and watch, breathing hard and slow. All of the furniture has been ripped to shreds, most likely done by a knife. There's cotton everywhere. All of my mother's decorations are broken. The Christmas wreaths are cut into pieces. The twinkling lights are unplugged and stomped on. I can tell by the way they're crushed. My entire cabin smells of gasoline.

"Whoever did this was going to burn the house to the ground," Matt states, clearly just as pissed as I am. He heads down the hallways, leaving me alone. "Even with the Sleepy Coldwater Serial Killer copycat locked up, this town still wants to torture you." He shakes his head, pissed off.

Whoever was in my house tore it apart and made sure to remind me of why I live alone up in these mountains, far away from everyone. The massive portrait I have of a deployment overseas, standing with my team, has been written on with red paint or marker. I'm not sure.

MURDERER.

Someone from Sleepy Coldwater did this. Maya is dead. So, the only suspects are the civilians who live here. This town will never forget what my father did, and they will never let me live in peace.

TWO MONTHS LATER

CHAPTER 38
GAVIN

Grief. Another day going through this alone.

In the end, everyone dies. We're a blip in time; our small molecular imprint in this world comes and goes so quickly. Too quickly. One minute, we're here, surviving, and then the next, we're corpses. In my forty years of life, I've realized that life is too short to spend it in fear. Everyone has it all wrong about what it means to be rich. It's not about money, material things, or how big your house is. Being wealthy is to wake up next to the love of your life. To be rich is to sleep next to the one who makes you smile just by sitting next to them. To find someone who will protect you and make you feel safe is a blessing. Not everyone gets to find their soulmate. That's what being rich means to me. It's in the memories, showing up for each other, and encouragement when times get rough.

She made me laugh.

She made me see the world differently.

She made me see that life is still worth living.

I stare at my phone screen. Drunk. Numb. Yearning and craving to hear her voice again. Coraline doesn't want anything to do with me. It fucking hurts. Sitting on my porch, I stare at the sun setting on the March sky. The air is still cold, but I can't feel it on my flesh. I can't feel anything but dread since she left me.

Spring is around the corner, one of my favorite times of the year, because it means more animals will shed their antlers.

A rock forms in my throat.

Coraline.

I want to go shed hunting, go back to my regular scheduled programming as a lonely broken man with a routine that keeps me sane…but I can't do it anymore. Not when I don't have her next to me to help hold them while I collect and search. I want to hear about her next art piece.

I'm in love.

This is the first time I've fallen in love.

It's love because even though I'm angry, hurt, and broken, I still want her to be happy. I'm still grateful for everything we shared, and her absence has left a hole inside me that nothing and no one will fill.

It was fast for me because I had known about her a long time before she knew me.

Coraline fell in love with me, too. I know she did. I felt it.

Holding a bottle of whiskey, I stare at the amber liquid still in my all-black suit, which I wore from visiting Merelyn's resting place today. When we buried her, Matt and Georgia were the only ones in attendance besides me. I wished things were different. I wanted Coraline there. Merelyn fell in love with her, too.

I feel like I'm going insane without her. I have to grieve Merelyn and also go through Cora slipping through my fingers.

The only time I see her now is in my dreams. So I drink, and I drink until I pass out just so I can see her—every day since she's left. Before I know what I'm doing, I dial her number without looking it up, because I have it memorized. I want to say things I didn't get to say when she was here.

I hope she didn't change numbers.

It rings and rings while my heart pumps out of my tight chest. What the hell do I do when she answers? I'm already losing my train of thought. The whole world is blurry. I'm too drunk for this. I didn't think it through. My knee bounces anxiously, my fingers sweating, making my cell phone slippery.

"Hi, you've reached Coraline. I'm not available at the moment, but please leave a message, and I'll get back to you as soon as I can!"

Beep.

Her beautiful, soft voice.

I'm so choked up hearing it again, I forget why I called in the first place. So, I stay seated, with the phone to my ear, and look at the mountains until my head clears again.

"Hey."

I focus on the snow in front of me as silence envelopes me again.

"It's been almost two months since we laid Merelyn to rest."

It's also been about two months since I last felt okay—since I last felt like the sun wasn't the only thing in this world to brighten my days.

I shut my eyes tight, feeling lost, but I continue. I'm already here, and it's already recording.

Get your shit together, Gavin.

"I'm going to say it. I miss you, sweetheart." My shoulders rise and fall. "I told you when you were here that I would share the story of my injury, but I guess I never got a chance to, so I'll do it now."

My whole body trembles as I go back into my past and replay one of the most painful days of my life.

"I was thirty-three years old on a deployment. I was close friends with my superior. Long story short, I took a bomb for him. He had a mama who wrote him a letter every day. A brother and sister who would send him weekly care packages. A father who would remind him he was there for him for anything he needed. He had a family. So when I saw he was about to step on an IED, I pushed him out of the way. He fell and survived with minor injuries, and I...well, I lost my leg. I would make the same choice again. I was ready to die that day. I had no one when he had a whole family waiting for him. I was going to make sure he came back home to them."

I take another gulp of whiskey.

"You know what I keep thinking to myself, sweetheart? I want to tell you about the day I first met you. Reasonably so. I know you're angry and confused, but I want to be clear about my feelings for you, if I wasn't before. I've been yearning for you every day and every night since I first saw you. It was a rainy day in Northern California. I took the first flight out with little to no planning. I just wanted to see my favorite person in person. I don't do shit like this. I don't go to concerts to see my favorite band. I don't go to basketball games to watch my favorite team play. I don't travel to see my favorite place. But I wanted to see you. The brilliant dreamer and mastermind behind the brush and pencil." I suck in a breath, my throat thickening.

"Beautiful. That nine-letter word was all I could think about when my eyes landed on you for the first time. You looked so beautiful doing what you loved. It took my fucking breath away. I couldn't move. I couldn't do anything but look at you. And when a thought finally did cross my mind, I realized that I had to have you. I want to go back to that day all the time and wish I could go up to you like a normal man would and ask you out on a date...but it would have been a lie. I could never worship you the way a nice man would. So I stayed away, paralyzed from your presence. I was shocked that I didn't realize I was spilling my coffee all over myself." I chuckle lightly but force the fleeting good feeling in my chest away. "Someone handed me a napkin." I stare at the screen, realizing it's already five minutes long. I could go on forever, but I'll keep it short. "I kept thinking to myself, I'm one lucky man just to be in the same room as you. You were standing next to your husband and friends." I grit my teeth at the thought of those miserable people around her. They were disguised as supportive people, but on the inside, they were snakes.

"Every single painting you did was mesmerizing. I couldn't fucking choose, so I bought them all. I didn't want anyone else to have them. It was like finding gold amongst stars. That night on the plane home, I realized something. I was done yearning. I didn't want to long for you. I didn't want to feel like you weren't within my reach. I didn't want to think about all the things I would do and say to you if you were mine. No, sweetheart. I was going to take a chance."

I press the red button.

CHAPTER 39
CORALINE

*I*t's official. I'm no longer married.

And tonight I'm celebrating being free from Liam.

A single divorced woman who may have left her heart in Alaska and came back to Texas with the ability to see ghosts. Ever since the car crash, I see ghosts all the time. I've gone to multiple doctors and therapists about it, but no one can give me a clear reason as to why I have this ability.

Some spirits are nice and just seem lonely or lost. Either way, they're always fleeting. It's rare for one to linger longer than a few minutes. Others carry evil and darkness. I found a way to shut those out for the most part, just by singing my favorite song in my head or out loud. It silences the bad ghosts.

They all have one thing in common: they don't speak.

My sister, Everly, hasn't left my side since I got back home. We moved in together, renting a home near my parents' place on the outskirts of San Antonio. It's a three-bedroom house in a quiet neighborhood. Everly lets me use the third room for my art.

Thanks to a handsome man named Gavin Ariksen, I create

again. I draw. I write. And most importantly, I dream. My muse inspired me to find myself. My art is flourishing.

Those few weeks in Alaska changed me in amazing ways.

There hasn't been one day that I don't think about him. Every time I'm at a grocery store, or in the car, or whenever I spot a deer on the side of the road…when I'm doing anything really, I think of him. Most of the time, I think: this moment would be so much better if he were next to me.

It was only supposed to be a few days of space. Then one week turned into a month, then two months turned into six. It's been six months since I left Alaska. We didn't even get to exchange numbers. I left after he poured his heart out to me. He deserves a better woman.

Someone who isn't scared.

And yet the thought of him with another woman eats at me on the inside. I don't want him to move on. I don't want to picture him kissing another person. I selfishly hope he still thinks of me as much as I think about him. I hope he remembers every single detail of the way he felt while inside me because I remember it. I've tried to move on and tell myself he'll get bored. He'll leave me just like my ex-husband did. I'm scared to get attached because of it. Yet, as time went by, the more I lied to myself, the more I realized I fell in love with Gavin.

Our connection was on a soul level, and when it came to our lustful chemistry, it felt like fireworks every time we collided and clawed at each other.

Months have gone by, and I haven't heard from him. This convinced me he moved on, too. Why wouldn't he? I broke his heart after he begged me to stay. He lost Merelyn. He's going through a hard time, and I left him. Why would he still want me after that? Maybe he hasn't moved on. Maybe, he's thinking about me, too?

Is he back at work in the middle of the ocean? Or is he home? I do miss the cute little town of Sleepy Coldwater, where

I could drink the best coffee I've ever had on gloomy days that felt perfect for getting lost in a book. My lips lift into a small smile.

Still, I meant it when I said I needed a break when all the truths came to light, after weeks of bliss.

Gavin lured me in secretly and threatened to keep me with him.

Merelyn and Maya are dead.

I need to heal on my own. I need to believe in myself on my own, even if it means walking away from a man who is a force of nature. He's been in love with me long before we met. It makes sense why he felt so strong and profound when it came to me. It kills me inside to know he's alone up in those mountains.

I kept my promise. I sought help after I left and came back to San Antonio. I have a therapist I see weekly; I let my family in on days I don't feel the strongest. I run one mile every day. I don't stop dreaming.

Learning to love myself without depending on another person for my happiness brought me peace. I knew I needed to work hard independently, so my happiness isn't placed in another person.

My phone vibrates just as soon as I'm done applying a red lip. My hair is more curly than usual after taking it out of an overnight braid. After being in a relationship with a man who condemned my curves, it did something to my brain after hearing it every single day. I lost myself, but just one night of Gavin worshipping my body snapped me out of that insecure mindset. There was never anything wrong with me. I love my curvy body, bigger breasts, and stretch marks. I'm wearing bell-bottom jeans with a belt, cowgirl boots, and a white V-neck blouse.

EVERLY:

Hurry. We have to leave for the rodeo in the
next five minutes.

ME:

Just finished. I just need to grab my purse.

EVERLY:

I'll wait for you in the car.

I press the button on the side of my phone and tuck it into my back pocket. Closing my lipstick, I saunter into my office. My boots clack against the tile as I walk past ten oil paintings of Sleepy Coldwater, a portrait of Merelyn, another one of Gavin drinking black coffee, the mountains I saw every night and every morning, and finally his home. I call it: The Cabin in the Storm.

I run my hands over it. These pieces are for me. I promised I'd draw Merelyn, and I kept it.

Life is good. Life is okay again. But it's dull, and I know exactly why. The reason? A tall man with glowing blue eyes and a smile that always holds me hostage. He probably wants nothing to do with me after I left.

I...miss him. I miss him so bad it hurts, and even if I wanted to reach out, I don't have a way to.

My sister's car horn blares through the walls. She's so impatient. The drive is about thirty minutes away, but even so, we're still going to make it on time. I grab my purse off my desk and swoop it over my shoulder.

THE SMELL OF DIRT, popcorn, and beer surrounds us while we sit on the metal stands. With a Shiner Bock in hand, I straighten, looking at the last bull rider leaving the arena. The chaps at the bottom of his jeans are flowing in the summer wind. It's a packed night, with hardly any room to move, let alone breathe in the Texas humidity.

"He was so good!" Everly exclaims, throwing a handful of buttered popcorn in her mouth. "There's one more bull rider before it moves on to the next event."

"What's next?" I ask, taking another swig.

"Bareback riding," she replies, shifting in her seat, already looking at the cowboys lining up. George Strait plays loudly through the speakers behind the announcer's voice. He's introducing each contender by name and where they're from.

Suddenly, that same cold, paralyzing feeling spears through me. Goosebumps prick my skin, as everything around me feels eerie. I remember this like deja vu.

The feeling of being watched.

I lean into Everly until my shoulder brushes against hers.

"What's wrong?" She quirks a brow. Her tone is already shifting into a protective one. After everything that happened, it brought my older sister closer to me.

I shrug to reassure her.

"Nothing. It's nothing," I say loosely.

The horn blares, signaling the last bull rider. It pulls our attention and distracts me from that familiar feeling I only got when I was in the cabin. The mad bull bursts through the gate, kicking, doing everything and anything to get the cowboy off his back. Its hooves blast off from the ground each time, bucking and moving. Just watching this happen to the man riding *hurts my back.*

The seconds feel like minutes as I watch from a distance. Slow and agonizing. Everyone begins clapping, whistling, and cheering, encouraging the man below. If this is the way I feel, I can't imagine how it feels for the one riding. Once it hits four seconds on the massive digital clock, the bull flings the rider into the air. I cover my mouth with my palm as the entire arena echoes with "ooos". His body hits the ground, but it doesn't take him long to scurry off the dirt. He climbs the gate and is over it in seconds with a look of relief all over his sweaty, gleaming face. His mouth gapes open as he clutches his ribs.

The next rider is up. I sit down scrolling through e-mails when my heart seizes in my chest at the next words that come out of the speakers.

"Gavin Ariksen. From Sleepy Coldwater, Alaska."

CHAPTER 40
CORALINE

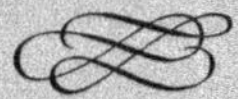

There's no way.

There's no way it can be *my* Gavin Ariksen. The man who's been haunting my dreams ever since I left. It has to be a weird coincidence.

But no, it isn't at all.

With my palm on my chest, I can feel my heart beating against my bones. My blood heats when I spot him in a black button-up and that same brown cowboy hat he wore all the time. He's behind the gate, ready to ride, looking so good. He has more silver in his beard, and he's put on more muscle than the last time I saw him. It's definitely him. I would recognize those dashing blue eyes anywhere. He still has that effect on me. He pulls me in like a raging storm in the oceans. Every time I look at him, I'm always caught in his current.

It feels like a spear to the chest—a gut punch of heartache the longer my eyes linger on him, because I have no right to shout out his name from the stands. I feel it on the tip of my tongue, wanting to pour out of my mouth and cheer him on, but then it leaves as soon as I remember I left.

I left him.

I let the fear of everything get to me.

Still…what is he doing here?

"Coraline," my sister whispers into my ear and shakes my shoulders. "Is that who I think it is?" she implores, her lips pressed together.

I nod.

"Yes," I murmur, sniffling. "I didn't know—" I shake my head, trying to gather my thoughts as I try to talk over the crowd's applause and cheers. "I didn't know he would be here. He saved my life in so many ways, and I never got to thank him." A tear streaks down my face when I blink. Everly rubs my arms with her palms, comforting me.

I'm so proud of him.

I feel purely and genuinely happy for him. He's here, back in Texas—his mother's hometown and favorite place to be stationed when he was on active duty. I thought he would never leave, but he did. He made it out of Alaska.

He left the cabin.

He's doing what he loves.

"Cowboys from all over the world compete at this rodeo every year," she informs me.

"I know." A hopeful smile plays across my face.

He raises his arm, making my lungs squeeze until I feel like I can't breathe. The horn blares, and he's off.

My hands curl around my face. If he gets hurt, I won't be able to stomach it. I close my eyes, but still keep my head facing in his direction. A small worried whimper slips out.

"Three. Four. Five. He's still on!" My sister jumps in her seat excitedly.

I'm going to throw up.

"Six. Seven. EIGHT!" my sister shouts, and my eyes explode open. Jumping with her, I watch Gavin launch himself off the bucking horse and reunite with the others behind the gate. "He did it! He did it!"

Still with my hands on my face, I can't help but smile so hard it hurts. The crowd goes wild, cheering the cowboy from Alaska on. I turn toward Everly. She wipes away the mascara that's run down my face.

"I thought I'd never see him again."

"Well, you have." She places her hands on her hips. "Cora. Are you going to stand here, or are you going to tell him all the things you've been wanting to say?"

"What are you talking about?" I retort, my cheeks reddening.

"Cora. There's something I have to tell you," she says, making that same mischievous look on her face when she has a confession to make. I know it all too well; it's been engraved into my mind since we were children. Every time she's about to admit to a wrongdoing, her eyes widen, and she looks everywhere but in my eyes. Bringing her fingers into her mouth, she starts to nip at her nails and rocks on her heels.

"What did you do?" I'm not sure I want the answer.

"He left a voicemail for you a couple of months ago...but I deleted it from your phone before you came out of the shower."

Fury blows through my veins.

"What?!" I thought all this time, he was mad at me for walking away. I thought he forgot about us.

"He left a message?" I bellow.

She nods, ashamed.

"What did he say?"

"I don't know. I just saw it and deleted it because he's your stalker!"

"Everly!" I snap, backing away from her. The crowd is still cheering Gavin on. "What the hell? That's not your place!" I scowl.

"I'm sorry! Okay? I thought I was doing the right thing as your sister. But watching you drown yourself in sorrow every day because you miss him has been hard. I just wanted to protect you from him. *From everyone*, after everything you've been through. But it may have been a mistake. You fell for him! I hear you cry every other night, and you don't think I've seen that damn shrine of paintings you have in your office? Get your ass down there. Don't make me drag you!" Her dark brown eyes narrow at me, raking my face in a scolding manner.

This is my second chance, and I'm not going to let fear steal away something good from me ever again. Gavin might be a lot of things, but a bad person isn't one of them. Giving my sister my back, I push past the crowd. Weaving and slithering between sweaty bodies, I head toward the bottom.

I'M WAITING for him to walk by the hallway, every cowboy does after they're done. With my hat in my hands, I tug at my lip nervously. Then the doors open.

He's not alone. Another rider walks beside him. They're both lost in conversation, covered in dirt and sweat, unaware that I'm here. I forgot how tall and broad he is. He's wearing that same gold cross chain; it glints underneath the white lights.

Before I can take one step, a group of women rushes around me. One of them knocks into my shoulder brutally. They circle them, completely blocking my view of his body entirely. I stand by the wall, unable to move as I watch them surround him like hungry fans. I heard about women throwing themselves at the men after the rodeo, but I thought it was an exaggeration.

One of them hooks her arm through Gavin's. He looks down at her. She plays with his cowboy hat and puts it on the top of her head. Those same blue eyes gleam at her...the way he used to look at me.

It's Georgia.

He moved...on?

My throat thickens, the air suddenly unbreathable, my chest and lungs burning the more I watch them together. She leans into him, grabbing hold of that same gold cross necklace I used to touch. Before their lips can connect, I run.

I do what I'm best at and run away.

The tears are falling, ruining my makeup, my eyes burning from the mascara, but I don't care. It hurt all these months to wake up without him. Every night I scream from the nightmares—his story—the blood—the shootout—the ghosts…everything, and yet Gavin made me feel safe and protected through it all.

And I threw it all away.

Threw it all away and pushed him into the arms of another woman.

I escaped the darkness with his help. I found my inspiration and started to love myself—I owe it all to him. Now another person gets to kiss him and experience the most amazing man in the world.

I thought I was in hell before, but now that I've gotten closure with an outcome I didn't see coming…I really am, and I don't know if I'll be able to survive this new storm.

CHAPTER 41
CORALINE

efore my horrid date can lean in and his lips collide with mine, I take a step back. Placing my hand on his chest, I squirm away.

"No…" I mutter. "I'm sorry, but no."

After seeing Gavin and Georgia, Everly made us go to the local bar just outside the rodeo. I didn't want to go; I just wanted to go back home and wallow, but she insisted. The first cowboy to ask for a dance, I said yes. I'm here for a good time, but I'm drawing the line at kissing.

I want to forget what I saw hours ago and stop crying for once…but I'm already regretting it.

"Come on, sweet thing." Chase wraps his arm around my waist as I smell the liquor on his breath. It makes my stomach coil. He's drunk way too much tonight, and I'm not some buckle bunny. He was boasting about all the girls who lined up for him after each rodeo. That should have been the first and last strike, but I continued. "Just one kiss." He's eager and desperate in all the ways that turn me off. His black cowboy hat pokes my forehead, and his stubble rakes my face painfully as he tries to fight his way to my lips.

He isn't taking no for an answer.

Instead, he leans in deeper, but I keep shielding myself with my cheeks, turning and eager to give him a knee to the groin.

"I said no." I use my arms to push his chest away, but he isn't getting the message.

Where is Everly?

Before I can kick him in the balls, someone's large fist sends him to the ground. Chase lands hard on the floor, dazed and halfway to unconsciousness. My hands shoot up to my mouth, completely taken aback in shock.

"No way in fucking hell," the man who punched him snarls.

That voice.

That scent.

It paralyzes me and sends an electric shock of heat into my blood.

Gavin.

The bar's bouncers intervene and pull him up to his feet.

"We were already on our way to you anyway," one of them says. "Let's go, Chase."

Gavin's hand curls around my forearm and hauls me deeper into the crowd.

Isn't he with Georgia? What the hell is going on? How did he find me?

"Gavin! What the?" I stumble but palm the walls to keep myself from falling. "What are you doing here?" I pull myself from his tight hold, and he lets go.

"I'm here to drink. Celebrate," he says nonchalantly. I can't even look at him without seeing the image of him being with someone else in my head. It hurts, and he's only making this harder. He has no right to be here or to fight off my first date in months.

He stalks forward, a toothpick in between his teeth. I keep taking step after step back until I hit the wall. Fire courses through my veins, and something inside of me twitches with need. He's dressed in all black from head to toe, easily towering over me as he used to before. Everyone around us is dancing or drinking the night away, completely oblivious to us.

"I saw you." *With Georgia.* "You moved on." I shake my head in disbelief. "You don't get to do this." I breathe softly, my voice quivering. I give him my back before he can see or hear me choke up. Blinking away the heartbroken tears, I locate the exit. "You're with someone else. I'm going to try and move on now."

I walk away because I don't want to break down in public or cause a scene more than we already have. I'll text Everly that I'm waiting for her at the car. I just need to breathe before I break. I weave through the dancing crowd and head for the neon sign that leads to the parking lot.

As soon as I'm out the door, the summer Texas air wraps around me like a comforting blanket. The humidity calms my nerves. The parking lot is half empty. The building's roof is the only source of light.

"Coraline."

Why is he still here? I know he's not anything like Liam, but for some reason, seeing him with Georgia, with my own eyes, I got that familiar ugly feeling in my chest when I caught my ex-husband cheating on me with my best friend. I know Gavin is single and so am I, but he's had my heart since we first met. I belong to him even though I left. I've been trying to convince myself that I'm not in love with him, but it hasn't been a choice for me; it's been an unfair, permanent attraction that no time or distance can sever.

"No!" I shout without looking at him. I stop walking over the gravel and search for Everly's jeep. "Don't say my name."

I've missed it too much.

"Stop running," he keeps tracking me.

"You don't get to tell me what to do!" I retort. Stopping, my boots skid across the gravel momentarily before I spin around to face him. I fold my arms across my chest.

Where the hell is my sister's car?!

"I fucking do," he growls.

My stupid heart does backflips as he gets closer. I hate that he still has this effect on my body. My pussy is already weeping for him. My flesh is already missing the way it feels when we collide. But he doesn't get to do this to me. Not after witnessing Georgia and him together—clearly happy. Well, I get to try to be happy too.

A few silent long beats pass as we stare at each other. His nostrils flare, and the veins in his arms bulge. Losing my internal emotional battle, a tear escapes my lashes. Heartache is written between us. I can feel it.

"You left me," he says with a broken tone. "You fucking left me, Coraline." I drink him in fully this time, my chin dropping as my vision blurs. He's lost weight. He's still built and muscular, but he's leaner, and the fire in his eyes has turned into something cruel.

"I don't sleep," he starts, then pauses.

I don't either.

"Merelyn died, and *you made me let you go*. I had to grieve alone. I lost her and you. These past few months have been hell."

I think about it all the time. I think about him and Merelyn every day and pray that he doesn't lose himself alone in Alaska. I thought I was making the right choice.

"I'm sorry," I whisper, agony painting every syllable.

He takes another step closer, but I'm too weak to step back—*to run*.

"I wanted to forget about you. I wanted to learn how to let you go. I wanted to grieve without having to take pills and drink myself until I died in that cabin, too."

I swallow. Guilt gnawing at me. Georgia helped him learn how to let me go.

"I saw you with her. With Georgia." I accuse.

"Yes," he confirms, simply with a slow nod.

Fuck. It hurts. This hurts too much. I smile and mirror his nod with my own, looking at the sky instead of his handsome face.

"You think I was going to wait for the woman who left without even saying goodbye? What did you expect? Huh? That I wasn't going to stay angry at you? That I was just going to deteriorate in that cabin and feel sorry for myself?" His brows narrow.

I look down, unable to meet his sad blue eyes. Something twists inside my chest. I can physically feel the hope I had when I dreamed of him turning into agony. She was there for him when I chose to leave. It makes sense.

"The answer is no." His voice deepens.

He's stabbing me in the chest with his words. Hearing and seeing him happy with someone else is a slap in the face, but I did this to myself. I chose to be scared of the one person who brings me to life.

I turn to walk away, holding my chin high. I don't want anyone to see me fall apart...*especially him*. What did I expect? I hurt him.

Suddenly, his hand curls around my hand.

"I'm not going to wait around, Cora. I'm not going to be angry." His hands wrap around my face, cupping the back of my head. "I'm going to reclaim what never should've left."

My brows knit together. An electrocution of hope is reborn in my soul. Warmth travels through me, and my eyes widen. Did I hear him right?

"But Georgia?" I shake my head. "I saw you together tonight. She—"

"She was being Georgia," he cuts me off. "She flew out here to support me. She knows my heart belongs to another woman, and she's having a hard time accepting it."

I shake my head in disbelief.

"But I saw her try to—"

"Kiss me? Didn't happen. These lips belong to you. No one else. Forever. I meant every word I said to you the day you left. There hasn't been anyone for months, and there won't be anyone for the rest of my life. I'm yours."

He's mine.

He's really back, and I don't want to blink.

He came back for me?

I don't realize I'm crying again until he swipes a tear away.

"Do you believe in coincidences?" I ask.

"No." He pulls the toothpick out of his front teeth. "I believe if you want something so bad, you go after it. No matter what that looks like. If it means letting go of the past and chasing after the future that I want, then that's what I have to do."

"I thought the city life wasn't for you."

"Coraline. You are for me. Wherever you go, I will follow." He pulls me in by the small of my back until our bodies connect. "You are my future. I found you again, and I'm not letting you go. Accept that you belong to me, or you can fight me every step of the way down the aisle at our wedding."

I grin for the first time in six months. Everything is warm again.

"I'm sorry for leaving you. It was stupid. I regretted it. I've been wanting to tell you that since the day I left. In the car ride, on the plane, and when I got home. I—"

He shuts me up with a fiery kiss. I sag in his arms, submitting myself to him.

"I needed it. You needed it. I had a lot of healing to do myself, baby." He cups my head again. "I needed to let you go so I could heal from my demons and be a better man on my own. I need to be the best version of myself so I can be a good boyfriend, husband, and father. All for you."

I sniffle, grasping onto the nape of his neck tighter.

"There was a lot of work to get done. Fuck, Coraline. I sold the cabin and got back on the bull. I thought it wasn't possible to be a cowboy again after I lost my leg, but it is. And…" he pauses as we lock eyes, "I'm going to do whatever it takes to be the man you deserve."

Sometimes, being alone to weather the storm is what other people need to survive and come out of it stronger. It's what we both needed. But now that I know without a single doubt this man is mine, I never want to survive any type of storm alone again. I want to do it with him and only him. *Together.*

"I love you." I sob. "I've been wanting to say it since I left. I'm in love with you, Gavin Ariksen."

He smiles. God, I love it when he smiles.

"You owe me a dance," he says against my lips. God, I've missed the way his beard tickles me. I listen to the song playing in the background, and I recognize it right away. "You Look Like You Love Me" by Ella Langley and Riley Green plays through the speakers.

"What are you talking about?" I ask, dazed and hot. That sizzling feeling between my thighs ignites, remembering just how well he stretches me.

"I dared you to dance with me, and you ran," he points out, the tip of his nose brushing against mine. Still with his eyes closed, a deep hum reverberates through his chest. It feels so good to have him in my arms again.

"So, Coraline. Will you dance with me?"

Another sting hits my eyes.

"Don't you run away from me this time."

"Or what?" I tease, a high-pitched sound escapes me when he pulls me in tighter.

"You run, and I'll make it hurt when I get you. You'll regret it when my cock is so far down your throat, no one can hear you scream for God when I'm so deep, making you mine in all the ways you crave."

"Don't tempt me." I press my lips, stealing his taste again. He makes me feel like the most beautiful girl in the world when he looks at me like this.

"Let's dance, sweetheart." He grabs his cowboy hat and places it on top of my head. Blushing, I let him lead the way to the middle of the dance floor. My phone vibrates in my pocket when we stop. I pull it out to set it to "Do Not Disturb" when the text message has me smirking.

EVERLY:

I may have played Cupid and found him after the rodeo while you were waiting in the car for me. I told him which bar we'd be at…I didn't have to pee. ;)

Of course, she did.

Gavin grabs my phone from my hands before I can reply. He holds down the button on the side until my screen turns black. Then, he tucks it into his back pocket.

"No more interruptions. No more waiting. No more fear."

Threading our fingers together, he pulls me into his chest. I feel all of his muscles around me, making me remember how good it feels to be pressed up against this sinful man. He smells like he always does. Radiating charming masculinity, with a dash of cigarettes and signature cologne.

"No more fear," I parrot as we dance to the music. We're both smiling so hard it reaches our eyes. And just like that, I'm back to square one, falling so hard for a man I met in a cabin in the middle of a snowstorm. The instant connection we share grows stronger, and I feel like I can suddenly dance all night.

"Gavin, you made me realize a lot."

He hums, egging me to tell him more. I love that about him. He listens to everything I have to say, even if it's just about the weather or the smallest wins or losses of my day; *he listens* with a smile on his face.

"I want to dream, but only with you by my side. Art is my

passion, but you are my soulmate. I am not hollow without art, I am empty if I lose you."

I love him. He opened my eyes to the possibility of trusting again. He reminded me that even though the world is cruel, I must hold onto my light no matter how much darkness wants to wreck it.

As soon as the song ends, he grabs me, cups my face with both of his large hands, and pulls me in for another soul-altering kiss. His tongue licks mine, and I let him in. We move perfectly in sync. He turns his head to the side so he can get deeper. I hold onto his back muscles as he continues to dominate my mouth.

"I choose you, Coraline Rosa, but now, you need to choose me." He presses his forehead to mine.

Easy.

"I choose you. I choose us."

He crashes his lips to mine. It's a passionate kiss. His lips slowly move against mine. His tongue sweeps in between my lips, and I immediately react to his familiar, addictive taste. Cigarettes, beer, and just...*Gavin*.

"Does your leg hurt?" I ask softly, looking up at him. "From riding the bull?"

He shakes his head. "Nothing hurts anymore, sweetheart. Now that I have you, everything is painless."

I smile as he twirls me around. Then, I'm resting my cheek on his chest again, listening to his heart beat.

"Nothing hurts anymore for me either," I tell him.

I wish I could stay in this moment forever.

"By the way, sweetheart. If you want me to cut off that man's lips for trying to kiss you, I will. Let another man hold what's mine again, and I'll deliver his arms to you with a bouquet of flowers."

A shiver rolls down my spine, and I look around the bar, searching for a solution. I shake my head and glare at Gavin's icy eyes. If there's one thing I've learned about Gavin during that snowstorm, it's that he's capable of anything and everything to keep himself tethered to me.

"Gavin Ariksen, are you jealous?" I tease.

"I'm *murderous*. You let him touch you," he says, anger intertwined in his deep, possessive tone. "Now, let's go to my truck, sweetheart."

"Right now?" I squeak, already blushing hard.

"Yes, *now*. I have to remind you who you belong to."

EPILOGUE

 Haunted by Isabela Rosa

One Year Later

I'm being chased, running through the grass, up and down the hills. My shoes crunch over stickers and twigs. The ends of my dress dance with the wind as I run. I squint over the sun, perspiration leaking down my chest and face as I weave through the trees.

Gavin loves to push the boundaries.

His prosthetic leg allows him to continue doing what he loves, such as riding horses, bull riding, and *chasing me*.

I'm deep in the woods when I feel his arm wrap around my waist. He tugs me into his chest with a wicked, hot grin that reaches his blue eyes. He was hiding behind a bush.

"Cora," he croons. "I like chasing you. I like it when you run from me, and your weeping pussy calls to me. Because now that I've caught you, I get to make you scream out here, and no one can hear us. No one can hear what my girl sounds like when she's getting fucked."

I smirk, taunting him as I rock my hips into his as I feel his hard-on through his jeans. Huge and harder than a rock.

Gavin sold his home in Alaska and bought a one-hundred-acre ranch in Texas. We moved all of his horses here and bought more. He's happy here.

We're happy here.

I'm a full-time artist creating for local business owners and gaming companies.

Gavin takes care of the ranch with my father from morning to night.

"I'm not wet," I lie. I'm turned on. I'm turned on so high that it makes me hate myself. I like the thrill of being hunted by him. Dark desires haunt me without remorse. I don't have to be ashamed of what I want.

He dips his fingers, running them through my slit and smirks. His fingers dip into his mouth, and he sucks on them. Humming deep, he looks me in the eyes and ghosts the shell of my ear. My blood runs hot, knowing he's caught me in a lie. This man is walking sex.

"Your wet pussy is begging to be fucked."

He lifts my hands and secures them together with a rope. He ties it in a knot, making my flesh burn.

Using a knife, he slices my panties off me. He flips me so I'm palming the tree, holding onto it, as he exposes me. Pulling my ass up, I'm on my tiptoes.

The man who stalked me. Watched me. Bought all my art all along.

My muse is my stalker.

"No one knows your body like I do. Say it," he growls.

"I'm made for you," I breathe.

"This is what you like, isn't it?" he taunts.

"Yes," I moan.

He brings the darkness out of me, but doesn't make it an ugly thing. We can be ourselves with each other. He worships me, and that scares the hell out of me because I've never had that before. I don't know what to do with a man who is *choosing* me every day. We both understand that a relationship isn't going to be sunshine with butterflies every day; it's a choice you make every day to selflessly love one another through the lowest of lows and highest of highs. To care for one another in every version we transform into with time. The most important thing is that we grow together and not apart.

He runs his hand over my chest and kneads my breasts. My nipples peak and pebble underneath his sensual grip. He places my other boob in his mouth, his lips wrap around it, his illegal, perfect tongue circling my nipple right before he sucks. Mewling, I arch my back and push my breast deeper into his mouth, chasing the euphoria he's planting inside my heart.

"Perfect. You're so fucking perfect," he groans against my nipple before he nips it and twists my other. "How do you want it?"

"Raw. I want every drop of your cum. I want to feel and see it drip out of me. Out of my ass." I'm ready for it. I smooth my palm over the scar on his chest. The bullet wound he took.

"Such a dirty whore. My whore."

Gavin

My wife is perfect.

Her pussy is divine...and I want her ass too. I want to fuck everything.

I lube the head with her slick, soft pussy, slapping her clit with my dick a couple of times, which causes her to tremble. She's so wet; she's making a mess of herself all over her thighs.

"You like it when I touch your ass like this, don't you?" I growl into her ear. She nods, nipping at her bottom lip, and I'm tempted to fuck her mouth. I bite her shoulder, and she yelps but doesn't run.

"Spit on my cock, baby."

She turns so I can see her brows narrow, and her angelic face contort into seduction. Everything about her reminds me of why I'll gladly lose my sanity. Hollowing her cheeks, she takes me instead, making it wet. Fuck, if she keeps doing that, I'm going to come down her throat.

"Turn around," her cheeks pinken further like she's ashamed to indulge in the sins I inflict as I rub her clit. I grip her breasts and squeeze until she's wiggling. She starts to fuck her pussy on my hand, and I grin sadistically as I continue to feel her insides.

"Has anyone had you here?" I push into her ass and fuck...it takes everything in me to stop the implosion that's knocking on my door. She's so fucking majestic and tight.

"No, Gavin..." She tenses up and tries to push away, but I hold onto her tighter.

"Fuck, Coraline." I stay still, waiting for her to fight me, but she just heaves and takes deeper breaths. "You're so tight here, too."

I push more of my length inside her, and she stops breathing.

"Beg for it. Let me hear your slutty voice tremble. Let me feel your pussy make a mess while it begs me to fuck it too."

"Fuck me hard, Gavin."

"Beg for it, *harder*." I command, huskily.

I pull my cock back, but not entirely out. She shivers as my body breaks out in goosebumps.

"Please."

"Please, what?" I push back in, and she clenches her tight little ass on my nerves.

Fucking hell.

I palm the tree and sink my teeth into her shoulder.

"Please, destroy me, Gavin, and don't hold back. *Now*," she demands like an order.

Jesus.

"I like it when you're so bossy and needy for my cock."

I sink back into her tight rim.

"It hurts, but I love it. I love you so much," she cries out, strumming her clit.

"I wish you could see your ass grip my cock like it was made for me."

She squeals as I pick up my movements. She's on her tiptoes, holding onto the tree for dear life. The white in her knuckles presents with each slow thrust I give her. I knead her breast as I thrust in and out of her deep and fast. Her breasts bounce in the palm of my hand.

"Oh my god," she moans, and just the sounds she makes when she's on the verge of an orgasm make me weak.

Ever since we met, I knew I was fucked. I knew if she asked me for something, I'd give it to her without hesitation. I knew that if I had to, I would burn down the world for Coraline.

Her arousal drips down her thighs, and I smirk. I grab it with my fingers, push it inside her, and pump it as her ass gets railed. Our skin slaps, and I give it to her the way she loves and desires.

Hard. Filthy. Dirty.

"So wet for me, sweetheart?" I pull my fingers out and suck on them, tasting her sweet honey and groaning from how good she tastes.

"Give me every drop of your cum, please. Oh!" she hisses, as I continue to stretch her ass slowly before I fuck her so hard she'll feel my cock inside her when she sits down.

More blood rushes down at the thought of her swallowing it.

"Where, Coraline? Where do you want it? Your face or inside?"

Thrust.

"Inside me. Inside my ass, right now, Gavin." She reaches over her shoulder and runs her fingers through my hair. God, my dick twitches whenever she's so needy.

I slap her breasts, and she wiggles.

I implode. We both reach our climaxes at the same time. My dick grows harder and bigger as I pulse inside her. She continues to chant my name as I kiss her neck. I fill her ass up, as she continues to squeeze it, flexing over it as it throbs.

I would love to see her carry my child one day, but Coraline and I are happy just the two of us. Maybe, one day, in the future, we'll come across that conversation again.

I spread her cheeks apart. My cum spills from her rim. Smirking, I collect it with two fingers and push it back in.

"This belongs inside you."

She tugs on her lip with her teeth and purrs, gripping the tree tighter.

"Yes, sir."

My cock stirs.

"Good girl."

Coraline finishes getting dressed. She smooths out the wrinkles in the dark brown dress and smiles at me. The sun is setting behind her, and the rays of burnt orange and yellow hit the golden flecks in her eyes. So beautiful. I lift her into my arms, and she places hers behind my nape, coaxing. Then she palms my scar on the chest. I will always gladly take a bullet for her and die happy knowing she isn't harmed.

I can't get enough of this woman.

I kiss her hard.

"I love you, Gavin," she breathes against my lips.

I will never get tired of her saying those three words. I need to hear her say it every day of our lives together. I glance around me as she combs her hair with her fingers.

When my eyes find the mechanical bull I practice on, adrenaline bubbles through my veins. Because of Coraline, I ride again. I practice again and truly live my life again. I rode the bull for the first time since my injury because of Coraline. She inspires me to live life to the fullest, even when the world seems against me.

I came to a realization. In the darkness, sometimes art is there to save you. Sometimes, it's a person, and sometimes it can be a song. As long as you find something good to hold onto, that's what matters.

Coraline did that for me. I left that cabin after years of reliving my trauma because I felt like if I left Alaska, I'd be leaving the only home I had left.

Coraline is my home now.

She hums sweetly and encases me with her arms. I hold her back tightly and press my lips to the top of her head.

"What's going through your mind, Gavin?"

I smile.

"You, sweetheart. Always you."

Gripping her face with both hands, I lock eyes with her.

"I fell in love with your art first. Then, I saw you and fell in love with your beauty. Then, I met you, and I fell in love with your soul." I press my lips against her one last time before we head back into our home.

It's a long walk. The smell of BBQ hits me, and my mouth waters. The sun is setting, and golden rays shine across her beautiful brown skin. We hold hands as we come out of the trees. Her parents are inside, watching the football game. Her family is my family now. I'm doing things with her parents I wish I could have done with mine. I get to speak to her father for advice on anything and everything. When I plan surprises for my wife, I call Cora's mom, and she answers on the first ring. And when her sister is around, we all laugh together.

"It smells good. Your dad should come every single weekend, if you ask me."

She giggles.

Coraline stops walking. Her honey eyes widen as she stares directly at something beside me. It's a spirit. Ever since she had her injury, she can see the dead. It explains why she thought my cabin was haunted.

Instead of reacting right away, I slowly stride toward her, giving her a short moment before I pry. She blinks slowly as she tracks it. Moving her hair to the back, I caress the small of her chin.

"Baby, what is it?"

"I see her, Gavin."

"See who, sweetheart?" I ask patiently.

"Your mother. She's here…with Merelyn," she murmurs with a comforting half-smile.

"Is she saying anything to you?"

I always thought about this moment. If I ever saw my mother again, what would I say to her? Ever since she passed, I have always longed to see her again in my dreams, but she never comes. I whirl on one foot, hoping to see what my wife is seeing, but all I get is mesquite, trees, and the horses in the distance. The grass is empty. No footsteps, no floating orbs she talks about. Everything seems normal.

"No."

She grabs my hand and threads her fingers with mine.

"What are they doing?" I ask, worriedly.

"They're okay, Gavin. They're happy."

I swallow the growing boulder in my throat. I cough, clearing it so I don't lose it.

"She wants you to know that she's proud of you. And that, she never left you. She's always been with you, by your side through everything. Her presence wasn't just in the cabin. She has always been with you and will always be."

My brows furrow.

"I thought you said they can't talk?"

"I did, but trust me."

I nod, itching for a cigarette. I pat down my jeans because I don't remember which pocket I put them in. Finally, I snag it out of my back pocket and light one.

She's here. In Texas. *With us.*

My mother was the biggest reason why I couldn't leave the cabin. I always felt her around, and it was the place she died in. We stand in silence, listening to birds chirp and bugs sing in the tall grass. The grief doesn't follow me anymore. We're all going to die one day, and I will be reunited with Mer and my mother and introduce her to the most beautiful woman—my wife.

"Gavin!" Coraline's father, Estaban, shouts. His mitted hand holds a plate wrapped in aluminum foil with an uncut brisket in the center. He has one foot out the back door and one still inside. "Coraline! Food is ready!"

"Let's go eat." She walks in front of me, the wind swooping through her long curly hair.

"I told you." I smile, walking after her.

"Told me what?"

"My cabin wasn't haunted. It's just always been you haunting me."

THE END

ACKNOWLEDGMENTS

Firstly, thank you to my readers. Thank you for being here and reading, The Cabin In The Storm. This was one of my lighter romances, and I absolutely fell in love with Gavin and Coraline! If you enjoyed it, please consider leaving a review and sharing it with a friend. To my family, thank you for always surrounding me with your love. To my Patreon members, thank you for helping me choose a book title! You all are incredible. To Dani and Blake, thank you for being here. To my cover designers, Jay and Austin, thank you for these incredible art pieces. To my BETA readers, thank you so much for helping me bring this story to life.

ALSO BY LEXIE AXELSON

See You Soon

I Promise You

Pretend

The Depraved Prince

Mariposa

The Cabin In The Storm

Wild Silver And Lead

ABOUT THE AUTHOR

Lexie Axelson is a Hispanic author from South Texas. She is a military spouse currently residing on the East Coast. She loves to pen angsty, heartbreaking love stories. When she isn't reading a book, she loves to watch horror movies and travel with her family.

Website: www.lexieaxelson.com

On my website, you can sign up for my newsletter, view my signing schedule, and visit my shop for signed books and special editions.

instagram.com/lexieaxelson

tiktok.com/@authorlexieaxelson

goodreads.com/lexieaxelson

patreon.com/lexieaxelson